*L*uanna looked at the man standing across from her, and her body fizzed as if she'd been dunked in champagne.

She'd like to dunk *him* in champagne....

Dark, nearly black hair, neatly cut. Swarthy and Latin-looking, but with intensely blue eyes instead of the deep brown the rest of his coloring suggested. His jaw—a strong jaw, but not Superman-square—sported a hint of stubble, not like he hadn't shaved, but like his beard was just that determined. A small gold hoop earring glinted in the lantern light, making him look like a tasteful pirate.

Luanna had always been fond of pirates....

love,
IN STITCHES

a hollywood spice novel

sophie mouette

LKP

LITTLE KISSES
PRESS

LOVE, IN STITCHES

Sophie Mouette

Print edition published 2017 by Little Kisses Press

ISBN-13: 978-1-946462-02-2 (trade paperback)
ISBN-10: 1-946462-02-0 (trade paperback)

Inquiries should be addressed to
Little Kisses Press
littlekissespress@gmail.com
http://www.littlekissespress.com

Cover image © inarik / Bigstockphoto.com
Cover design by Allyson Longueira
Little Kisses Press logo by Dayle Dermatis

For Ken & Jeff,
my own personal pirates

love,
IN STITCHES

Chapter 1

*I*f Luanna Devenaux had known what kind of day she was going to have, she would have worn a different blouse.

More than a year in southern California and she still couldn't get a handle on the weather. She was a Southern girl born and bred, but even the South cooled down *some* in autumn and winter.

With the arid Santa Ana winds sucking the moisture out of her very eyeballs and nearly eighty degrees at 9 a.m., her choice of three-quarter sleeves and a rayon-linen blend that apparently had more rayon in it than she recalled meant she was sweating like a whore in church, as her daddy would say.

She sighed with relief when she stepped into Luscious Couture's blessed air conditioning and sighed again with sheer joy (and some astonishment) that, more than a year later, she had a fashion design job here.

The sound of Los Angeles traffic was replaced by the hubbub of the warehouse. The two-story industrial ceiling meant all the discussions the designers had about their ideas had to be at a higher volume or their words would be swallowed by the space. Plus Tad, one of the other junior designers, always insisted on having Pandora radio on his favorite station, an unsettling mix of modern pop, Mexican pop, and Asian pop, and they had to raise their voices over that as well.

Luanna loved it.

She loved the smell of fabric, draped across mannequins or on bolts along one wall: sweet silk and sheepy wool and crisp linen.

She loved the enormous mood board that took up much of another wall, a crazy collage of fabric swatches and color chips and sketches and inspirational pictures.

The announced colors for two years hence—because next year's designs were already being produced—were Directoire Blue, Seashell Pink, and Mirage Gray.

Luanna privately thought of them as Barbie's Eyeball Blue, Hoohah Pink, and Confederate Gray, because by God, that gray *was* the official true gray of the fine soldiers of the South.

So the pictures, torn out of magazines or printed off the Internet, included ocean and sky and cornflowers for the blue, seashells and babies' bottoms and cats' noses for the pink, industrial punk and old pewter dishes for the gray.

The whole place thrummed with a creative energy that jittered her up better than crack. Not that she'd ever tried crack—she just didn't think she'd ever need drugs as long as she could shoot this crackling artistic energy into her veins.

She dropped her purse in a bottom drawer of her drafting table/desk and wished, not for the first time, that the vending machine in the break room dispensed real honest-to-God sweet tea. Not that weak lemony swill every else thought constituted proper iced tea.

Still, that was the only thing she didn't love about working at Luscious.

Before she could sit down and review the sketches she'd done yesterday in preparation for a mockup today—yay for getting to do some hands-on sewing!—she heard her boss's voice cut through the hum of work.

"Luanna, may I see you in my office?"

The hum stopped as everyone else pretended to be focusing on work when they really wanted to hear the gossip.

Diane, Luanna's boss, stood on the metal catwalk that provided access to the offices lining the upper half of one wall. She'd had the sense to wear a sleeveless sheath dress in royal blue. With her spectacularly slim figure and jet-black hair, middle-aged Diane could've passed for half her age.

Luanna wanted to be Diane when she grew up. Only curvy and blond, because there wasn't much she could do about her curviness, and she *liked* being blond.

Without waiting for a response, Diane disappeared into her office. Luanna trudged up the metal staircase to the offices that lined the upper half of one wall. She might be in blissful air conditioning, but she was still wilted from the walk from the parking garage to the studio through the Santa Ana hellwinds.

Diane usually worked on the floor with the junior designers, but as a senior designer, she warranted an actual office, which she went into only when she needed to make a phone call or do some computer work.

Luanna knew she wasn't late, knew she'd gotten raves at her one-year review, so she was only mildly unsettled—until she stepped into the office and saw someone else there. That guy from HR. What was his name? Hernando? Something like that. All she knew was that she'd seen Tad and Hernando, who'd clearly had a little too much to drink, stumble out of the electrical closet at last year's holiday party looking adorably mussed.

It was never good to find HR waiting when you've been summoned to your boss's office.

Diane, now behind her chic black metal desk, said, "Close the door behind you, please."

Luanna mentally straightened her spine. Whatever it was, she was confident it would all get sorted out, so she fell back on her Southern politeness, which called for her to comment on the weather.

"Whoo!" she said, sitting down in the padded chair across from Diane. The office was so tiny that her knees knocked against the back of Diane's desk, and she could smell Hernando's too-sweet aftershave because he was so close to her that if he tripped, he'd be in her lap. "It's hotter than Satan's housecat out there, isn't it?"

Diane normally loved Luanna's "Southernisms," as she called them, but not this time.

Hernando didn't crack a smile. Dayum.

"Luanna," Diane said, "we've got a situation that needs addressing. I'm sure it's a misunderstanding, something we can get cleared up quickly, but I do need to remind you of the legal forms you signed when you came to work for Luscious Couture."

She put a hand on a green manila folder on her desk, which Luanna guessed was her employment file.

"Of course," Luanna said, remembering the confidentiality agreement and raft of other forms she'd run by her best friend Chloe Montiero's brother Curt the lawyer before signing. They'd all been pretty straightforward; nothing she'd had a problem with.

So what *was* the problem? Why did Diane sound as if she were reading from a script? They'd always gotten along well, Luanna thought.

"It's come to our attention that you might be doing some design work on the side," Diane said, "which would violate the noncompete clause you signed."

Luanna felt her stomach spin faster than a NASCAR crash.

Now she knew what this was about.

She wasn't, in fact, doing any wrong. She was sewing on the side, and it was for money, but it wasn't couture design.

And it wasn't anything she could ever, ever tell Diane, or anyone else.

She might've signed a confidentiality clause with Luscious Couture, but her oath to the famous and high-powered crossdressing men she made women's clothing for went deeper than legalese.

She'd made them a promise. She'd made her friend Ray Stark—beefy action hero Ray Stark—a promise. And Luanna Devenaux would sooner sell her momma to the devil than break her promises.

"Oh, no," she said truthfully, "I'm not working for any other designer or company. I just do a little sewing for friends, you know, for pin money, and because that's what you do for friends. My best friend, Chloe—she came out with me from Boston—just got engaged, and of course I told her I'd make her wedding dress. Probably the bridesmaids dresses, too, because Lord knows I don't want to be caught in one of those hideous off-the-rack monstrosities. But I've never used any supplies from here, or sewn for friends on company time."

She suspected she had crossed the line into "talking too much to cover up your hedging the truth." She suspected Diane knew it, too. Diane was no fool.

Hernando probably wasn't, either, except when he had too much to drink. But who didn't do foolish things then?

Diane drummed her manicured nails on the file folder, black flashing against the green. "Luscious has a very narrow view of what constitutes a noncompete violation. We're going to need to see everything you've made, and a list of who you've sewn anything for."

Luanna felt like that time the horse she'd been riding had bolted.

She hated that out-of-control feeling more than anything in the world.

Blinking her big baby blues sometimes worked with men, and some particularly inclined women—she hated stooping to that, but if it got her out of a parking ticket, so be it—but she knew it wouldn't work with Diane, who was married and straight as a road in Kansas, nor Hernando, because, office indiscretion with Tad, duh.

Stuck between a rock and a hard place, that's what she was.

Screwed was another way of putting it. Seriously screwed.

She licked lips gone as dry as her eyeballs in those hot, arid winds. "I'm afraid I can't do that," she said. She was about to say more but stopped. Every word she added would bring her closer to dropping a hint about *why* she couldn't say anything, about *whom* she couldn't say anything.

Slippery slope.

And Lord knew, slippery slopes always ended you up ass-first into a swamp, eye to eye with a hungry gator.

She tried again. "Diane, I can assure you—I can swear on a stack of bibles a mile high—that I'm not doing anything that violates any of the agreements I signed with Luscious. You know me, you've worked with me for more than a year now. I'm asking you to go on my word and my honor."

That was how the world should work, anyway.

Diane glanced at Hernando, then shook her head, and Luanna saw regret in her soon-to-be-former boss's eyes.

"I'm sorry, Luanna, I truly am," Diane said. "You're clearly a talented designer. But Luscious, like any professional designer, has to protect its brand, and we have no choice but to let you go, effective immediately."

No choice? Even when the bear had you backed up against the tree and your shotgun had jammed, there were options.

"A check to cover this pay period and any unused vacation days will be mailed to you within two weeks," Hernando said.

"Thank you," Luanna said, because she was raised to be polite and because she wasn't really listening anymore. Her brain was already trying to figure out how she and Evenrude, her Welsh corgi, would keep from starving.

Diane's words, "like any professional designer," were loaded ones. Getting fired from a couture firm—fashion was a cutthroat and yet tight industry—would make it difficult to get a new job. Luanna could spin her leaving any number of ways, and HR wouldn't be allowed to give specifics, but Hernando's tone of voice could convey everything.

Hernando was highly unlikely to sound perky when he confirmed the dates of her employment. Even if Tad was…

Nope, not gonna go there.

"And again, I'm sorry, but I'm required to say this," Diane went on. "You're still bound by the confidentiality clause. If any Luscious designs show up somewhere, you'll be prosecuted to the fullest extent of the law."

Luanna tamped down her panic, stood, and held out her hand. "I understand. Thank you, Diane. It's truly been a pleasure working with you."

Diane followed her out of the office and stood at the railing. Luanna made her way down the stairs, followed closely by Hernando. As he watched—and her colleagues all pretended not to watch—she got her big gooshy purse out of the drawer and dumped her personal belongings into it. The framed photo of Evenrude and her beloved peacocks. The Paula Deen bobblehead, a gift from Chloe. The packet of ramen, which would've made Chloe shudder if she knew.

It made Luanna shudder, in truth, but she believed in being prepared, and she never knew when she'd have to pull an all-nighter. Or when there'd be an earthquake, but if she were trapped by an earthquake, the microwave probably wouldn't work. She could crunch the noodles, though.

She hadn't really brought any other personal effects to her workspace because every inch had been taken up with sketches and fabric swatches and pens and pins.

She looked longingly at her most recent sketch, the one she'd planned to mock up today, and pressed her lips together to keep them from trembling. Then she squared her shoulders and left her dream job behind as she went back outside into the hellish heat to figure out how to get her ass out of the swamp before the alligator chomped on it.

*

The heat slowed Luanna's steps, like an inappropriate faux-fur stole edged with lead weights dragging her down. The fabric shops, their wares spilling out onto the sidewalk, pushed bolts of orange and black and skulls and spiderwebs.

Halloween might have been her favorite holiday when she was growing up—oh, the costume opportunities!—but in this heat, it seemed ridiculous.

As in, you had to trick-or-treat as a surfer or bronze-bikini Leia just to stay cool.

She tried to take a deep, calming breath in through her nose, then remembered why that wasn't the best of ideas.

This part of Los Angeles never smelled good. Even though the streets were wide—two lanes in each direction—cars always clogged the streets, and the tall buildings trapped the exhaust. Combined with something unidentifiable she didn't want to think about (it wasn't the cleanest section of town), there was always a funky cast to the air.

Luanna fought off her churning emotions by focusing on the next step: get to her car and crank the AC.

One thing at a time.

She was tempted to stop at Starbucks, a familiar one between the parking garage and Luscious Couture, but the usual barista didn't know how to make proper sweet tea, and technically Luanna couldn't even afford a bottle of water right now. Tap water for this girl, damn the contaminants, full steam ahead.

Tears prickled behind her eyes (where had she found the moisture?), but she fought them back, pressing her lips firmly together and straightening her back. Her parents wouldn't approve of her getting hysterical in public, though they'd have different reasons for it. Daddy would remind her that she'd made the honorable choice, even if it was hard, and that meant there was no point in crying. He'd also recommend a bourbon and branch water once she got home to make the hard choice easier to swallow.

She was more of a margarita girl herself, but the general principle was sound. It would be noon in Louisiana by the time she made it home.

Momma, on the other hand, was the queen of making scenes, but she'd point out that Luanna was in the middle of Los Angeles, surrounded by strangers; with no one to hug her or fuss over her distress, it wasn't worth ruining her makeup. (Not that Luanna ever wore Momma-level makeup, with mascara on the false eyelashes, but again, the principle was sound.)

And thinking of Momma brought the briefest of smiles. Luanna's mother was, under her fluffy, flamboyant, big-haired costume, one of the smartest and toughest people Luanna knew, but she was an old-school Southern belle and mostly used her brains to get Daddy and other men to do her bidding.

She reached the parking garage, trudged up the cement stairs to the roof. And that's when she started to crumble again.

The way the rooftop garage worked was that early arrivals (for example, employees) got boxed in by later arrivals (for example, shoppers looking for fabric bargains). So Luanna had to stand in the heat—the flaming ball of evil pounding down in the cloudless blue expanse of hell—while the attendant found her car, moved the one in front of it, moved hers to escape position, and returned with her keys.

Waiting screwed up the plan of *Get to her car and crank the AC.* Waiting gave her time to think.

This was a poor time to think. No good could come of it.

By the time the attendant rescued her car and handed her her keys, she was practicing every deep breathing exercise she knew and a couple she'd made up on the fly.

She slid into the front seat of her beloved hunter-green Mini, and when the air conditioning, ancient but loyal, kicked in, the tears threatened again.

Next step: drive home.

It would have been an easy step except for the blurring tears and overall distraction, which meant that as she eased the Mini down the tight, narrow turns of the garage, she might have just drifted the tiniest bit toward the center, and when the driver of the car zooming up the ramp leaned on their horn, she probably jerked to the right a little too suddenly.

The fender of her car slammed into the steel post looming out of the concrete, placed to point drivers down the ramp. She hadn't been going fast, but the sudden jolting stop still had a whiplash effect, and her head bounced off the headrest, making the world spin for a moment.

The crunching of metal made her stomach lurch.

The other driver zoomed past, and if Luanna hadn't been such a positive person, she was sure she would've seen the driver flashing her the bird.

Not terribly charitable, but maybe they were having a worse day than she was.

Luanna rested her forehead against the steering wheel. Not likely.

Especially not when she tried to drive away, and her wheels wouldn't turn.

Okay, this was now officially the Worst. Day. Ever.

Luanna decided to blame the blouse.

Chapter 2

The only tiny positive factor to Luanna's day was that it was a Monday, which was Chloe's day off from the restaurant.

Hearing her best friend's voice on the phone saying of course she'll come and pick Luanna up, don't you worry, nearly sent Luanna into another bout of tears.

Chloe was there for her when the tow truck arrived and the driver had to hammer on the poor Mini to get the fender away from the tire so that the car could be coasted down the ramp to the truck outside.

In fact, Chloe was the one who stood at the curve in the ramp and directed cars so nobody had a head-on collision, while Luanna waited outside (in the shade of a shop awning, clutching the cold bottle of water Chloe had brought for her) for the tow truck.

And because Chloe was constitutionally incapable of not taking care of everyone around her, Chloe was also the one who insisted on stopping at the grocery store on the way home to pick up the fixings for margaritas (although she offered to get bourbon).

Luanna stayed in the Nissan and indulged in a brief bout of weeping, partly in gratitude.

She was finished and powdering her nose by the time Chloe crossed the parking lot again. Chloe, her curly dark hair piled on her head, her short, curvy form poured into a sleeveless white-with-red-polka-dots sundress, was a force of nature, and Luanna adored her.

"When you called to say you were leaving work, I was afraid you were sick," Chloe admitted as she eased her new-to-her car onto the 405 freeway. She and Luanna had driven the Mini from Boston to Los Angeles, but now they both had to drive to work. (Well, until today, that was.) Traffic was moving, but a bit slow; lunchtime in Los Angeles, yippee. "I'm so glad you're not sick. Sandrine's been reading WebMD—God only knows why—and if she found out you were sick, you know she'd quarantine us. And then forget that she did it, knowing her."

That choked a laugh out of Luanna, because Chloe wasn't really exaggerating all that much. Sandrine Moss, on whose estate they lived, was what Chloe termed "fruit-bat crazy." (Although Chloe had been trying to break herself of that habit, because she was engaged to Sandrine's older brother, Brand Mossiman. While Brand might not disagree with the description, refraining was the polite thing to do.)

In truth, Sandrine was a sweetheart. A little nutty, sure, but deep down she had a heart of gold. When you were one of the highest-paid actresses in Hollywood, you had a right to be a little eccentric.

Luanna was from the South: eccentric was practically what you aspired to be.

She'd already told Chloe about being fired—Chloe also already knew about Ray's proclivities and Luanna's side job, although she didn't know the other men Luanna made women's wear for—and about how her car insurance would be shooting up thanks to her little fender bender.

"So how's your day been so far?" she asked, deflecting Chloe away from being sympathetic and helpful. Luanna didn't think she could take much more of that.

They were going slowly enough that Chloe could take her hands off the wheel and fling them into the air.

"Sandrine called at four a.m. because she forgot about the time difference, wanting to give some wedding suggestions." Chloe made a sound, something like a strangled moan. From that noise alone, Luanna figured Chloe might need the margaritas as much as she did.

"What now?" Luanna asked.

"She wanted to talk about the wedding theme," Chloe said, and Luanna was pretty sure her friend was clenching her teeth. "We haven't even decided whether to have it here or in Rhode Island, but Sandrine's already talked to some friend of hers, Valerie, who's some sort of socialite party planner. There was talk of clowns." She drew in a deep breath through her nose. "I do not want clowns at my wedding. The idea of clowns at my wedding just makes me want to elope."

"You don't have to have clowns at your wedding," Luanna said, projecting as much *soothing* as she could. "Sandrine will understand."

"Oh, I know she will, in the end," Chloe said. "I just wasn't ready for the clown suggestion at effing four in the morning. And I know I have an enormous family and all, but I guess I never thought my wedding would be so…enormous. Or complicated."

"Your wedding should be what you want it to be," Luanna said. "Big or small." Southern weddings tended to be complicated, and while Luanna loved the dramatic aspect of them, that didn't mean it was what Chloe wanted.

More's the pity. Luanna was on Sandrine's side about this one.

Well, within reason. She was kind of horrified about clowns, too.

"You're right, of course." Chloe sighed, but she was smiling. "After that call, I had about five seconds when I thought about eloping to Vegas. We'd never do it—weddings should involve your families, and the estate really is a dream venue. It's just challenging at times."

"Darlin', just give me a heads-up if I have to make spangly Elvis jumpsuits for everybody," Luanna said.

Chloe snorted as she took the freeway exit. "It'll never happen. For one thing, I am way too short to rock an Elvis jumpsuit."

Now they were on the shaded, quiet streets of Beverly Hills, home to the stars who were Really Stars and had more money than sense.

They stopped at the ornate, twisty wrought-iron gates, and Luanna looked out at the tall, leafy, black cottonwood trees with their rough, gray bark, similar enough to the poplars of Louisiana that they made her a little homesick.

"Oh, dear sweet Lord in heaven," Luanna said.

Chloe punched in the gate code and pulled her head back in. "What's wrong?"

"I can*not* tell my parents about this. About any of this."

Chloe patted her hand and put the car in gear. "Don't worry, sweetheart. You'll have a new job before you know it."

"I don't want to think about it anymore," Luanna admitted. "Not for the rest of today, at least."

"Perfect," Chloe said. "We're going to have our own personal spa day." She pointed out the window at the Arabian Nights fantasy of the estate pool and cabana. "We'll lounge by the pool, sit in the hot tub, drink margaritas, and convince Lance to make us something spectacular and decadent to eat."

Actually, what sounded even better was stripping off all her sticky clothes and diving into the cool blue water of the pool. Except other people lived on the estate, so Luanna knew it behooved her to actually put on a bathing suit first.

"Didn't Lance ban you from the kitchen?" Luanna asked.

Chloe rolled her dark eyes. "It was a misunderstanding."

The whole reason they lived on the estate—Luanna still in the guest house, and Chloe recently almost-completely-moved into the gatehouse where Brand lived—was that Chloe had been Sandrine's personal chef.

Well, to be honest, Sandrine had kind of blackmailed Chloe into being her personal chef. Semantics.

But when Chloe got the chance at her dream job, working at M. DesJardins' new restaurant, Sandrine had graciously released her from her contract and promptly hired a startled Lance, who'd helped as a sous chef a couple of times.

Young Lance, still wet behind the ears, with his tattoos and piercings and bad-boy swaggering, hadn't seemed the type to put up with Sandrine's admittedly wacky eating habits (which changed on a near-daily basis), but he'd settled in surprisingly well.

It had just taken Chloe a little while to get used to the fact that Sandrine's kitchen was no longer "her" kitchen.

Still, Sandrine never minded when Lance made a little extra food for his friends, because they were her friends, too.

Luanna shook her head. Friends with *the* Sandrine Moss. Who would've thunk it?

If Sandrine weren't on location in Romania, she'd probably have joined them for drinks by the pool.

She would even have brought them all tiaras to wear. Sandrine did like her tiaras.

Chloe pulled up in front of the guest house. "Go change into something more comfortable. I'll do the same and be back in a few minutes."

"You know you still have clothes here, right?" Luanna said as she got out, her purse and the bag of margarita fixings in hand.

"Yeah, I know, I'm sorry. Thank God Brand and I are going to look for a bigger place after the wedding. This living in two places is driving me a little bonkers." Chloe sighed. "*É o que é.*"

It is what it is. Luanna had learned that much Portuguese because it was Chloe's mantra.

Chloe pulled away and Luanna bent to scritch Evenrude behind the ears. The corgi was on a long lead so she could get from the shaded, relatively cool patio around to the grassy area on the side of the cottage to do her business. The two estate peacocks, Brad and George, who had some sort of platonic ménage romance with Evenrude, dozed on the lawn chairs.

The guest cottage was about three times as big as the apartment Luanna and Chloe had shared when they first moved to LA, and it was a hell of a lot nicer, too. Luanna kicked off her shoes by the front door and let the gushy-soft hunter-green Berber carpet perform better pressure-point massage than any shiatsu master. She set the liquor store plastic bag on the coffee table—a faux-distressed off-white piece with a glass top that was the farthest from Luanna's style, but Sandrine had decorated—next to the cereal bowl she'd neglected to put away this morning.

She took two steps toward her small bedroom, one of two in the place (she'd turned Chloe's old room into a sewing studio), and stopped dead in her tracks, quivering like a hound dog who'd sniffed out a coon.

Sandrine might be a friend, but Luanna was living rent-free in her guest house, a situation that had come about when Chloe worked for Sandrine. Chloe no longer worked for Sandrine, and was planning to move off the estate entirely, which left Luanna with no real reason to be mooching off Sandrine.

So on top of everything else, she might have to find a place to live, too.

She swore she heard an audible *chomp* and a swish of air as the alligator just missed chowing down on her ass.

She turned back, twisted the top off the tequila, and took a long swig.

Then she peeled off her unlucky, sweaty, evil blouse and tossed it in the direction of the kitchen trash.

*

Several months later, things were not better.

Things were *dire*.

But it was New Year's Eve, and she was determined to enjoy it.

She got to the party late—it had been relatively cheaper to fly on New Year's Eve, so the shuttle from LAX dropped her off at the estate close to 11 p.m. She quickly dropped her bags in the guest house, refreshed her makeup, and slipped into a glittery silver, low-necked top that did wonders for her cleavage and clung to her curves. She paired it with black capri pants and silver slip-on ballet-type shoes, because the festivities were being held outside, around the pool area.

Just a casual get-together for Sandrine and Ray and fifty or so of their closest friends, although Brand had friends in the area, too, and Chloe had invited a few people from work.

Luanna would've mentioned it to some of her co-workers—if she'd had a job, that is.

She shook her head and flicked her fingers to release the negative energy.

New Year's Eve. A time for celebration. A time to reboot and start fresh, dammitall.

She stepped out onto the patio. Cool air brushed her bare arms, but there would be heat lamps around the pool, and body heat, and hot food and warming alcohol.

Evenrude gazed up at her with hopeful, liquid eyes, and she dropped to her knees to hug her stupid, lovable Welsh corgi.

"No, you can't come with me, darlin'," she explained, scratching behind Evenrude's ears. "Too many people to trip over you—and we can't have you y'all getting loose again."

She tried not to feel guilty for being in Louisiana for the holidays when Evenrude decided to go frolicking with the peacocks…and forgot she couldn't fly like the peacocks, which meant she'd ended up in the cactus garden. As in, cactus spines in *her*. Chloe and Brand had rushed her to the emergency vet, and Evenrude was pretty much already all healed up.

Still, Luanna felt something awful for not being there.

"You celebrate here with Brad and George," she added.

Brad the peacock fanned out his tail upon hearing his name. George chose to scream, and Luanna screamed and fell back on her ass.

"Dammit, George." She stood up, checked to make sure her capris were fine. "I'll be bringing back a treat for Evenrude"—the corgi thumped her tail against the tile—"and Brad, but not for you, you loud bastard."

George made an annoyed clucking noise and fluttered up to the back of a lawn chair.

Luanna gave Evenrude one last affectionate rub and headed to the party.

The noise greeted her before anything else: a frothy champagne bubble of voices, the big-band swing music from an incredibly good sound system.

Then lights. Strings of fairy lights draped everywhere, creating a magical sparkle on the Arabian Nights fantasy of the cabana, all brightly colored tile and minarets.

She spotted Chloe and Brand, headed their way. Chloe squealed and ran up to hug her, almost knocking her off her feet. Chloe might be five-foot-nothing, but she made up for it with enthusiasm.

Brand had his cell phone to his ear, giving someone the gate code, so Chloe grabbed her arm and dragged her a few steps away.

"I'm *so* glad you're back," Chloe said. "How was Louisiana? How's your family?"

Luanna had promised herself she wouldn't complain, wouldn't even think about it all, not on New Year's Eve, but Chloe's take-care-of-everyone superpower loosened her tongue.

"Oh, dear Lord," she said. "We were all playing cribbage one night, and we'd all had one too many drinks—cribbage just isn't worth it without alcohol—and Grand-mère asked me how Luscious was, and I accidentally might have made some remark that might have led them to figure out I was no longer employed by that lofty establishment."

"What did you say?" Chloe asked, her brown eyes wide with sympathy.

"I said Luscious could kiss my fine Southern ass."

"Oh," Chloe said. "Oops."

"*Oops* is right." Luanna closed her eyes, trying not to remember everybody's faces. "So of course they spent the rest of the time trying to convince me to come home, that there were perfectly good design jobs in Baton Rouge. My family is exceptionally good at guilt."

"Yours and mine both, sister." Chloe hugged her again. "Come on, let's get you some champagne—although whisky is traditional on New Year's Eve, if you want something stronger. Are you hungry? There's a ton of food."

"I can manage to get myself food, darlin'." Luanna smiled, loving how much her friend loved to make everyone feel at home.

"I know, but I thought I'd check to make sure we weren't running out of—"

"You don't work here anymore," Luanna reminded her.

"But Lance—"

"I'll wager you dollars to doughnuts he's doing just fine. You go find your sweetie. It's bad luck if you miss kissing him at the stroke of midnight."

"Yeah, where did he go off to?" Chloe left in search of Brand.

Lance was, in fact, competently dealing with the buffet of food in the outdoor kitchen, which was almost the size of the guest house. Heated serving dishes lined up on white-cloth-covered tables, with cold food arranged on the granite prep space. Candles in punched-metal lanterns gave the covered area a cozy feel.

"Hey," Luanna said, grabbing a plate.

"Hey yourself, gorgeous," Lance said, winking. Flirting was like breathing for him, and Luanna was used to it. His spiky hair, normally bleach-tipped, glowed electric blue in the lantern-light. Apparently that was his idea of dressing to the party theme. He wore his usual tight jeans and T-shirt combo; Luanna doubted anyone would ever talk him into chef's whites.

Something smelled both delicious and familiar, making her stomach rumble even as it panged for the South she'd just left. "Hoppin' John!" she exclaimed, making a beeline for the pork, beans, and greens dish.

"Sandrine, via Olive, gave me a list of traditional New Year's Eve dishes from around the world," Lance said, mentioning Sandrine's extraordinarily efficient and unflappable personal assistant (she'd have to be, working for Sandrine, who changed plans faster than it took to drive a lap at Talladega). He pointed. "Hoppin' John and cornbread from the South. Fresh fruit is Mexican, although the pomegranate is…Turkish, I think. Noodles are an Asian custom, big surprise."

"What's this?" Luanna pointed her fork at something that did *not* smell good.

"Pickled herring," Lance said. "A tradition of people from the land of crazy."

Luanna filled her plate with the edible food, then snagged a glass of champagne. It was cool and tart and bubbly, and she wasn't at all surprised to need a second glass almost immediately. Wisely, she then went in search of a place to eat that wasn't next to the champagne fountain.

She found herself smiling again. The food was tasty, the mood was infectious, and the champagne helped numb the nagging worry in her belly.

Fact was, she still hadn't found a job. Her car insurance had gone up, only for her car to be pronounced unfixable. (Brand, who fixed classic cars as a hobby, said the suspension was borked. Well, he'd used a more technical term, but the bottom line was that fixing the Mini would cost well more than the car was worth.) Chloe said she didn't need to be paid back for Evenrude's emergency vet, because Evenrude was practically her dog, too, but Luanna's parents had taught her never to owe money to friends. Speaking of parents, she'd racked up her credit card flying home for the holidays.

None of the design firms had openings. Or it was possible Hernando from HR was adopting a frosty tone when anyone called about a reference. Fact was, she didn't *have* any good current references, because Luscious had been her first real design job. Her favorite professor had retired to a small village in Italy and was hard to get hold of.

She'd even applied for a spot on *Project Runway*, but hadn't heard back from them. Yet. There was always hope.

A busboy swept away her plate and cutlery, and she went back for a third glass of champagne—this one she intended to save for midnight, which she was pretty sure would be soon. She'd left her phone in the guest house, and there were no clocks out here in fantasy pool land.

Rank the positives, that's what her daddy would say. Okay. She was healthy, her family was healthy, Evenrude had recovered. She had never been convicted of a felony. She had all her own teeth. And…

And oh, my goodness gracious, but that was a fine specimen of manhood also reaching for champagne.

Chapter 3

Luanna looked past the champagne fountain to the man standing across from her, and her body fizzed as if she'd been dunked in champagne.

She'd like to dunk *him* in champagne…

Dark, nearly black hair, neatly cut. Swarthy and Latin-looking, but with intensely blue eyes instead of the deep brown the rest of his coloring suggested. His jaw—a strong jaw, but not Superman-square—sported a hint of stubble, not like he hadn't shaved, but like his beard was just that determined. A small gold hoop earring glinted in the lantern light, making him look like a tasteful pirate.

Luanna had always been fond of pirates.

His button-down shirt was deep red, and while Luanna's fashion-oriented brain would have normally picked out the price range, the fiber content, and which big-name designer had been dimly imitated in its creation, she couldn't get beyond the way it draped across his broad shoulders and how great the color was against his dusky skin. The sleeves were rolled up. He had muscular arms, dusted with dark hair.

Yo ho ho, y'all.

She gestured with her champagne flute. "Having trouble choosing?" Along with his own champagne, he held a short glass of what looked like a fine whisky.

He glanced down as if he'd forgotten he was a two-fisted drinker. Then he laughed, a sound like the honeyed whisky she'd had in a British pub once. "Oh, this? I was planning to be the first-footer. Not that there's a doorway to come through, of course."

"That's a Scottish custom, right?" she asked. "It's good luck if a dark-haired man is the first person through the door after midnight, especially if he's got whisky."

"You're correct. I knew a Scottish exchange student in college who taught me the mysteries of her lands." He winked, and it was a completely different wink from Lance's.

Lance was young, cocky, and even flirted with middle-aged, married, scary-efficient Olive. Hell, Lance practically flirted with Evenrude. It was just automatic for him.

Luanna's pirate, on the other hand, winked in a way that made her feel as if she were the only person at the party. That wink was for her and her alone, and it was confident, not cocky. It promised things…seductive, naughty things the pirate knew he could deliver.

Well. Whew. She resisted the urge to fan herself. If she fanned herself, she might very well accidentally flutter her eyelashes, too.

Luanna had no place in her life right now for a relationship. It would just complicate things that were already way too messy and uncertain.

As much as her body yearned in that direction, she was probably too jet-lagged and in too much of a state of upheaval to even invite him back to the guest house for a fun romp.

But she liked meeting new people, and he seemed like a smart, mouth-wateringly gorgeous (stop that) guy, and the perfect distraction on New Year's Eve so she didn't think about how her life felt like the ground did when an earthquake rolled through.

"I'm Luanna," she said, holding out her hand.

He set down the whisky and took it. "Derek," he said. "I'm friends with Brand Mossiman."

She laughed. "Get out," she said. "My best friend, Chloe, is Brand's fiancé. You and Brand went to UCLA together, right? I've heard some stories."

"Only the good parts are true. Besides, it was a long time ago."

She smiled what she hoped was a knowing, slightly flirtatious grin. Given the combination of jet lag, exhaustion, and just enough champagne that without the first two factors she'd just be feeling pleasantly relaxed, it was probably either demented or leering, but with luck he'd take it as teasing. "Part of what I heard about you involved a guys' night out last week. You'd just gotten back from…somewhere."

"I'd been doing a lot of travel for work, and then went home to New Mexico for the holidays." He looked grave, briefly, but then the pirate gleam returned to those intense blue eyes. "As for the guys' night, only a little mayhem resulted and everyone got home safely."

"Nothin' wrong with a little mayhem, sugar. No worse than Chloe and I would be if we had a few months to catch up on. But since you're friends with my best friend's fiancé, I feel entitled to tease you."

"Well, it does make us practically cousins," Derek said, and crooked his arm. "Shall we find a place to watch the fireworks?"

She didn't want to think of him as a cousin. Unless you counted kissing cousins. That, she could get behind.

No, she reminded herself, you have no time for such foolishness.

Her body ignored her brain's reminders, to the point of blowing a virtual raspberry.

They settled on the low, wide, brightly tiled wall that bordered the pool area. It wasn't high enough to keep anyone out (except maybe Evenrude, who along with having short legs was a bit on the stout side), but rather served as a visual delineation and a place to put towels and sunglasses and other swimming paraphernalia.

"Actually," Derek said, swirling the whisky in the lowball glass before setting it down next to him, "I'm also celebrating tonight. Our Kickstarter campaign funded this evening, which means my production company is officially making a movie."

"Well, congratulations to you!" Luanna held out her flute, and they clinked and sipped. "Tell me more." Gorgeous *and* an entrepreneur. She was a sucker for the combination of sexy and brainy.

"Well, Graham and I are producers, and I wrote the screenplay," he said. His eyes unfocused a little. Luanna recognized the look: Chloe got the same expression when she was planning a menu. "It's about the Civil War."

"Well, butter my butt and call me a biscuit!" Luanna said. "I'm all over the Civil War like white on rice." She pointed a thumb at herself. "Louisiana, born and bred."

"I had a feeling, from your accent," Derek said. His smile made her insides fizz again. "But enough about me. What do *you* do, friend of a friend's fiancée?"

"I'm not even going to try to parse that," she said, shaking her head. "I'm in fashion."

It wasn't a lie, not exactly. She *was* in fashion. It wasn't as if she said she *worked* in fashion. With any luck, that would be true very soon. Fingers, toes, etc., crossed.

"Huh," Derek murmured, half to himself. "Brand said something to Graham about—"

But before Luanna could learn what the menfolk had been chatting about, everyone else shouted "Ten!"

They were not, in fact, judging ice dancing. The countdown to midnight had begun.

Luanna and Derek stood. He was close enough to her that she could feel the heat of him, even though they weren't touching. He smelled like the sun-kissed ocean, and she wondered if he tasted salty.

Stop that.

"Seven!"

"I believe it's also a tradition," Derek said, "and good luck to kiss someone at midnight."

"Four!"

Luanna turned to him. They locked eyes. It seemed to take a long time for the other partygoers to shout "Three!" and "Two!" and, in fact, she thought they'd never get to one.

She didn't have a place in her life right now for this kind of involvement.

But she really, really wanted Derek to kiss her.

The fireworks banged and popped and whistled, but she had no eyes for the multicolored display of lights.

Derek took her hand in his, still watching her, and raised it to his lips.

And then this rakish pirate of a man kissed the back of her hand, gallant and yet undeniably the sexiest dayum thing anyone had ever done to her.

It was just the press of his lips against her flesh, but he took his time, never breaking his gaze.

There was that promise again. The promise of what those lips would feel like elsewhere on her body.

Luanna quivered; her legs started to melt out from under her.

Screw her uncertain life.

He lowered their hands but didn't let go yet.

"Happy New Year, Luanna," he said, a hint of a smile on his lips. "Here's to a sensational start to the year."

Before she could say anything, someone shouted "Happy New Year!" and Brand walked up accompanied by a stockily built red-haired guy—stocky in a solid, appealing way but not built right for the skinny black jeans he sported—with impressive sideburns that were either straight out of the nineteenth century or the latest hipster thing, a faux-vintage sports coat several shades more red than his hair, and an affable face with a smile that wasn't hipster-sardonic at all. (The empty cocktail glass he gripped might have had something to do with the warmth of that grin.) Kind of cute, but Luanna itched to redress him in something perhaps less fashionable but more flattering. A guy like him needed a subdued, classic look to offset the vibrant hair and the square build. Then he might turn a few heads in a good way, not get second looks because his outfit was just a bit off.

"Oh, hey," Brand said to Luanna, his wire-framed glasses glinting in the flicker of a nearby lamp. "You've met Derek. This is Graham. The two of them are doing a movie and they're looking for an assistant costume designer, and I was going to introduce you."

She wasn't a film costume designer, Luanna wanted to protest. She worked in haute couture fashion. Or she should be. Would be, soon, surely.

But her brain refused to connect with her vocal cords, and she wasn't sure she could even form words, much less coherent sentences. All thanks to that seemingly innocuous, but really oh so erotic, kiss on the back of her hand.

She took a sip of champagne to wet her suddenly dry mouth, trying to ignore her suddenly wet panties.

One: it was a job offer, in a barren wasteland of zero job offers.

Two: it would mean she'd get to work with sexy pirate Derek.

What little was left of her brain told her that the answer really was a no-brainer.

"Um, okay," she said, and gulped the rest of her champagne.

"Stellar!" Graham said. "So, we won't start filming for a few months, but—"

"Now, now," Derek interrupted, plucking the flute from Luanna's hand. "This is a party, not the time for work details. We can talk about things like timeline and salary later."

A white-shirted member of the wait staff swung by with a tray of champagne, and Derek replaced Luanna's empty glass with a full one.

He raised his own glass. "I would, however, like to propose a toast to Luanna joining the *Magnolia Road* team!"

Well, if they were going to drink on it, it must be official.

The champagne was crisp and cold, the night air was soft, and laughter drifted across the lawn and pool area. She might just have a new job. She was flirting with—and possibly going to be working with—an incredibly sexy and charming man. What else could she want?

A conversation about fashion and costuming, apparently.

It was her own fault, really. Well, the fault of jet lag and the champagne she couldn't stop sipping, and the distraction of Derek that made her giddy and weak-legged every time she caught his eye.

"Derek says the movie's about the Civil War?" she said to Graham. "I suppose you could say that's one of my specialties, given that I'm from the South—from a long line of proud Rebels."

"Excellent!" Graham said, knocking his own champagne flute into hers so enthusiastically, she feared the glasses might shatter. Thankfully they did not. "You'll be working under Yancy McMillan. She's mostly done TV—she worked on *The Young Vikings* and *Bloody Revolutionaries*, so she's totally up with period pieces."

Luanna had heard of the latter show—vampires in the Revolutionary War. She resolved to stream some episodes of both shows and check Yancy's credits on imdb.com.

She knew nothing about costuming for film and TV, but it sounded like now was the right time to get going on some learning.

Brand said something about going to find Chloe and escaped. Luanna didn't blame him. He didn't care about costumes unless they were part of the special effects he created.

Graham was still talking. "You're on Pinterest, right? I'll share my Pinterest board of ideas with you. Yancy's added a few things, too. Some sketches, some examples... I'm envisioning a specific look. The movie's a romance—"

"It's not a romance," Derek interrupted, in the world-weary tone of someone who's said the same thing a thousand times but still isn't being heard. "It's a period piece that includes a romance."

"Thomas and Adelia fall in love," Graham said, in the world-weary tone of someone who's defended his position before. "So the costumes... they have to be sexy, you know? The audience has to understand what they see in each other."

"Civil War costumes are terribly sexy," Luanna agreed. "Those tight uniform pants." She fanned herself. "Lord a-mercy."

"And cleavage," Graham said.

"Well, not so much," Luanna said. "It was more about the nipped-in waists from the corsets, the wide sweep of the skirt...the flash of a forbidden ankle..." She smiled dreamily, lost in the fantasy of crinoline-wide skirts belling side to side as ladies danced.

"And cleavage," Graham repeated. "That's what corsets are for."

Derek muttered something about character development and not all attraction being purely sexual.

Through her champagne-hazed state—she wasn't walking on a slant, but her head was surely bubbling like her drinks—Luanna realized this was not the time nor the place to debate the issue with Graham, who very well might be signing her paychecks soon. But her champagne-hazed state meant she couldn't stop the next words that insisted on fleeing from her lips: "Well, bless your heart."

He wouldn't know most Southerners considered that to be less than complimentary, right?

Before Graham could react, or she could clap her hands over her mouth in horror, Derek said, "There's something else I'd like to talk to you about, Luanna."

"Oh?" Please let it be sex.

"I write and host a monthly show about societal trends throughout history—how ideas and concepts and mores changed over the centuries, and what caused the changes. Or how things haven't changed. Did you know that in early Ireland, they complained about the youths wearing baggy pants and their hair in their eyes?"

"No, I did not." Even though the topic hadn't been about sex, it was still kind of fascinating. She'd become far too numb to the ridiculous reality shows on TV—and the ridiculous reality of the Hollywood elite—that someone talking about actual research and scholarship was more fascinating than it ought to be.

Especially when it came from the lips of a hot pirate.

"Well," Derek said. "I'm trying to pull something together about men's clothing trends throughout history…" He waved his hands to indicate the idea wasn't fully formed yet. "It sounds as though you might be able to give me some great information."

"That sounds right up my bayou," Luanna agreed. A warmth suffused her belly. She could sense they had things they could talk about, which was always a good thing.

"I was hoping you'd say that," Derek said, and the warmth in her belly moved south at the sight of his smile. "I'm also hoping you'll join me on a little tradition of mine."

"Oh, God," Graham said. "Here we go again. I'm outta here." He headed in the direction of the bar.

"Sorry," Derek said. "He's had to put up with me on New Year's Eve before."

"Now I'm really intrigued," Luanna said.

"Did you know," Derek said, "that the tradition of making resolutions on New Year's Eve can be dated back to the Roman times?"

"I did not," Luanna said, fascinated.

"Every year, I make it a habit of asking people on New Year's Eve what their resolutions are," he said, and held out his arm. "Would you like to join me on this quest?"

She tucked her hand in the warm crook of his elbow. "Let me pick up a bottle of water on the way, and I'd be delighted to accompany you."

Chapter 4

$\mathcal{L}$ate the next morning—almost afternoon, really, given the hour when Luanna, Chloe, and Brand had staggered across the estate to their respective homes—Luanna headed back to the mansion, a spring in her step because she knew Derek would still be there. About twenty guests had stayed the night rather than drive the LA freeways home, and so brunch was on the agenda.

The temperature was in the low 60s, with a briskness in the air. The winter desert climate was a nice change from Louisiana where, even at similar temperatures at Christmas last month, the humidity had been ridiculous. The air still smelled a little like sulfur from last night's fireworks.

Evenrude strained at her leash, the back half of her body wiggling as she wagged her tail even as she plowed ahead with excitement at all the new smells in the world. "New" as in "she'd forgotten them overnight," but still, Luanna had missed her beloved corgi and didn't mind the workout.

She'd tried on and rejected a dozen outfits, which wasn't her usual method of operation. Because she worked in fashion, she was always thinking about it, even subconsciously—which meant she was decisive when it came time to choose what to wear. But today she felt like a giddy schoolgirl, excited to catch a glimpse of her crush in the halls. She'd finally decided on a gray knit dress and a long, swingy burgundy cardigan, topped with a chiffon scarf looped several times around her neck, and her sparkly silver flats from the night before. Casual, comfortable, and nice to her curves.

When she got to the mansion, she left Evenrude tied to a long lead on the side patio, then headed inside.

Luanna hadn't been in Sandrine's massive home for a month, maybe two, but in that time, Sandrine had completely redecorated the main living room. Replacing the stark white with pops of color that had been so trendy yesterday were shades of grass green and copper, with bamboo and Asian accents.

"Matcha green tea," said Olive, appearing at Luanna's right elbow. "It's all the rage right now; full of antioxidants. Eleventh-century Japanese Zen priests drank it. There's a whole ceremonial brewing process. Sandrine is very committed. Even Ray thinks it's making his workouts more efficient…as long as there's a medium-rare steak involved."

Olive said all of this in the patient, nonjudgmental tones of someone who worked for an impulsive, unpredictable starlet who changed her dietary needs, décor, wardrobe, and vacation plans faster than designer shoes fly out of a store during a half-price sale.

If Luanna had less self-confidence, she might've felt overwhelmed by a woman both better-put-together and better-organized on New Year's morning than, well, almost everyone. But in truth, Luanna was a little in awe of Olive.

Plus she was hilarious once you got a couple of shots of tequila into her.

Although she was in her early fifties, Olive (pronounced Ah-*leave*, and nobody, not even Sandrine, argued with that) Welsh had the smooth, soft skin of a woman half her age. "Hazelnut" was how Chloe had first described Olive's skin tone to Luanna, because Chloe always described things in relation to food—but it was apt. Rich, dark hazelnut. Short and shaped like something resembling a fireplug, Olive had impeccable taste when it came to clothes that flattered her figure, tending toward suits in dark jewel tones. Today's, in fact, looked a lot like Directoire Blue.

Luanna wondered whether she'd ever again find a job in which knowing the colors of the year would be required, or even useful.

She was also barely listening to Olive's explanation of Sandrine's decorating choices, because she was trying to process what was *happening* in the ceremonial Zen tea room.

She counted twelve or thirteen guests sitting around Sandrine's living room, each attached to a nearby portable IV unit by lines leading to their arms. A petite young woman with red hair in a cute pixie cut, wearing carnation-pink scrubs, moved among them, checking the bags of clear solution.

"Lord have mercy," Luanna said. "What…?" She flapped a hand, unable to continue.

"IV vitamin drip for hangovers," Olive said. "It's all the rage right now."

"Full of antioxidants?"

"And it's liver cleansing. All those nasty toxins."

"Isn't it the liver's *job* to cleanse the body of toxins?"

Olive just looked at her, and they shared a quiet bonding moment.

"Well," Luanna said finally, "Sandrine certainly spares no expense."

Olive gave a hint of a snort. She was far too polite to rip out a real one, especially when it came to commentary about her employer. "Did you *see* the fireworks last night? This is nothing."

To Luanna's relief, Derek wasn't one of the guests partaking in the IV cure. Not that she judged them, really, but she wasn't sure she could have a meaningful relationship with someone who bought into the latest fad like that.

Then again, what was she doing, thinking about meaningful relationships? Complicated life right now, she reminded herself. Too messy and uncertain. Plus, unless last night had been an alcohol-induced hallucination, she was going to be working with him. (For him? She wasn't even sure how the chain of command laid out.)

Well, logic could just take a big ol' jump off a short pier, if her emotions had any say in the matter. And right now they did. Her stomach gave a little happy jump as she spotted Derek across the room, up a few steps in the dining room.

He turned his head slightly away from the person he was talking to, caught her eye, and smiled, and her insides turned to mush.

He wore a soft-looking, long-sleeved cotton Henley in a dark blue that was almost purple, and faded jeans. Both molded to his body as if they'd been custom made for him, accentuating his trim physique. She imagined the blue of his shirt highlighted the blue of his eyes.

She headed across the living room, but before she could get to the three shallow steps, a mountainous shadow crossed her path.

Ray Stark. Sandrine's partner, American Action Movie Awards winner several times over, and Luanna's client. One of her very, very confidential clients.

"Hey, pretty lady," Ray rumbled his personal name for her. "Happy New Year."

She let herself be swept up in a generous hug. Ray looked like a cross between Vin Diesel and Brad Pitt. Muscular, bald, and a Midwestern farm boy with the sweet personality to go with it…and a closet cross-dresser. Luanna was one of the few who knew his closely guarded secret, which was that he loved the way satin and silk swished and thought it was a damn shame only women were supposed to be able to enjoy it.

Luanna knew because she was his personal seamstress. Him, and a number of other high-powered Hollywood men who required absolute discretion.

"Happy New Year to you, too!" she squeaked, because he didn't know his own strength.

He set her back on her feet. "Let's get together soon. I have a couple of…requests."

"Absolutely," she said, because not only did she love the challenge of making striking and feminine women's wear for a man shaped like a tank, but because he paid well and she wanted to pay Chloe back for Evenrude's vet bills. "Have Olive text me your next available time."

"You're a peach," Ray said. He lowered his voice and added, "Meet me in the kitchen later. Lance promised to save some bacon."

Her stomach made a noise that agreed bacon was an excellent idea. "See you there," she said.

Ray moved away, and she caught Derek's eye again. He smiled, and with weak knees she finished crossing the living room, went up the steps, and he held out his hand, drew her closer. His hand was warm, and he gave hers a small squeeze. She liked touching him. A lot.

"Good morning," he said. His voice sounded a little rough, a little raspy, undeniably sexy.

"Good afternoon, almost," she said. "I didn't mean to interrupt you."

"You didn't," he said, and indeed, the two people he'd been talking to had moved away, joined another couple. "I'm glad you're here. How can you look so rested? I swear, you're glowing."

"I had jet lag," she said. "I barely remember making it to the bed. I slept hard. You?"

A wicked smile kissed his lips, and she realized what her words could mean and what he was thinking. She willed herself not to blush, even though she felt the heat, pooling down low. Then she willed herself not to wriggle her hips. Mmm.

"I slept…very well, thank you."

The "thank you" could mean many things, she decided, and she liked all of them.

"Not going to partake of the latest hangover cure?" he asked, gesturing down into the living room.

She laughed. "No, I'm going old-school: coffee strong enough to strip the hair off a hunting hound and the greasiest breakfast known to mankind, which is hopefully what Lance is putting together for the few of us who don't view 'fat' as a four-letter word."

"I like your style," Derek said. "Coffee's over there."

He pointed to a cappuccino machine that looked as if it belonged in a Starbucks. (It probably did.) Thankfully, it was staffed by a competent-looking young man with purple hair.

"Oh, thank sweet baby Jesus in his cradle," Luanna said, and made a beeline. She'd had a cup of coffee before she'd come over, but it couldn't hold a candle to this magical elixir.

She hadn't realized Derek hadn't let go of her hand until she started moving. Instead of letting go, he followed, his fingers entwining with hers.

Graham appeared out of nowhere, beating them to the coffee station.

"Oh, Luanna, you're here. Good. I talked to Yancy, and of course you'll have to meet with her before we can make the formal offer and sign the paperwork—how does Tuesday sound?"

It sounded as if Graham had had enough coffee already.

"Sounds perfect," she said. "In fact, I'm glad you both didn't wake up and realize you'd made a terrible mistake offering me the job."

She said it while looking at Derek. "I didn't if you didn't," he said, and somehow, she was sure they were no longer talking about the job.

"Not hardly," she said.

She made her coffee order, dropped a couple dollars in the tip jar, and watched the man hand Graham his request and start working on hers.

Then she remembered something. "I checked online, and there's a Civil War reenactment happening in Thousand Oaks in a few weeks. I was thinking we should go and look at the costumes and whatnot."

Derek sketched a bow. "Only if you accompany me, fair lady."

"Why, Mister…goodness, I don't even know your full name."

"Acosta. Derek Santiago Acosta."

"Mister Acosta, I'd love to accompany you. And Graham, you should go, too."

Graham rolled his eyes.

"Yes, you should go," Derek said. "We all will—it'll be fun."

At some point, he'd taken hold of Luanna's hand again, and now he squeezed it gently. Her entire body agreed that *fun* was in the cards, oh yes indeed.

She sipped her espresso to clear her throat as her innards fizzed with delight. "Perfect," she said.

The inclusion of Graham made sense on a professional level. But she suspected the perfection of the day would come from a certain pirate of a man.

*

Derek sat at his desk at Zombie Iguana Productions and stared at everything that needed doing. And did nothing.

The production offices were in an unprepossessing cement building in what passed for an office park in southern California. Long, low structures like storage units, with roll-up doors and shop or warehouse space on one side and offices on the other, all sharing a common parking lot. On one side was a guy who made custom motorcycle windshields; across the way, a guy who rented vintage costumes to movie studios. (He was low on Civil War–era pieces, but he was keeping an eye out.)

Zombie Iguana, in suite 109, was identified only by a small logo on the door, designed by Graham's sister, an artist. A cartoon iguana, wearing ragged clothing, its front claws extended as if it were shambling, its mouth open and tongue half out as if it were moaning "Braaaains!"

There was an open reception/brainstorming area, since they rarely had drop-in visitors and their PA, Rodrigo, served as their receptionist. Right now the walls were covered with whiteboards of schedules and notes and storyboards. The warehouse in back housed equipment, props, extra filing cabinets, and a ten-foot-high statue of their logo, which made children cry. In between was the small office Derek and Graham shared.

Pale blue walls covered with more white boards. Filing cabinets and two wooden desks purchased from an office supply warehouse, and everything permanently infused with the scent of cinnamon and cloves from the chai lattes Graham lived on, because the independent coffee shop was right around the corner and, Derek guessed, Graham was sweet on one of the baristas. He could hear the faint sounds of equipment from the motorcycle windshield shop; thankfully the concrete walls were thick, and if the industrial noise ever bothered them, streaming music was enough to block it out.

Derek had his laptop plugged into his wide desktop monitor, and the screensaver—also the Zombie Iguana logo—taunted him.

This was the problem with being away longer than you expected: everything piled up in your absence. And while he knew it was just a case of *pick one thing and do it*, he couldn't even seem to focus his brain on the *pick one thing* part.

There was a pile of pink phone message slips left by Rodrigo. A stack of scripts in his In Box, even though Zombie Iguana wasn't accepting scripts at this time—they had enough on their plate with *Magnolia Road* and Derek's show, not to mention Derek's new screenplay…which was also nagging at him as a To Do item. That and at least four show episodes in various stages of development.

He'd been able to keep up on email for the most part while he'd been away, but he'd had to shove some correspondence into an Answer Later folder.

This was crazy. He pushed back from the desk, his chair wheels spinning smoothly and silently on the low-pile, blue industrial carpet. The rest of the office might be low budget, but his chair was top of the line. He wasn't taking any chances with non-ergonomic furniture. Too many writing projects to finish in his lifetime.

He wished Rodrigo was the type to have a candy bowl on his reception desk, because he could really go for a Hershey's Kiss or something.

Did that constitute stress eating? In which case, maybe he ought to just accept it and get a burrito from the taco truck next to the coffee shop.

In truth, he didn't *have* to be here.

None of the phone messages were urgent. The unsolicited scripts certainly weren't. He could go home, see if he could revive his half-dead houseplants, and work on the new script, which was the only thing that really called to him right now.

Except…

"Bro," Graham said as he walked into the office, "go home. You don't have to be here."

They'd been friends long enough that Graham could read him well, and vice versa.

"I know. I just kind of—"

"—wanted to be here when Luanna comes in," Graham finished. "I know, I know." He propped his shiny gray low-laced boots on his desk, which—even though he'd worked in the time between Christmas and New Year's—was far more of a mess than Derek's. Although Graham seemed to have a method to his madness. His desk looked like chaos incarnate, but when he needed to put his hands on something, he could, surprisingly fast.

Well, most of the time.

"Well, I *am* a producer on the film we're hiring her for," Derek said, "so technically I should be here for the interview."

"You're so cute when you get huffy," Graham said. "We both know we're hiring Luanna unless Yancy takes some violent dislike to her, and Yancy's not the type to do that. The real question is, do we have to have the sexual-harassment-in-the-workplace lecture?"

Derek felt his hackles rise a moment before he realized Graham was trying to wind him up again. "We probably do," he said. "I have this co-worker who's making inappropriate comments about my love life."

"I have not said one inappropriate thing today," Graham retorted.

"'Today' being the operative word."

"Naturally." Graham swung his feet to the floor, leaned forward. "But seriously, is everything okay? I didn't want to say anything on New Year's Eve, but you still seem off, and taking extra vacation isn't like you…"

"In a weird way, yeah," Derek said, as all the conflicting emotions cascaded over him again. "It's never easy when your parents divorce, but honestly, they're both happier now. I guess I didn't expect the holidays would take so much longer because I had two homes to visit."

It was largely true, and if he were going to unload to anyone, it would be Graham or Brand, his two closest friends. But he came from a long line of people who valued personal privacy—you didn't air your dirty laundry—and a small town where everybody had an opinion, whether the topic was their business or not. He respected his parents' desire for discretion. That his friends knew his parents had recently gotten a divorce was enough. They didn't need the gory details.

The bell on the door jingled, and he heard voices out front: Yancy McMillan's throaty rasp and Luanna Devenaux's sultry drawl.

The latter sound in particular delighted him.

"Y'all didn't tell me how delightful this woman is," Luanna said when she saw Derek and Graham. "We met in the parking lot and I swear we're fast friends already."

She wore a simple linen dress, yellow with red edging and wide red belt, a style he imagined wouldn't look out of place in the 1950s. She'd paired it with red heels and red lipstick, and she looked casual-professional and confident. Her wavy blond hair trailed over one shoulder, and she had a garment bag slung over the other.

Yancy laughed. "Fabric nerds unite!"

She couldn't have made a better contrast to Luanna. A mix of Irish, African-American, and Greek, she had a round face with deep dimples, and today her yarn braids were candy-floss pink and lemon-yellow. She also looked as though she'd emerged from a fifties movie, but in her case, it was *Grease*, with her tight, calf-length pants and sleeveless button-down top, white with blue polka dots, knotted at her waist.

Sitting at the conference table in the front room, they got down to business. Luanna impressed Yancy (and Derek, and probably Graham) by opening the garment bag to reveal a muslin mockup of a Civil War woman's blouse, based on some quick research she'd done over the past couple of days.

"That's phenom," Yancy said. "I don't know Civil War costuming as well as I know other periods, and with being on the home stretch with *Belladonna*, I was worried I wouldn't have time to do the research. Tag, you're it."

"Now, Yance, one of the things I wanted to talk to you about is how period we want to go on this," Graham said. "This is a romance, after all."

"No, it's not," Derek said for what felt like the hundredth time. "It's a period movie with romantic elements."

"So it needs to be a little sexy, you know?" Graham continued, ignoring him. "Like, cleavage."

"I'm pretty sure Civil War–era dresses weren't the cleavage-baring type," Yancy said, and Luanna held up her hand. Without having to look, Yancy high-fived her. How, Derek wondered, had they had time to discuss that in the parking lot? "But we'll find other ways to make it clear they're hot for each other, costuming-wise. Sexiest scene I ever saw was in *The Age of Innocence* when Daniel Day-Lewis unbuttoned Michelle Pfeiffer's glove."

"Oh, lordy, yes." Luanna fanned herself.

Graham looked unconvinced.

Luanna mentioned the Civil War reenactment that was coming up in a few weeks.

"I'll still be embroiled with *Belladonna*, I'm afraid," Yancy said. "In fact…" She glanced at her phone. "Must dash. Hire her, you two."

She hurried out, and Graham pulled the hiring forms from a folder on the table. He didn't pass them to Luanna just yet, though. He stared at her thoughtfully, his lips pursed.

Derek saw the flicker of worry in Luanna's green eyes, but otherwise she stayed composed. He wasn't sure what Graham was up to, but if his partner didn't give Luanna the damn paperwork, they were going to have to go into the back and Have Words.

"I hired Yancy because I trust her vision," Graham said finally. "She doesn't bullshit me. And neither do you." He slid the forms across the table along with a pen. "Welcome to the team. It'll be a few months before we start actual filming. Anybody want coffee? My treat."

"I'm fine, thanks," Luanna said, looking up from the forms with a dazzling smile.

"Um…no, I'm okay," Derek said, distracted.

Graham snorted. "Don't make me give you the lecture," he said, and left.

When Luanna was done, Derek signed the papers and said, "Welcome to Zombie Iguana."

"I've been meaning to ask you…where'd the name Zombie Iguana come from?"

He winced. "It involved a bet. And way too much tequila."

She laughed. "Got it. But it's unique—I like it. Can I see the place? I've never been in a movie production office before. It seems so… Hollywood-exotic."

"Nothing exotic about it," he said. "But sure." A warmth curled in his stomach at the thought of spending more time with her.

In the office, she homed in on the photos in clear plastic slots that affixed with magnets to the filing cabinet next to his desk. "Oh, is this-all your family? Your momma's so pretty, and your daddy looks like an old-time movie star."

He pointed out his sisters—Rosa, in her college graduation gown, and Betsy, posed in front of her brand-spanking-new veterinary practice.

With a jolt, he wondered if he should add a new picture for his mother. After all, she was no longer the long-haired, house-dress-wearing woman in the current photo. Upon coming to the realization that she was, in fact, a lesbian, she'd cast off the traditionally feminine trappings that she'd held to only because it had been expected of her.

Just before Christmas, when Derek had walked into the house she and her partner, Beatrice, shared, he almost hadn't recognized her. Her hair was cropped short, she was wearing a sleeveless white T-shirt, cargo pants, and big stompy boots, and at that particular moment, she was holding a sledgehammer because she'd been knocking down a wall.

He loved his mother, wanted her to be happy no matter what, but he just hadn't been expecting *that* from a woman who, when he was growing up, had confined her redecorating to paint and curtains.

Then again, if he replaced her picture with how she looked now, how did that jive with her need and his father's need for privacy?

Really, the only people who came into the office were Graham and Rodrigo, although Yancy would be in and out once production actually started—the warehouse was big enough to store costumes—as would a few more people. Those people wouldn't know his family from before, though.

It made him sad that his mother had put on a front for so many years. She'd been raised in a traditional family and community, did what was "normal": married a man, wore dresses and makeup, raised a family. The family-raising part she loved, and she had loved his father, too—just not, she'd finally accepted last year, in *that* way.

Even if she'd been heterosexual, why did it matter to anyone but her whether she wore skirts and baked bread, or wore pants and demolished kitchen cabinets?

The whole experience had sent him down a rabbit hole of not only emotion, but ideas and musings on gender roles and clothing. The roles had pretty much stayed the same, up until recently, but the clothing hadn't, necessarily, when it came to the notions of feminine and masculine.

"So, y'all are producing *Magnolia Road*," Luanna said. "Is that it? Like, one thing at a time?"

"Actually, no," Derek said. "Most producers have multiple projects going on in different stages, just like writers. ZI produces the show I write and host—it airs on the ScHis Channel."

"Shizz?"

"ScHis. Science and History. It's a crappy name, I know. A lot of cable packages don't even offer it."

"Well, Sandrine has every channel known to mankind, and the whole estate has access, so I'll be sure to check it out." She smiled. "How exciting!"

"More exciting than living on the estate of one of the top movie stars of the decade?"

She waved a dismissive hand. "Apples and oranges, honey. So, the movie and the TV show."

"And I've just started another screenplay, so we'll produce that if we can pull it together," he said. "There's a lot of steps along the way. One thing at a time. Let's get *Magnolia Road* made first. I'm really glad you're with us on this, Luanna," he added.

For a lot of reasons.

Maybe Graham did need to give him the lecture…

Chapter 5

Contrary to popular belief, it *did* rain in Southern California. For about two weeks in January or February, often a near-constant barrage that closed freeways and flooded canyons.

Derek liked it anyway. Plants got watered, everybody momentarily stopped complaining about drought conditions, and when it was over, it was over.

Now it was indeed over, and the weather was back to relentlessly cheery, the sun bright in a cloudless dome of blue. But the ground couldn't handle the deluge, and was still frantically trying to soak all the moisture in. Thus dampness, even squishy in places, which meant…

"Great. I'm walking through a field on the one day this year when it's going to be muddy." Graham groused. "Which wouldn't be so bad if I'd been smart enough to *think* of that and wear different shoes."

He'd started complaining in the parking lot, with its pockets of muddy gravel. Now, as they tromped through a field of barely green grass toward the Civil War reenactment that was scheduled to be just over the rise, Graham was going for round two.

It was, in truth, a lovely day, and Derek swore to himself he wasn't just thinking that because this excursion had been orchestrated by Luanna.

And the fact that she'd grabbed his and Graham's hands and was towing them up the slope like a woman on a mission. Which she was, because if she let go of Graham's hand, he might just flee back to the parking lot.

Okay, in truth, he *was* interested in this new experience. For all his focus on historical trends, he'd never attended an historic reenactment event.

He was interested in any number of new experiences if they included the tall, curvy blond.

He shook his head, trying to dislodge at least some of the random thoughts and ideas bouncing around in his brain. Someone had once said that being a writer was like having fifty million website tabs open at the same time.

Okay, maybe "fifty million" was an exaggeration. But it sure felt that way sometimes.

Most people didn't understand that writers worked on multiple projects simultaneously, which is why the question "How's your show going?" was usually met with a blank stare. At any given time, he was brainstorming episode ideas, meeting with Graham and the rest of the team about episode ideas, researching episode ideas, and writing the damn episodes.

When he wasn't toying with his real love, screenplays, that was.

Thankfully, the nonfiction topics he focused on were ones that fired up his creativity and worked their way into his fiction projects.

Maybe an article about the types of people who were drawn to do historic reenactment as a hobby?

"Y'all know it rained," Luanna was saying to Graham. "You should've worn old shoes."

Derek pressed his lips together to stop a snort, knowing what was coming, but no more capable of stopping it than he would a runaway freight train.

Graham stopped dead in his tracks, his expression more appropriate on someone who'd just been told their grandmother was stripping at The Seventh Veil.

He actually shuddered.

"This is part of research for the film," he said. "I'm excited about the project, and I'll be talking it up to anyone who might be a resource, so I wanted to look professional, look like a producer. Which maybe wasn't my smartest idea ever because now I look like a soggy producer whose best shoes are covered with mud and squishing with each step I take. But you of all people should understand dressing the part."

"I do. But more importantly, I understand practicality," she said, lifting one rubber-booted foot. "Sometimes, and it pains me to say it, you have to sacrifice fashion for function." Luanna smiled so brightly Derek imagined the sun was coming out.

Graham sighed. "But the fashion served a function. Or at least it did in my head. Just didn't work so well in reality."

"Look at it this way. Wet feet are an authentic taste of the period. Do you have any idea how much it rains in parts of the South? And they wouldn't have dry boots to change into, let alone anything like this." She actually shook her boot this time. Muddy water and a few bits of grass flew off.

"If I owned rubber boots, I might have worn them." Then Graham snorted. "Who am I kidding? I'd still have worn the good leather shoes, but I'd feel even more like a dork because I'd know I'd left perfectly good boots in the closet so I could impress people with my shoes. Which are not going to impress anyone at this point."

Luanna had a point about the boots. Wellies were overkill for wet grass and a few patches of mud, but they were better than Graham's nice shoes or his own canvas sneakers, and Derek was charmed by the fact that they were garish green and pink plaid.

Her floppy straw hat might not be the height of fashion, but she had fair skin, so it made sense. Even in old jeans, she somehow managed to look put together and stylish in a funky, eclectic sort of way.

The way those faded jeans hugged her curves didn't hurt one bit. They made her butt look amazing, the way they lovingly cupped her cheeks.

He probably shouldn't be thinking about her butt, since they were going to be working together. But (ha!) the fact was that he was as intrigued by her brain as he was by her delightedly not-Hollywood-stick-thin body.

"Stop complaining," Luanna added, proving her point by striding forward again in her garish Wellies. "You're just trying to get out of seeing that I'm right."

"I never didn't believe you weren't right," Graham protested.

"There are so many double negatives in that sentence, even I don't know what you just said," Derek commented, liking the fact that Luanna wasn't going to pull any punches with Graham. Derek had been friends with Graham for years, and loved him like a brother—which meant he knew when Graham needed a whup upside the head.

Graham ignored him. "I just feel we need to take some liberties with minor historic details in order to serve the story we want to tell."

"No, you just want the actors to look hotter," Luanna said.

"Well, there's a romantic element to it," Derek said. "It helps if the leads are attractive."

"Whose side are you on, anyway?" Luanna demanded, turning on him.

"Art and beauty," he said. "At least when it comes to creative works. Journalism, on the other hand, requires truth and accuracy." She opened her mouth, and he held up a hand to forestall her. "Yes, it was hard not to fall down the rabbit hole of research when I wrote the screenplay. I finally reminded myself that I had a *story* to tell, and I had to honor that story, first and foremost.

"That said," he went on, now stopping Graham before his friend spoke, "I think this is an excellent educational opportunity."

"You sound like my mother," Graham grumbled. "You can't make me eat my peas, either. Neener-neener. And…"

As they'd walked, the sounds of a large group had grown louder: voices, laughter, the creak of wheels and bang of hammers. Now they reached the crest of the hill, and the tableau spread out before them.

"Whoa," Graham said, sounding stunned and impressed. "It's like a movie."

"Remind me," Luanna murmured, "never to take you to Medieval Times. *Ev*-er."

"Oh, we've been," Derek said, wishing the memory hadn't resurfaced. "We were seated in the priest-knight's section, and we got thrown out because *someone* kept standing up and shouting 'Less prayer, more practice!'"

"It's choreographed," Graham said, although it was a vague comment over his shoulder. "I didn't appreciate being seated in what was clearly the losing area."

Luanna leaned in close to Derek, so close he could smell the sunscreen she'd slathered on her face and arms. "He does know the outcome of the War Between the States, right?" she murmured, sotto voce. "Because otherwise, this is all going to end in tears."

He couldn't stifle his laugh, but it wasn't a problem because Graham was completely distracted right now.

The encampment was several clusters of canvas tents, and from one of them rose the smell of roasting meat. The battle hadn't started yet, but the reenactors all seemed to have duties to attend to—the bustle of movement was almost overwhelming.

"Look at those guns," Graham said. He shook his hand free of Luanna's and headed to the munitions area, seemingly having forgotten about getting his shoes muddy.

Derek was keenly aware that he was now left holding hands with Luanna, which might be weird, but apparently she hadn't noticed yet. He liked the feel of her skin against his and didn't want to let go.

He felt her move, saw her stand up a little straighter. In truth, even he felt the need to salute. This was the spectacle he'd had in mind when he wrote the script. Why had he never thought of coming to this? Damn, Luanna was savvy.

She'd had no background or training in costume design for film, yet here she was, hitting the ground running and trying to make a stand on what was accurate for the time period, artistic vision and budget be damned.

"Isn't that a spinning wheel?" he said, spotting a large wooden wheel at the edge of a canvas tent. He watched Luanna's eyes light up, watched the delight cross her face, and couldn't help but smile.

When they got to the booth, they found several women inside, making fabric and sewing. Derek didn't know what ninety percent of the activities going on were, but he was here to learn.

"Hey," Luanna said—not in an abrupt way, but as a drawn-out, almost musical word that Derek knew passed for a casual greeting in the South. When the women greeted her, Luanna beamed and immediately fell into explaining her interest in the clothes and peppering them with questions.

Derek had no idea what box pleating or cartridge pleating was, but apparently they merited a spirited debate. He was happy enough to let Luanna do her thing while he soaked up the atmosphere, and, when she took off her hat to lean closer to look at some fabric on the loom, it felt natural just to ease it out of her hand and hold it for her.

He realized his assumption that most of the dresses would be plain, dull grays and browns had been way off. Some dresses were sprigged with tiny flowers; others were surprisingly vibrant plaid. And, he had to admit, the way the huge skirts billowed out from tiny waists was kind of sexy.

He could absolutely envision Luanna in one of the dresses—one with green to accent her eyes. The rows of buttons did lead a man to think about unbuttoning them, making it part of the seduction….

The mental video screeched to a halt when he realized he had no idea what the correct undergarments looked like. Well, he was sure Luanna would find out. It occurred to him that the cultural significance of under-wear—practicality versus sexuality versus propriety—throughout history could make an interesting article.

He wanted to make a note on his phone, but figured if he whipped it out, one of the ladies would bean him on the head with a cast-iron frying pan for abusing technology.

So he filed away the idea to consider later, and watched, and listened, and enjoyed doing both. Luanna was…well, *vivacious* was a pretty damn perfect word to describe her.

She could talk easily with anyone, making them feel comfortable, as if they were already fast friends.

And yet, at the party on New Year's Eve, when he'd just barely met her, he'd sensed some reservation. He was sure there'd been a strong flare of attraction between them, and as the seconds to midnight had counted down, they'd locked eyes and he'd really, really wanted to kiss her.

But something in her eyes, some faint sense of distance or hesitation, had made him back off a tetch, and he'd kissed her hand instead.

From the way her breath had hitched and her nostrils had flared, he guessed he'd surprised her—in a good way.

At the time, he'd wondered whether the hesitation had been because he was a stranger, or because she was involved with someone (a discreet check with Brand provided the answer he'd hoped for: no), or because she wasn't interested in him, or men in general (the latter was also no, although, Graham had added, there was no reason she couldn't bat for both teams).

He sensed that she'd opened up a little since then, let her guard down some. He hoped it was because she felt more comfortable around him, now that he wasn't a complete stranger.

The noise in the direction of the battlefield increased; it sounded as though orders were being shouted, equipment was being moved.

Derek tapped Luanna on the arm. "I think the battle's going to start soon, if you want to see it."

"Oh!" Luanna bit her lip, looking longingly around the tent and then toward the battlefield, clearly torn. Derek was also torn, trying not to think about her luscious lower lip or her longing looks. "Yes, I do want to see it."

She made her good-byes to the women, some of whom hugged her, making her promise to come back after the reenactment on the field. As they left the tent, Derek handed her her hat.

"Why, thank you, darlin'," she said, favoring him with a brilliant smile. "Do you think we should find Graham?"

"I have a feeling he's already front and center," Derek said.

The next few hours were filled with cracking gunshots and the rotten-egg sulfur smell of gunpowder, the boom of cannons, and the cries of the soldiers as they fell, all overlain with the dust kicked up in the field. Which would have been a lot worse if it hadn't rained recently, and Derek was thankful for that.

They hooked back up with Graham and toured some of the other exhibits. Graham displayed a disturbing amount of enthusiasm over the surgery equipment in the medical tent until Derek told him under no uncertain terms was he adding any amputations to the screenplay. Luanna got the email addresses for seemingly every woman in the textiles tent and bought patterns at one of the mercantile booths, and Graham only grumbled a little at the fact that she was going to expense them.

He grumbled less when he decided he could pay for their lunches and write them off on taxes. Luanna had been mildly concerned the food was going to be authentic to an army encampment of the period; she wasn't quite sure what that would be, but she suspected it involved a lot of beans and salt pork and not much seasoning. Fortunately the food vendors offered a mix of hearty 19th-century home-style fare such as pot pies and more typical 21st-century California selections from burritos to hot dogs. Luanna, getting into the spirit of things, tried a chicken and ham pot pie and decided it wasn't bad.

Derek found himself caught up in the spectacle, disappointed when it was over. He wasn't sure whether he wanted to rewrite the script or start a new one. He did know he wasn't ready for the day with Luanna to end.

"So," he said as they walked down the hill to the parking lot. "Who's up for dinner?"

"Can't," Graham said, and Derek felt a little guilty for being glad that it wouldn't be a threesome. Bad friend, no biscuit. "I've got a ticket to the new Save the Bees exhibit at the Natural History Museum."

"I'm in, as long as it's somewhere cheap," Luanna said. "I've just started a new job and haven't gotten my first paycheck yet, so I'm so broke I couldn't jump over a nickel to save a dime."

"My treat," Derek said. "We'll talk about the movie for five minutes and then I can write it off as a business expense."

"Deal," Luanna said.

Despite knowing it was going to be a cheap-and-cheerful date, getting there felt more Hollywood than Derek's usual life, thanks to the fact they were riding in a sweet lemon-yellow 1966 Mustang. Luanna had apparently borrowed it from Brand, part of the car collection that was nominally Sandrine's but were more like Sandrine's gifts to her car-fiend brother, which she used occasionally. First time Derek had ever ridden in this one and he was enjoying it.

Of course, the driver might have had a little to do with that.

On the way to Graham's place to drop him off, they mostly talked about the movie, all speaking at once sometimes as they bounced ideas off each other. Graham and Luanna seemed to be getting along well, which made Derek happy. Graham was one of the brightest guys around, and full of ideas and ideals, but sometimes he rubbed people the wrong way by pushing those ideas and ideals too enthusiastically. Luanna, though, seemed to enjoy it and followed the way his brain jumped around from idea to idea, sometimes steering him back on topic when he went too off course. Good. She'd be working most closely with Yancey during the movie, but an ability to keep up with Graham would make her job a lot easier.

They waved Graham good-bye outside his building. For a second, Derek was silent, not in an awkward way (he hoped), but just looking at Luanna. She was rosy-cheeked from the sun despite her hat and sunscreen, and she was smiling, probably because just before he'd headed into his building, Graham had pulled up the website for the local big cat sanctuary (another of his pet causes) on his phone and shown them pictures of newborn ocelot cubs that were so cute Derek suspected he was grinning too.

Or maybe that grin was because he was finally alone with Luanna. They'd had a long, busy day and needed food soon. But there was something he wanted to do first.

Okay, there were several things he *wanted* to do first, many of them tasteless if not downright illegal to do in a car parked on a busy street. Especially if the car was Brand's Mustang, because people stared at it. But he'd settle for a small, simple gesture.

He took Luanna's hand and, as he'd done on New Year's Eve, raised it to his lips. Her green eyes widened as he kissed the back of her hand—and when he turned her hand and placed a kiss in her palm, she sighed. "I'm glad you could join me for dinner. It'll be fun."

Her laugh was soft and throaty. "I'm getting gladder by the second. But you're going to have to tell me where I'm going."

Chapter 6

*D*erek guided her to a small restaurant with a Spanish name in a part of town she didn't know at all—which wasn't a surprise given the breadth of the Los Angeles area.

It was unprepossessing on the outside, a real little hole in the wall, in a strip mall with a pot-holed parking lot and flickering streetlights, but that might actually be a good sign. She wasn't a foodie, not like Chloe, but she loved good food, and some of the best meals she'd ever eaten had been at simple mom-and-pop places, from backwoods Cajun joints to Chloe's parents' Portuguese restaurant and her uncle's seafood shack in Rhode Island.

Plus, she could see between the lettering and cartoon logo of an ear of corn dancing with a jalapeño on the plate-glass window that the place was crowded. You want a good meal, you go where everyone else knows to go.

And her optimism was rewarded quickly. Rich, spicy smells accosted her as soon as Derek opened the door. Not Mexican—she was used to those scents at this point of her sojourn in LA, even if she still needed help navigating anything but the simplest taqueria menu—though the name was definitely Spanish and so were most of the voices she heard. The interior looked like it might have been a pizza place in some past life, with the standard pizza-place photos of Italy replaced with ones that had to be of Latin America somewhere—ruins, folkloric dancers in masks, a startlingly blue lake in a volcanic crater, city scenes focused on white buildings that must date back to the colonial period. The Formica-and-chrome tables had seen better days, but the few empty ones were sparkling clean, as was the cooler full of pop and beers with unfamiliar names.

Her mouth watered and her stomach took the opportunity to growl loudly in a break between sprightly Latin pop songs.

Momma would have told her to pretend it hadn't happened, but since it obviously had, Luanna just laughed. "Seems we got here right on time. I'm about hungry enough to take a bite out of a table, and Formica's nasty even with hot sauce and an Abita, or so my cousin Jackson says."

"I want to hear that story once you're not likely to start eating furniture. Have you ever had Salvadoran food?"

She shook her head. "Don't think so. Is it like Mexican?"

"Some of the dishes are similar: tamales and flan and tres leches cake. But don't let my abuelita hear me say that."

"You're Salvadoran?"

"Half, which is enough I can give you a guided tour of the menu here. This is mostly a pupuseria, and you have a choice of fillings…"

A pupusa turned out to be sort of like a dumpling made of corn tortillas, and Derek put together a shareable plate of them and other treats that sounded like it would be a very satisfying meal—and one that didn't make Luanna feel like she was spending too much of Derek's money. Very good food, but not date food or a date restaurant.

That was good, right? This was a not-date, she'd decided on the drive over, when she was feeling bad about how quickly she'd agreed to Derek paying. But the bottom line was, she really was broke, and she really wanted to hang out with Derek some more. This hadn't been pre-planned like a proper date.

But there was that shiver-inducing romantic kiss on the hand to consider.

So she was calling this a "pre-date" so they could both deny it was anything but new acquaintances getting to know each other better if it went horribly wrong—or even if it went all right, but with no real spark without champagne and fireworks.

Though Luanna suspected lack of spark wasn't going to be an issue. Simply walking next to him, or catching a glimpse of that piratical smile, made her feel tingly where it counted.

Her life might be crazy and unsettled. It might be a crappy time to get into a serious relationship. But she was a strong believer in putting the positive out into the universe, and if the universe said now was the time to flirt with this man and see where it went, even if it went no further than a non-serious-but-seriously-fun fling, so be it.

And really, her life *was* looking up. Even though the Zombie Iguana job technically didn't start for a few months, because she was going to do research, they'd given her some up-front money from the discretionary fund. That would keep Evenrude in kibble for a bit longer while Luanna hustled to get a temp job and some commissions from her clients.

She'd been so worried about Zombie Iguana—worried that Graham would talk to someone from Luscious who'd badmouth her. But she'd told him and Derek as much of the story as she could without actually saying too much about her side projects, and Graham's response had been to say unprintable but rather amusing things about corporate types shackling the creative spirit.

Things were sunny indeed, and she was going to focus on the good things.

Such as this-here food, which was *delicious*. The enticing smells hadn't lied, not one bit. She'd have to tell Chloe about this place, if she could remember the name, let alone how to find it; she'd have to write it down and they could Google it later.

Such as the fact that she and Derek were leaning ever closer over the shared platter of unfamiliar, delicious food, and when they brushed each other's hand not exactly by accident, they'd freeze as if something stupendous had happened. And at least for Luanna it was pretty stupendous, each innocent contact sending shivers and heat surges through her and making her flash back to New Year's Eve. A kiss on the hand, something even an 1860s gentleman could get away with bestowing on a lady, and yet it was as sensual as some sex Luanna had enjoyed and more memorable than a lot of said sex.

Derek was looking a little rumpled and windblown, his usually sleek hair looking like it would wave exuberantly if it were just a little longer. She liked the effect; it made him look even more piratical.

Liked the way he savored his food, closing his eyes as if it helped him focus on the explosion of flavors from each bite of pupusa or empanada. Chloe would approve, Luanna thought.

Liked watching the muscles of his tanned throat as he swallowed his drink, not one of the pops from the cooler, but something called horchata that they made in-house. (She'd chickened out and settled for a diet Coke, which she now regretted.)

Liked, once they'd eaten enough they were willing and able to slow down, the sound of his voice as he talked a little bit about the family she'd seen in pictures in his office, mostly about his sisters. When she asked about his parents, his expression turned dark briefly, and he muttered something about a divorce so recent everyone including Derek was still shell-shocked. Then he quickly asked her about her family.

Right. Didn't want to talk about the divorce. She had a lot of family stories to tell and most of them were funny, so that might take his mind off any unhappy thoughts.

"I'm from a small town outside Baton Rouge. My daddy's family's Cajun."

"Are they alligator hunters or vampires? Based on TV, you'd think every Cajun was one or the other." He was so clearly teasing that she laughed and gave him a tongue-in-cheek answer with a serious expression on her face.

"We do know folks who hunt gators for a living, but my daddy's a lawyer. A small-town lawyer, but a lawyer, and his maman was a nurse. No vampires in the family as far as I know, though I wouldn't put it past some of my relatives on my momma's side…that would be the Beauregards… who are odd even by Louisiana standards."

"And what does your mother do?"

Luanna laughed. "Momma *lives*, that's what she does. Lives large, lives as elegantly as she can in a town that didn't even have a Walmart of its own until a few years back, let alone fancy stores or nice restaurants, and keeps my daddy wrapped around her manicured little finger. She was the Sweet Potato Queen of her home parish back in high school and she never lets you forget it."

Derek, halfway through a swallow of horchata, sputtered, then gulped. "Sweet Potato Queen?" he managed to say after a bit of choked laughter. "Do you know how hard it is for me not to start taking notes? There has to be a show in that!"

Luanna shrugged. She'd never gotten that particular reaction before, but life as a Louisiana girl in LA, and before that, Boston, had taught her things that were perfectly normal in the world she grew up in seemed exotic, even funny, to Yankees. But she liked the gleam in his eyes, the enthusiasm.

"I mean, the whole idea of a Sweet Potato Queen is iconic Americana," he said. "It ties in to changing views of small town life and agriculture and even the changing role of women. Like, it was obviously a big deal to your mom, but is it still a big deal for a girl today?"

Yeah, she definitely liked the enthusiasm. "It is in Momma's hometown, but that's because the Sweet Potato Festival became a way of rebuilding community spirit after Katrina—they're closer to the Gulf than we are and got hit pretty hard. Which is another angle for you."

He grinned. "That's better than the one I thought of, which is how these food-related titles tie into Americans' changing eating habits. Though the higher-ups might like that one better; foodie stuff always gets an audience."

"If you go with that one, you know you should talk to Chloe."

He whipped out his phone, made a note. "That's a great idea—thanks. Between the two of you, I could make a great head start. And you and I still need to talk about men's clothing trends throughout history."

Luanna laughed. "That's going to take more than the five minutes you said you needed to write this off on taxes, darlin'."

He looked up, clearly a little distracted. It was a look she'd seen before, when Chloe was planning a menu and was interrupted, and when Sandrine or Ray was studying a script. Luanna was sure she'd had the same expression on her own face when someone tried to talk to her when she was thinking about dress design.

"I'm sorry," he said, reaching across the table and covering her hand with his. "I didn't mean right now. I just got caught up…"

"I understand completely," Luanna said, patting his hand and very, very much enjoying the warmth and pressure of his, sending little shivers up and down her spine. "If you don't write things down, you might forget them, what with all the projects you have going on."

"Anybody reading my to-do list would think I was insane," he admitted, glancing at the screen again. "Pick up dry cleaning. Review *Magnolia Road* production schedule. Write ten pages on new script. Find a heterosexual crossdresser to interview."

Luanna froze. There was no way he could know about her clients…right?

Right. It was a coincidence. But just to be sure she didn't blurt something out, she veered the conversation in a different direction. "Goodness, I'm just glad you were able to find the time to take me out to dinner."

At that, he turned off the phone, placed it face down on the table. "I've actually gotten a lot done in the past few weeks," he said. "Plus, some things are more important than to-do lists." He squeezed her hand and winked.

"Like food," she said teasingly, even as her insides fluttered.

"Like food with a pretty, funny, interesting woman," he countered. "Someone I'd like to spend all night talking to—but there's a line of people waiting to eat, so we should probably free up this table."

As they dumped their trash in the receptacle by the door, then headed outside into the cool spring night, Luanna shook off any lingering concerns.

And decided to focus on the good things.

Chapter 7

$\mathcal{I}$t was a lovely night and the loveliness extended into Derek's neighborhood in Studio City. Or maybe that was the company, because the neighborhood, one of small single-family homes she guessed dated from the '30s or '40s, was nice enough, but lacked the funky charm of someplace like Venice Beach, let alone the over-the-top grandeur of Sandrine's Lifestyles of the Rich and Excessive…well, you couldn't really call it a neighborhood when the properties were so huge you couldn't see any of the other houses, could you?

She parked the Mustang in front of the indicated house, a cute 1940s one-story, the stucco painted a pale shade she couldn't quite make out in the dark. They were only two blocks from the hustle and bustle of Ventura Boulevard (cue Tom Petty), but here it was quiet. The tree-shaded street was lined with cars—she guessed most of the houses had one-car garages, accessible from alleys running behind them, so second vehicles got left outside. She'd been lucky to find a spot so close.

Derek's house had a big bay window in the front, and a neat lawn and a curved sidewalk. The porch light glowed over a red door, and it looked as though the house was bordered by a narrow flower bed.

It wasn't easy keeping plants and grass alive in what basically amounted to a desert, and she figured he probably had a gardener, unless he magically had the time (and the green thumb) to tend to the patch of grass and flora himself.

She didn't ask, because that would be rude, and her momma hadn't raised her to be rude.

She had also been raised by a momma with a brown thumb (Daddy liked to putter in the garden, grow big fat tomatoes and endless zucchini, but that was the extent of it), so starting a conversation about gardening amounted to madness.

Neither of them had raised her to be a shrinking violet, either, so she drew in a breath and said what she wanted to say. "I really enjoyed today," she said. "Unfortunately, I'm getting together with Chloe for wedding planning early tomorrow. Mornings work best for her work schedule, and it's the only time Sandrine can Skype from Eastern Europe where she's shooting." Which she wouldn't have mentioned to just anyone…the fact she and Chloe were buds with a Major Movie Star was just weird…but Derek knew the Major Movie Star was Brand's beloved sister, his only living relative, and so bound to be up to her gorgeous eyebrows in the wedding.

"Tomorrow's crazy for me too, unfortunately." He smiled, and it was that rakish, piratical smile that tickled over her skin and let her know he didn't think she was brushing him off. "I'd like to see you again. Without Graham." He said it without rancor; Luanna could hear the fondness in his voice. "I love Graham, but he can be annoying in large doses, and he was worse than usual today."

Luanna shrugged. "I know his type. He's all right. A little pretentious and concerned about putting across the right hip image, but I bet that's because he's insecure at heart and Hollywood'll just make that worse. And he's not the only smart person I've met who figured that because he knew a lot, he knew everything about everything. So I'll be really enthusiastic about the things we agree on, then distract him with something shiny and take care of the things he doesn't understand so well while he's distracted."

Derek laughed, and the laugh tickled her in some interesting places. "Took me years to figure out Graham-herding that well, and we've been friends since middle school."

She lowered her voice to a conspiratorial whisper, even though her new boss was in another part of town getting his hipster party on. "I bet he was a big ol' dork back then."

"He still kind of is, but he's learned to make it work for him. The whole hipster thing helps. It's semi-cool now to be dorky and fascinated with obscure things if you do it in a fun way."

While she was chuckling at that thought, Derek whispered, "But that's more than enough about Graham," and leaned closer, across an expanse of plush, pale yellow leather interior that expanded to the Grand Canyon.

Time slowed to a crawl. Luanna was moving herself, but the air was suddenly thick as sorghum syrup, heated and moist as August on the bayou, and it was fighting her efforts to reach her objective, which was getting her hands and lips on the delicious pirate in the passenger seat.

But he didn't kiss her, not yet. He reached out, cupped her cheek in one capable hand as if her face was something precious and fragile, his flesh warm against hers despite the car's air conditioning, which was trailing off and ticking now that she'd killed the engine. Or maybe she was hot enough for both of them, creating contact sizzle. She couldn't really think, her thoughts melting like snowflakes in that slow-burning fire, and besides, all she wanted to do was savor the sensation of his touch.

When he dragged his thumb slowly across her full lower lip, as if pondering how it would feel to kiss her, or getting a lay of the land, deciding how best to put his mouth on hers, she forgot how to breathe. When he raised his gaze to hers, she saw his pupils dilate. One corner of his mouth tugged up, just a hint. She remembered how he'd kissed her hand (she hadn't really stopped thinking about how he'd kissed her hand). A deceptively languid action, full of promise. If he could make her knuckles tingle like that… make her lip tingle just from a stroke of his thumb…she was in big trouble.

She'd never been one to run from trouble.

Right now, she wanted to leap up onto trouble and lock her arms and legs around it and not let go.

He touched her lip again, stroked, and she caught her breath. And thankfully, although it was an involuntary reaction on her part, he took it as an invitation. Or maybe he did that *because* it was an involuntary reaction on her part. He clearly was behind the space-time glitch that was making everything move in excruciatingly sexy slow motion. Everything except her heart, which sped up as he leaned toward her and finally, *finally* covered her mouth with his.

She hadn't realized how badly she wanted it, how badly she needed it, until it happened. She'd always thought of a kiss as the first step, but now it felt like a culmination, a coming home, and she didn't want it to end. She wanted to experience every last lingering sensation that came with it.

Slow, deep kisses paired with light, teasing ones, the barest touch of a tongue against hers. Every move deliberate, coaxing out her response until she matched the tempo of their erotic dance. Not a tango, but a slow, seductive ballet.

Warmth curled through her, teased the butterflies in her belly, pooled lower.

She reached out, caressed his face in a mirror image action of his hand on hers. His stubble was rough against her palm. It would be teasingly rough between her thighs. Her core fluttered at the thought.

Still he kept on kissing her, savoring her as if she tasted better than the finest dark chocolate, the richest port, the most decadent meal. And that made her even hungrier for him.

He took her lower lip gently between his teeth, tugged, then his tongue slid over the same flesh, soothing. He pulled back, his mouth hovering so very close to hers, and she heard her own ragged breath.

How could such languorous kisses bring her to this? By this time, she was used to going faster, harder, devouring each other's mouths, hands tangled in hair or roaming, caressing, exploring.

He'd touched only her face and she was already melting, throbbing.

"You taste," he murmured, "like smoked paprika. Hot, spicy, like an oak fire."

He tasted the same—she guessed because of the dinner—but it was the way he said it that locked her own words in her throat. He'd said what she'd been thinking…no, feeling. Thinking was a thing of the past.

Then he trailed kisses across her cheek, found her ear. As on her lower lip, a nip, then a swirl of tongue to soothe. Now her neck, where his kisses heated, the fading air conditioning cooled the spot, and then his breath mixed both together.

She tilted her head to give him easier access, because the feel of him kissing, licking, nuzzling in the hollow where shoulder met collarbone was lighting her body on fire. Every inch of her flesh tingled, not just where he explored, because she could imagine his mouth on every inch, what it would feel like.

The thought of him spending the same attention on every inch of her flesh, before he even got to her breasts, her clit, made her breath slide out on a low moan. She wasn't sure she'd ever made a sound like that before, but she couldn't not. She was already so wet, so needy, and she'd take him right now if he wanted, but at the same time, the sweet torture was heady, thrilling.

"You smell," he paused to say, his voice rough with lust, "like sunshine."

Then he was back at her mouth, the kisses a little deeper this time, and every graze of his teeth was like a graze of teeth against her budded, aching nipples, and every caress of his tongue was like a caress against her pulsing clit.

It wasn't as if he didn't want her, too, she could tell. Any time he pulled away, his breath was ragged, and when she slid her hand down and placed it on his chest, she could feel the erratic pounding of his heart.

She was pretty sure if she reached lower, she'd find out just how badly he wanted her.

She wanted to touch him there, feel his hardness. Wrap her hand around his cock, make him lose the ability to speak, to think. Another time, in another relationship, she might've done just that. But where it would have felt perfectly fine then to dive in, speed things up, skip a few steps because clearly their bodies had skipped those steps already…now it felt…rushed.

She didn't want to skip those steps. She wanted to linger over every single one of those steps. Learn about her rakish pirate by slow, careful exploration. The treasure was the ultimate goal, but there was adventure to be had along the way.

It was her turn to explore his face, his neck, to curl her tongue around the glittering gold hoop in his ear and hear, with a shudder of delight, the low growl of enjoyment he made in response.

All that mattered was this moment, and Derek's lips on hers, and their hands on each other's skin. Innocent skin that had become one massive erogenous zone.

His hand strayed from her face to play with her hair. Not tugging or using it like reins to control the action, but caressing until her blond waves seemed to have nerve endings of their own, and those nerve endings were all aflutter. Her mouth felt swollen with the kisses, alive in a new way. Like kissing was all that could possibly matter.

When they pulled apart, she felt bereft.

They gazed at each other. Luanna imagined she looked half-crazed with lust, whereas Derek's half-lidded eyes spoke of a long, slow slide into lust. It was, she was pretty sure, the sexiest anyone had ever looked at her.

"You're driving me crazy," Derek said. "I can't quite think straight when I'm around you."

"There's supposed to be thinking?" Luanna was amazed she made a complete sentence, with words and everything.

He trailed his fingers across her face again. "Not when kissing you feels like this."

She realized he was giving her a choice. Acting the gentleman, making sure yes meant yes.

"If it weren't for this stick shift—and the fact that it's not my car—I'd be all over you like white on rice," Luanna confessed.

Derek laughed softly, and it felt like that La Perla silk robe she loved so much whispering on after a long, hot bath with rose-scented bubbles. He ran one finger along the line where her shirt met her skin, and that was enough to make her clench. Then he leaned in and murmured in her ear, "Luanna, I'm hoping we'll enjoy each other's bodies in every imaginable way and a few no one's even thought of yet. But we're not going to do it all tonight." He nuzzled his lips down the curve of her throat again, making her sigh. Then he worked his way up to her ear and a moan seemed insufficient, but it was all she could manage to do. "We're going to take it slow and easy, explore each other. When we take each other, it's going to be because we can't not, because if I don't slide my cock into you, we'll both die from the need. When we have sex, Luanna, I promise you…it will be *phenomenal*."

He slipped out of the car before she could respond, cut across his own lawn, fished keys out of his pocked. After he unlocked the door, he glanced back, touched his lips, and gave a little shiver.

Then he was gone, yet his presence lingered in the car: in the tenderness of her lips, in the throb of her clit.

She started the car, but didn't trust herself to drive yet. She sat, breathing steadily, trying to calm her pounding heart, her sensitized flesh. The air conditioner wasn't helping; the flow of air across her skin made her feel hotter, edgier.

Damn the man. He was right. It was going to be beyond phenomenal when they got to it. If the getting to it didn't drive her into erotic madness on the way.

As experienced as she might be now, the evening brought her back to her teenaged years, those hot-and-heavy petting sessions just down the road from her house, the night thick with sultry air and Spanish moss and the promise of passion to come.

She'd walk in the house afterward, lips swollen, body flushed, a scarf artfully tied around her neck to hide any hint of love-bites, to find her momma waiting up for her. One eyebrow raised, Momma would look her up and down, leaving Luanna guiltily suspecting Momma not only knew the scarf trick, but had invented it.

"This boy," Momma would finally say, "is he gonna be trouble?"

"Oh Momma," Luanna said, easing the car away from the curb, hearing the engine's sexy, purring growl, "you have no idea."

Chapter 8

*T*his, Luanna thought. *This* was crazy mayhem, and yet, somehow, it worked.

The one-bedroom gatehouse didn't look much different than before Chloe had moved in with Brand a few months ago. The main area was one room, with a prep island separating the kitchen from the rest of the space. The biggest changes, unsurprisingly, were in the galley-style kitchen, which now sported a Henckel knife block and a cherry-red KitchenAid mixer, not to mention actual real cloth dish towels. Otherwise, the space still felt like a bachelor pad, with an oversized black leather couch and chairs, and science fiction memorabilia from the movies Brand had done CGI effects for.

The light saber, Chloe had confided to Luanna, made an excellent flashlight in an emergency.

Luanna didn't want to know what constituted a light saber emergency.

Luanna was there for the planning extravaganza about Chloe and Brand's upcoming wedding…whenever "upcoming" might be. Between his work and Chloe's crazy hours at DesJardins LA, it would be a miracle if they ever set a firm date.

If Sandrine had been in town, she'd have insisted on having the planning session in the mansion, but they were making do with Sandrine on Skype from Romania, fed through Brand's enormous TV screen.

Truth be told, Sandrine's head—albeit stunning with her coppery-red hair, turquoise eyes, and diamond-cutting cheekbones—was a little too large for comfort on that screen.

It was one thing to watch her on a movie screen because, well, that was fiction.

This was a giant head talking directly to them.

Meanwhile, Chloe hadn't been able to stop herself from making crazy-good breakfast nibblies for the planning session: individual quiches, fresh grapes in three colors, farmers' market strawberries with a juicy, intense flavor all out of proportion to their size, pepper-crusted bacon from happy heritage pigs that had apparently blessed their meat with extra deliciousness before they moved on to a loftier plane of existence, and steamed asparagus and artichoke hearts drizzled with Hollandaise such a lovely shade of pale yellow Luanna snapped a picture so she could match it in fabric, maybe with a scarf of the soft springtime green.

To accommodate Sandrine and her early on-set call time the next day, they were meeting at 9 a.m., which was 7 p.m. in Romania. Truth be told, Sandrine didn't *need* to be part of the preliminary planning, but she wanted to be, and with the high-strung but deep-down sweet starlet, you picked your battles.

Kinda like what they said about wrestling with a pig in shit.

Plus Chloe had to work that afternoon.

Chloe handed Luanna a glass of orange juice fresh squeezed from the small grove outside. "Oh! I keep forgetting to ask: How did it go yesterday? Was Graham crazy?" She turned back to the kitchen island to grab more nibblies to put out.

Luanna swallowed a mouthful of the juice, amazingly cold and tart and sweet, and said, "Oh, darlin', Graham's a sweetheart. I know how to handle him."

"You say everyone's a sweetheart," Chloe pointed out.

"Well, everyone I meet is," Luanna said.

Chloe moved to stand directly in front of her, hands on her hips. She might have been short, but she was feisty. "More importantly, how was *Derek*?"

The mention of his name shocked Luanna as if she'd stuck her finger in an erotic light socket. Her entire body heated up and tingled at the memory of his lips…everywhere…and those talented fingers dancing enticingly slowly across her skin…

"Um…" she said, stalling. "I actually like him a lot. We went out to dinner afterward—"

"You went on a *date*?" Chloe's eyes widened. "Details. Now."

Before Luanna could respond (or even process how much to reveal— if it had been just Chloe, she could share more, but as much as she adored Sandrine…), Olive arrived. She'd agreed to be Chloe's wedding coordinator, which had made everyone heave a sigh of relief. Olive's unflappable competence made you feel wrapped in a warm quilt while a hurricane howled outside.

"Good morning!" Olive said. She and Luanna exchanged air kisses, which necessitated Luanna leaning down a little because Olive wasn't a particularly tall woman.

"Luanna was just telling us about her date last night," Chloe said.

Olive made one of those "say *what* now?" moves with her head. "A *date*? With whom?"

"Brand's darling friend Derek," Sandrine's giant head supplied.

"Y'all, it wasn't really a date," Luanna protested, although she'd been up half the night wondering whether it was or not. Well, and thinking about Derek and doing naughty things while thinking about Derek. She'd had to replace the rechargeable batteries in Sweet Boy, even.

"I needed to do some research on Civil War costumes," she went on, "and Derek was doing some research for a show he does, and Graham needed to see the costumes, too, so we all went to a reenactment out in Moorpark."

"Ooh, fun!" Olive said. "I've been to one of those. The Ren Faire was more my thing, though."

They all stared at Olive for a moment, but she just smiled and spread her hands and said, "Luanna? Your not-a-date?"

"Graham had a thing to go to afterward, so Derek and I grabbed dinner together, and then I drove him home," Luanna said with what she hoped was a casual shrug. "He's charming, and…I think we click." The smile grew on her face despite every effort she made to stop it. "And he's a good kisser, and that's all that happened, and we're here to focus on Chloe. So let's do this, y'all."

She refused to tell them anything else, no matter how much they begged.

Luanna had a fold-up cart she used when she shopped in LA's Fabric District, and she'd used it to haul over design books, the latest wedding magazines, and her laptop and sketchbook.

On the way over, she'd been feeling a little smug about being so organized.

Now, in the blink of an eye, Olive had her favorite flipchart set up and a fistful of Sharpies in various colors and pointer at hand, along with her usual iPad and iPhone.

And, no doubt, a list of contacts and links for everything a girl getting married could possibly need: bridal boutiques, florists, and caterers, oh my!

"Oh, Olive, while I've got you here," Sandrine said, "did you get my text about my body wash?"

"Already being couriered to you; you should have it by tomorrow morning." Olive accepted a glass of orange juice from Chloe without missing a beat.

"Okay!" The word burst out of Chloe on a puff of air as she plopped down on the man-cave-esque sofa. "You guys are *awesome*! Thank you for being here. I…I have no idea where to begin."

"Setting a date might be a good idea," Olive said, standing next to the flipchart page that said SCHEDULE in large purple letters.

"Well, it can't be when either Ray or I are away on a shoot," Sandrine said. "Olive, you have our schedules, right?"

No surprise that Sandrine thought of her own schedule first—but then, she *had* offered to host the wedding on the grounds of one of the most phenomenal mansions in Hollywood, as well as the use of her personal chef.

Poor Lance. Luanna wondered whether anyone had told him about that plan yet—and whether smelling salts should be kept at the ready when he did find out.

And maybe a therapist.

"Of course," Olive said with a reassuring smile.

"It can't be during bluefish season, or that would knock out half of my relatives," Chloe said.

"So that leaves out July through early September, yes?" Olive said with a glance at her calendar.

Olive knew when bluefish season in Rhode Island was? Really, Luanna couldn't muster up any surprise at that.

"And it'll have to be after Brand finishes his current movie," Chloe added.

"Do you have those dates?" Olive asked.

"Crap," Chloe said. "I'm not sure. Let me text him… I think it's September? Same time as the end of the bluefish run."

"So, a late autumn wedding?" Olive said.

"Ooh!" Sandrine said. "How about a Halloween wedding? Everyone could dress as their favorite movie character. I think I'd be Savannah Starr."

"Isn't it cheating to come as the character *you* played in a movie?" Luanna asked.

"Oh." Sandrine's giant, perfect, pale brow furrowed delicately. Then she brightened. "So, Chloe can be Savannah, and I'll go as Thelma. Or maybe Louise. Ooh, I can't decide."

"I think we're putting the cart before the horse," Olive said. "It's up to the bride and groom to decide if they want a themed wedding."

Chloe clutched an enormous mug of coffee against her chest and said in a small voice, "We haven't really discussed it, but I think we'd like to go a little simpler."

"Once we decide on the date, we can send save-the-date notices so people have time to make plans," Olive pointed out. "I'll put that on the schedule to revisit in two weeks." She made a note on her iPad, then flipped the chart, the large paper crinkling as it revealed the next page: COLORS.

"Oh, thank God, I know this one!" Chloe said. "Nautical blue and kind of a sandy beige—beachy colors."

"Wonderful!" Sandrine said. "I look good in those colors."

Again, it was a remark that could almost be interpreted as selfish, but Sandrine had a point: she was a bridesmaid, and her photograph would likely end up in the media, and it behooved her to look her best. (Unless it was for a role like in *Too Solid Flesh*, in which she'd played a leper. Then again, Luanna had to admit, Sandrine had been an awfully pretty leper.)

"That *is* a lovely color scheme," Olive said. "Are you going to carry the beach feel into everything else, like the cake and the invitations?"

"We don't want to get too kitschy, but probably a little bit," Chloe said.

"Maybe a cake shaped like a sand castle?" Luanna said, because she had a vision board forming in her head.

"Huh," Chloe said. "I hadn't thought of that, but it's kind of a cool idea. Definite maybe."

"And it could be set up inside this whole network of fountains and ice sculptures, and *oh!* I can finally put in that wave pool I've always wanted, like at Mandalay Bay in Vegas!" Sandrine said.

Granted, the ocean was at least an hour away, given LA traffic, but a wave pool on the estate? Luanna decided not to go there.

Except a portion of her brain—the libido-controlled portion—supplied the idea of midnight skinny-dipping with Derek. She shifted in her seat.

"Great start," Olive said. "I'll send you some links to wedding sites so you can look at other beachy-themed weddings and get some ideas, and then we can narrow down some details. There's probably some good boards on Pinterest."

"I'd suggest starting a vision board, either on Pinterest or by hand," Luanna said. "It's what we…well, not we right now, but normally we…do in fashion design. Stick up anything that catches your eye or inspires you."

"That's a really good idea," Chloe said.

They moved on past CAKE and FLOWERS, and had a brief run-down of the wedding party. Luanna was maid of honor, with Sandrine and Joannie, Chloe's cousin, as bridesmaids. On Brand's side, Derek would be his best man, with Ray and maybe one of Chloe's brothers—if she could figure out how to choose one of five without causing a family ruckus—as groomsmen.

Evenrude, of course, would be the ringCorgi.

Luanna was just spreading her books and materials out on the coffee table when Ray arrived.

"Honey, you're just in time for the best part—wedding dresses!" Sandrine said.

"Ooh!" he said, sounding gleefully excited even with his bass rumble of a voice. The warmth of his smile filled his brown eyes as he blew a kiss at Sandrine.

Chloe and Brand might still be in the throes of new love, but Sandrine and Ray…Luanna couldn't keep a smile off her own lips. The two had been together for just over two years and the depth of their love for each other was still apparent. On paper, they looked like opposites, but the oppositions they'd weathered, including the private admission of Ray's crossdressing, had brought them only closer.

Ray snagged one of the magazines and settled his chiseled bulk into an easy chair, stretched out his long legs, and said, "Don't let me interrupt anything."

Of course, the occasional small, happy noises he made while perusing the magazine made it hard to keep a straight face—everyone in the room knew Ray's secret and loved him all the more for it—and it turned out that Chloe had even less of an idea what she wanted for a dress than what date was good, so the planning session dissolved soon thereafter.

Olive told them she'd email them all schedules, broken down by what needed to be done each month assuming the wedding was around Halloween, and began packing away her Tower of Organization. Sandrine, after making kissy cooing noises at Ray, signed off to get her beauty sleep. And Chloe turned to Luanna and said, "Okay, now we have time to talk— tell me *all* about your date!"

Olive stopped sliding Sharpies into their color-coordinated organizer and said, "Yes, details?"

"No time," Luanna said, pointing at Ray. "I have another meeting."

"We need a girls' night," Chloe said, a little wistfully.

"We'll have to wait until Sandrine gets back," Olive commented. "That way we can borrow her tiaras."

*

The master bedroom suite in Sandrine and Ray's mansion boasted enormous his-and-hers closets—if "closet" was the right term for a clothing-storage and dressing room that was half the size of the entire guest house Luanna lived in. And that guest house was nothing to be sneezed at, size-wise.

Luanna thought it was half-magical—well, Sandrine's closet, anyway. So many pretty dresses! So many couture designers, all in one place! A silky and satiny and sparkly rainbow of fashion!

As Chloe would say, *Squee!*

Although the fact that Ray's had a secret compartment closet for the "special clothes" she designed for him made her so happy, she practically had to hire someone to help her enjoy it.

Ray had some country music on: the peppy kind, not the morose kind, thank goodness. She'd grown up listening to the blues thanks to her father, and that had been bad enough. (At least it had been tempered by her mother's jazz habit.) She hummed along as she unzipped the garment bag and freed the dress she'd been working on.

Ray sat on a fainting couch just like a muscled action hero would—as if it were a bad guy he'd just wrestled into submission—except for the fact that he was wearing a black slip and a pair of three-inch pumps. (To help preserve his secret, Luanna ordered his extra-extra-large women's shoes for him. It made for some interesting messages in her Spam folder, that was for sure.)

She was just about to ask him to step up on the padded stool so she could pin the dress on him and check the fit when her phone buzzed in her jeans pocket. She didn't recognize the number, but her gut told her it was important, and she always listened to her gut.

Don't go into that house; even if it's not haunted, it's probably unsafe. Order the beef, because something's not right with the chicken. And if the little voice tells you to answer the phone, you answer the phone.

"Hello?"

"Hi. I hope it's not too forward if I say I miss you already."

Oh, sweet Lord. The sound of Derek's voice caressed her as surely and sexily as his mouth and hands had. Luanna bit her lip and locked her knees to keep from sinking to the ground.

She glanced at Ray, who smiled indulgently, made a "go on" motion with one hand, and went back to whatever he had been intently doing on his own phone.

He was either reading a script or playing Candy Crush; she couldn't be sure.

"I wouldn't call that forward," Luanna drawled. "I'd call that sweet."

"How did the wedding planning go? I hope I'm not interrupting."

"No, it's over—for now, anyway. I'd call it organized chaos, really. Chloe has some ideas of what she wants, but scheduling's going to be an issue. And Sandrine, bless her heart, has no end of ideas."

She glanced at Ray again. He smiled fondly, so she felt fine with continuing. "She may or may not be installing a wave pool on the grounds in case the wedding has a beach theme."

Derek laughed, a full, unabashed sound of delight that made her stomach do a little flip-flop of happiness. "I've met her only a few times, but that sounds like Sandrine. Thinking outside the box."

"That's her to a T," Luanna agreed. "So what are you up to?"

"I have a few minutes to kill before an interview, so I thought I'd call the woman who haunted my dreams last night. Couldn't get her out of my head…kept thinking about how she kisses, how her lips feel against mine. How she makes these little breathy moans…"

Thank the good Lord for a dressing table and chair, because Luanna's knees up and gave out on her. She didn't drop so much as melted onto the chair.

"Well, I was up half the night thinking of a man with magic hands," Luanna said. "Couldn't get him out of my head, either…even when—"

Ray cleared his throat, a spectacular reminder that she was about to engage in phone flirting—goodness, just call a hound dog a hound dog and admit it bordered on phone sex—in front of a uninvolved third party.

"Sorry," she said, regret coursing over her like a cold shower. "I'm actually, um, meeting with another client…about to meet with a client. My client's here."

There was a long enough pause that she started to wonder whether Derek had hung up, and what that might mean. But then he said, "Are you all right, Luanna?"

"Yes, sorry, I'm fine," she said quickly, quicker than her normal response, which made her feel vaguely guilty even though she had nothing to feel guilty about. Except for the fact that she was keeping a client waiting, and that was the height of rudeness and unprofessionalism.

And the fact that she couldn't really say anything else to Derek without running the risk of more questions about why she was meeting with a client and who that client might be.

"Thank you for calling," she said sincerely. "It…makes me really happy. I'll talk to you soon. Good luck with your interview."

Then she hit End before she lost her last nerve.

Oh, goodness, she felt more addled than a cat trying to cover up poo on a marble floor.

Chapter 9

*L*uanna stood in her sewing studio, holding her phone, her lower lip caught in her teeth.

The "studio" was—especially compared to Luscious Couture—miniscule. It was the size of an average bedroom…because it *was* a bedroom.

The guesthouse was bigger than most people's first apartments. (Not surprising because the main house was big enough to include a planetarium.) Two bedrooms, a bathroom, and a galley kitchen open to the living room…yet Chloe's vacated bedroom, with the queen-sized bed shoved against the wall, provided enough room for a sewing machine, an overlock machine, a small cutting table, and the dress form Luanna was currently pondering.

Bolts of fabric were piled on the bed. Woe betide anyone who might want to sleep in this room again. Thank goodness Chloe and Brand were engaged, lessening the chances of Chloe wanting to return.

Luanna missed her, but being thrilled for Chloe absolutely trumped that.

The dress form was draped with her latest creation for Ray now that they'd had the fitting. It would be a challenge to create a vintage-looking rust-red linen fit-and-flare dress with a white-piped portrait collar for anyone, let alone for someone Ray's build, but he'd fallen in love with a costume in some Audrey Hepburn movie he'd been half-watching while curled up with Sandrine. She thought she was doing a good job meeting the challenge, though the bodice would take a few more rounds of fitting to get just right and she kept staring at it trying to figure out why the collar didn't fall quite the way she wanted it to. Unfortunately, she stared at it without really seeing it. She'd stalked around it three times before she'd realized that.

She didn't want to work on this project, or add to her own vision board for Chloe's wedding dress, or do more research on Civil War clothing so she could gently guide Graham's costume choices for the movie.

She wanted to call Derek.

Well, if she wanted to accept the gods' honest truth, she wanted to tackle Derek and soundly fuck him, and be soundly fucked by him, but she also knew that was part of the wanting, the slow burn leading up to the conflagration.

Hearing his voice earlier today, even when she couldn't say much, had reflamed the erotic itch that hadn't gone away, despite her best efforts last night after their date with a few choice toys in her nightstand drawer.

Oh, she'd come, and come hard, remembering how his lips felt on hers, on her neck, and thinking about his lips and tongue everywhere else.

Especially *there*.

But the orgasm, while glorious as always, hadn't been…satisfying.

It had scratched the erotic itch, a short-term relief, but the source of that itch still eluded her.

This wasn't a release she could achieve on her own, a realization that dumbfounded her, knocked her back for a long, hard loop.

She could bring herself off all she wanted—and no mistake about it, boy howdy, she *wanted*—but it was Derek who held the key to true gratification.

Damn him.

She shook her head, chuckling. No, fuck him. Ideally multiple times.

Well, the cock won't crow if the sun don't rise. She hit redial on the number he'd called her from earlier today.

"Luanna." His voice stroked her intimately. "I'm glad you called."

"I'm sorry about this morning," she said, her eyes on the dress form. "Picky client."

"I respect your work," he said. "No apologies needed. We couldn't have talked long anyway. I had to rush off to do an interview."

Okay, that was settled. "Thanks. How did the interview go?"

"It was fascinating. The interview was for a side project, an article for one of the arts weeklies about a performance art company. They do a lot of work that plays with gender issues, and it turns out the company director is genderfluid; note to self: make sure the copy editor at the magazine knows Ash's preferred pronoun is *they*. Mostly we talked about the company, but talking about their work morphed into self-presentation when you're genderfluid. Great conversation, only now it's raised questions I'd like to investigate down the road and the last thing I need is more ideas." He laughed. "I have enough to keep us going for the next four years even without input from Graham or the rest of the team. No way I'll get to them all."

Oh, did she know all about that challenge. "Oh, lordy, sounds like my sketchbook of designs I'll probably never take from paper to fabric because there are only so many hours, not to mention only so much money for fabric. How do you choose which projects to work on?"

She was genuinely interested in his answer, but Derek's words had gotten her brain cranking in ways she couldn't discuss with him: about the sartorial challenges of not being exactly a guy or a girl and whether that might be a potential market for her design skills. Gender-neutral clothing existed, of course, but what about clothes that had elements of both? A man's suit, but with a peplum on the jacket? Or an interesting collar? It would still have to flatter a broader shoulder; not all men were shaped the same, of course, but the likelihood of a wider collarbone was high.

Her gaze trailed over to the dress form. *That* was what was wrong with the collar on Ray's dress. The original pattern had assumed more slope to the upper shoulder.

That was when she realized she hadn't been listening to Derek's response at all, and with a sinking feeling she realized he'd stopped speaking.

"I'm sorry, sugar," she said, and she *was* sorry. Apparently the only thing that could distract her from a man finer than frog hair split three times was puzzling out a particularly thorny sewing problem—and that was a problem when she didn't *want* to be distracted from a man as fine as that. "I just faded right out on you, didn't I? I called you to take a break from figuring out a problem, and I guess you're my lucky charm because my subconscious just started providing the answers I needed."

His laugh was like warm chocolate drizzled on peanut-butter pie. "Well, I guess that means I have a free pass the next time I do the same thing to you. Brand says I do it all the time. As if he isn't just as guilty of it."

Her own laugh released her guilt and tension. "The curse of being creative," she said.

"I can think of worse things," he said. "Do you need to get back to work?"

"In a moment. I know how to move forward now, at least." She paused, truly not ready to stop hearing his voice. Unfortunately, she hadn't planned anything past the opening gambit. What now? "I'd like to see you again," she said, because it was true.

"You're reading my mind, then," he said. "I know it's kind of last-minute, but I'm going to the Nuart's double feature of *La Cage aux Folles* and *The Birdcage* on Tuesday night. It's a midnight showing of *The Birdcage*, so if you can't stay that late…"

"No, that sounds sweeter than rock sugar," she said. "*The Birdcage* is one of those movies I can't stop watching if I catch it on TV, no matter where I started watching. I've never seen the original, though."

"Me, neither," he said. "And I love *The Birdcage*, too. I'll be honest: I'm going as research for an episode I'm working on. So it's a date, but…"

"It's a date, and no buts about it," Luanna said. "Text me the details, and I'll meet you there."

"I'm looking forward to it, Luanna," he said, and she could hear that piratical timbre in his voice. Mmmm.

She hit End on her phone, feeling like a weight had lifted. Sometimes the clichés were true. Knowing specifically when she'd see him again felt like a relief—now she knew what she was looking forward to. She did a little dance in place.

And at that moment, it also became abundantly obvious how to fix Ray's dress, without nearly as much fussing as she'd thought. Grinning, Luanna plugged her phone into the set of small speakers, selected her Happy Sewing playlist, grabbed a fabric marking pen, and went to town.

*

"Expecting the apocalypse to happen while we're watching the movie?" Derek asked, picking up Luanna's enormous tub of popcorn so she had her hands free for her bottle of water and box of M&M's and fistful of napkins. Seriously, the tub had to be the size of his own head.

"Don't be silly," she said. "Popcorn and candy is part of the movie-going experience; it's too easy to sit at home in your underwear watching a DVD and eating leftovers."

His brain immediately supplied him with several mental pictures of Luanna in her underwear. Different colors and styles, as if he were perusing a lingerie catalogue and she was the only model.

He chose all of them. Or none at all. If she liked sexy underthings, that was a bonus, but if she was more comfortable in Jockey for Her, he was fine with that, too. He was more interested in Luanna the person, and that included her fashion choices.

Tonight she had on a pair of jeans, knee-high brown boots with a low heel, and a long-sleeved, vee-necked, mint green top that brought out her eyes and flirted around her curves. She'd piled her long blond hair up in a messy updo he knew took ages to perfect, but more importantly it exposed the soft skin at the nape of her neck, and he wanted to nuzzle her there, breathe in that sunshine smell of hers, hear her soft noises of pleasure.

Then he wanted to do other things that would make her noises of pleasure get a lot louder.

Not right now, though. Later. Now he wanted to hang out and watch movies with her, get to know her better while they waited for the films to start, find out what parts of *The Birdcage* made her laugh out loud.

"Besides," she added, because all of his thoughts had happened in a flash, and they were still having a conversation, "it's a double feature—and the popcorn's for sharing. It's only fair."

He'd bought the tickets, noting that it was a work expenditure.

"I bow to your superior logic," he said. "Shall we?"

They got their tickets ripped, went into the theater, and settled into comfy seats about halfway down the aisle but off to the side. There was a smattering of patrons—not too bad for a Tuesday night foreign film with subtitles—and none of them were nearby.

The walls of the Art Deco theater were draped with pleated, cardinal-red fabric, and the ceiling shimmered with gilt medallions and molding. The seats, however, were modern, and quite comfortable, with a bit of a rocking motion.

Derek tucked a small flip-top notebook and a pen in his cup holder.

"You can write in the dark?" Luanna asked dubiously.

He clicked the pen. At the end of it, just above the tip, glowed a ring of light. "It's not nearly as intrusive as a cell phone," he said, "but I still like to sit away from people if I can, so I don't distract them."

"Whoa!" She took it from him and played with it, flicking the light on and off. "That's slicker than Satan's skating rink!"

He loved her crazy metaphors, and the way her nose crinkled when she laughed. So many women in LA felt they had to act a certain way, be a certain way, but Luanna was just Luanna, damn the torpedoes, full speed ahead.

Damn, now *he* was doing the metaphor.

The lights went down, and during the reminders to silence your cell phone and STFU, Derek reached over for a handful of that buttery popcorn that smelled like heaven in a cardboard tub.

His hand collided, mid-scoop, with Luanna's.

Instant electricity.

He drew his hand back slowly, deliberately sliding his now-buttery fingers against hers.

"Sorry," he murmured.

In the dim light of the theater advertisements, he saw the corner of her mouth quirk. "I'm not," she said, and slipped a piece of popcorn into her mouth.

That would have been enough. But she followed it up by delicately licking the butter from her fingertips, and he could have assumed it was an automatic response except for the way she kept her eyes on his as she did it.

He was massively turned on by the fact that she gave as good as she got. He'd had his share of women, and not all had understood the long game. Those that had, had been more passive, not just letting him set the pace but expecting him to, waiting for him to make the next move.

Luanna, he sensed, got it.

It wasn't about teasing…more about flirting. Seduction. Stoking the fire so when the time was right, the conflagration would roar and singe your ever-loving eyebrows off.

He shifted in his seat, looking forward to setting her world on fire.

They didn't interact much during *La Cage aux Folles*. Subtitles required attention, plus he scribbled a few notes here and there, things he noticed were different between this movie and the remake they'd see next. And things that were the same, that caught his eye.

But still, Luanna was a constant presence, a heady, sweet distraction.

The line of her throat when she threw her head back and laughed. The concentration in her eyes, her face illuminated by the screen, as she took in a scene. The softness of her hair when he put an arm around her and toyed with a stray lock that tumbled down.

The feel of her hand against his thigh, where she rested it, comfortable and yet…not exactly sexy, but something he was constantly aware of. That she was touching him, the pressure of her hand through his jeans.

When the movie ended, she leapt up from her seat.

"Be right back," she said, waving her empty water bottle to explain the urgency of her departure.

She returned a few minutes later with two bottles of water, handed him one. She was giggling. He raised an eyebrow.

"I was just remembering," she said. "When *The Birdcage* came out, my parents decided to go see it because they liked Robin Williams…but they had no idea what the movie was about."

"And their reaction?"

"Daddy just said, 'Oh.' He was just overwhelmed, I think. He didn't have a problem with it, but it was so far from what he thought he was going to see that he couldn't process. Plus he's a polite man of few words. Momma, on the other hand, wanted to know where they found their false eyelashes." She laughed. "She said, 'Dayum, those drag queens have the best clothes!'"

"Your mother seems to have a handle on what's important in life," he said.

"She does have her opinions, and isn't hesitant to share them," Luanna agreed. "So, what did you think of the movie?"

He pondered how to pull his scattered thoughts together. Scattered not just because there was a lot to consider about the movie, but also because of her presence.

"I'll have more figured out once I re-watch *The Birdcage*, because it's been a while since I've seen it," he said. "Right now, I think the ending is one of the most striking differences. In this one, it's the father who takes off his partner's wig and says 'He has two fathers: us.' If I'm remembering correctly, in *The Birdcage*, the son is the one who reveals the truth."

"You're right! I'd forgotten that," Luanna said. "Now I'm looking forward to the second movie even more, to compare it. The daughter's relationship with her father seemed different, too, but I'm with you—I need to see *The Birdcage* again to really get a sense of it. This is fun! I can't wait to talk about it afterward."

"Me, too," he said, genuinely happy. He leaned over, kissed her. He'd meant it to be just a brush on the lips, but realized almost immediately that he was an idiot for thinking that. Luanna caused a reaction in him that he imagined was similar to how women reacted to chocolate: he wasn't satisfied with a quick taste.

He had to indulge, savor.

She tasted of butter and salt, and he thought, vaguely, that he'd never be able to go to the movies again without getting a hint of an erection.

Which was going to be awkward, because he went to the movies fairly often.

But right now, he didn't care. All he cared about was Luanna's soft lips, and the silky feel of her hair in his fingers, and the delicious tight feeling he got in his groin any time he touched her.

He was so, so tempted to say screw it, we can watch the movie on Netflix later, let's go back to my place so I can explore every inch of your luscious body. And it would be good, so very good.

He wanted it to be better than that. He wanted it to be explosive, off the charts. To the point of needing each other so badly, they couldn't stop even if the apocalypse happened.

He knew it would be. He'd had the first sense of it the night they met, on New Year's Eve, when he'd kissed her hand. He'd kissed other women's hands as a greeting, and not all of them got it. Not all of them reacted with the new, dawning understanding that their knuckles could be, with the right person, an erogenous zone. That any part of their body—every part of their body—could be.

He'd sensed Luanna got it, and she'd proven that the other night in the car. She'd agreed to wait; agreed, as near as he could tell, that she understood how good it could be, *would* be.

As if by mutual agreement, they both pulled back from the kiss at the same time. His body thrummed, his heart throbbing in time with his cock. Luanna made it worse by uncapping her bottle of water and taking a long swig.

Lucky damn bottle.

"Whew," Luanna said, a sparkle of amusement in her green eyes, "it's hotter in here than a goat's butt in a pepper patch."

"I'll…take that as a compliment," Derek said, because, in fact, the A/C seemed to be on the Decidedly Frosty setting.

"Before we do something that will get us kicked out of the theater, tell me about the episode you're researching for," she said. "What exactly will it be about?"

He hesitated.

Sometimes he didn't like talking too much about ideas until they were better formulated—but that wasn't the issue this time. This topic had become personal in a weird way and the interview he'd done the other day had thrown him for a loop. His brain was processing things that had nothing to do with work, but he wasn't ready to blurt about his mom's midlife shift from married-to-his-dad, ultra-girly homemaker to leather-clad butch dyke with a serious girlfriend. He'd be nothing but supportive if a random friend came out and made dramatic changes in their life and their look, but this was his *mom* and part of him wasn't coping all that well.

And Luanna had gotten really quiet when he'd talked about his interview with Ash. Luanna seemed like the type who'd be fine with someone's sexuality or gender identity once she actually knew them, but maybe the abstract idea threw her. Which might make things awkward as long as "Derek's mother" was an abstract idea, not an individual.

"I'm still in the information-gathering stage," he said carefully. "You know the show's about societal trends throughout history. For this episode, I've been thinking about how men's fashion changed throughout the years—what was considered 'masculine' in one time period can be entirely different in another. Hair length, for example. Or the frills and lace of the 17th century fops, which was briefly revisited again in the New Romantic movement in the 1980s. Not that the New Romantics were considered mainstream."

"Well," Luanna said, "keep in mind 'fop' was a pejorative term."

He blinked in surprise, and she tapped him on the knee.

Rested her hand there again, making him aware of that contact, that warmth, which radiated out.

"Clothing designer, remember?" she said. "I haven't studied fashion history in depth, but I have a passing knowledge of it. Took one semester in college and I've done a bit of research on my own, mostly when I saw a movie and the historical costumes looked about as crazy as a coat on a chicken. Anyway, you're right that 17th century men's clothing was a lot frillier than would be considered normal today. But a fop was a man overly concerned with his appearance, and usually kind of an airhead."

"Point taken," he said. Now the warmth he felt wasn't just because of physical contact. There weren't many people he could carry on a conversation like this with. "Anyway, I'm not sure yet how I'll narrow the big idea down into an episode. Especially since the conversation with that genderfluid performer added even more avenues to explore."

"I'm looking forward to seeing it when you do," she said. "And let me know if I can help with the research. I can dig out my reading list."

The big screen changed from silent advertisements to a second showing of the admonishments to be quiet as the lights dimmed again. Luanna glanced around.

"Well," she said, "guess your pen won't bother anyone."

Derek followed her gaze. She was right; the theater was empty except for the two of them. Midnight on a Tuesday (well, Wednesday now): not prime movie-watching scheduling.

The movie started, a swoop over the ocean to the glowing pastel skyline of South Beach and then right into the club and the drag show.

He pondered the difference in setting, especially the time: he didn't know what the French attitude toward gays was in the late 1970s, but in the late 1990s in America, it was still somewhat bleak, although there were pockets where it was more acceptable. Hence the movie's Miami setting.

He jotted a quick note, returned the notebook to the plastic cup holder.

During the first movie, he'd been aware of Luanna at his side, enjoyed her nearness. Now, again, she rested her hand on his thigh, and he felt the delicious heat of that contact.

They were the only people in the theater. And they'd both seen this movie before.

And she was intoxicating.

He slid his hand beneath hers, stroked his thumb across her palm, a slow, seductive movement. A moment later, she curled her hand to do the same to him, and he reveled in the sensation. Her hands were soft, but there was the hint of a callus on her finger, probably from sewing.

He felt like a teenager again, except now, blissfully, he knew what the hell he was doing. A heady combination.

An arm around her, a dip of his head to nuzzle her neck, gently nip her flesh, revel in the sound of her indrawn breath. Women sounded so sexy when they were aroused. He imagined the lush, drawn-out vowels of Luanna's speech laced with what she wanted him to do, what she wanted to do to him, and that erection he'd been trying to stave off surged fresh.

And Luanna, sweet Luanna, was clearly someone who never backed down from a challenge. She turned to him, nibbled on his jaw, found his earlobe. How could she be the first woman to discover the gold hoop in his ear made that area all the more sensitive, teaching him something he'd never realized himself?

He kissed, she licked. He licked, she nibbled. He nibbled…

Oh, sweet Jesus, she stroked. Her eyes were on the movie screen, but her hand first rested on his chest, then slipped to his pec, her fingers finding his hard nipple beneath the silk of his shirt. Gentle petting across the peaked nub, the sensations maddening.

"Minx," he breathed against her ear, and she turned her head and smiled at him, a wicked, knowing smile.

His arm around her, he stroked the side of her breast, deliberately avoiding her nipple, making her squirm just a little. Robin Williams and Nathan Lane blurred as he imagined her naked breasts, reddened peaks begging for the touch of his hands and mouth. She'd be glorious, arching into his caresses. Showing him what she liked, what she needed.

Mindful of the possibility of theater staff—exhibitionism had its place, but not on a first date—and aware of the exquisite end goal, he didn't push the game much farther than that. But the discovery that Luanna would play, and play with wicked confidence, was enough to drive him half-insane with lust.

He wasn't sure how he was going to get out of the theater when the movie was over.

Chapter 10

One morning the following week, when she pinned the right sleeve to Ray's dress inside-out for the third time, Luanna knew it was time for a break.

She set down the box of pins, draped the crisp linen back onto the dress form, and left her tiny sewing studio.

She hadn't realized how stuffy it had been in there until she stepped out onto the guest house patio with a snack. The patio wasn't much more than a flat area covered with crazy mosaic paving, arranged with a glass-topped table and four white wrought-iron chairs, and two incredibly comfortable lawn chairs with flowered cushions. The day was warming up, but the patio was still in shade, keeping the air at a reasonable temperature, unlike early afternoon when everyone sane would retreat into air-conditioned interiors.

Evenrude wiggled her butt in welcome, coming over for scritches behind her ears before returning to her favorite spot and settling back down for a hard day's nap.

Luanna took a moment to simply savor the tart Greek yogurt with fresh, sweet strawberries (the yogurt was homemade by Lance, a test batch that didn't quite meet his feeding-to-the-boss standards, but was still better than anything Luanna had gotten from a store) and take a few calming breaths. Neither the yogurt nor the breathing exercises fully cleared away the knot of stress that had taken up residence in her stomach, but they helped.

She'd been jolted awake ridiculously early that morning by a robocall from a creditor, and after that, sleep had been as far away as the moon, her heart thumping as if she were a treed coon with a pack of baying hounds below. So she'd given up and gone to work on Ray's rust linen masterpiece.

The stress wasn't all bad, though. She was also on pins and needles waiting for a callback from a small, up-and-coming athletic-wear design firm she'd interviewed with. It was a temp job, filling in for somebody for a few months—just enough time to fill the gap until Yancy needed her full time for *Magnolia Road*. They'd promised to get back to her with a response today. She felt good about how the interview had gone; they'd been impressed by her sketches and samples, and one of the ladies vetting her was originally from Atlanta, so they'd had a lovely chat about home.

A soft breeze kicked up, caressing her bare arms the way Derek's fingers caressed her flesh, and she shifted in the lawn chair, the heat between her legs a reminder of unfinished, unfulfilled business between them. Lordy, the way he could make a light caress on the inside of her forearm feel like something much more intimate.

She figured she deserved a few minutes to indulge herself in thoughts of Derek. Better that than fret about the email from the student loan people saying she didn't qualify for a hardship deferment and since she was already in arrears they'd need to see a payment ASAP, and a shockingly high quote on both the insurance and the part she needed to get the beater car that replaced the wrecked one back in running order.

She still couldn't get used to the idea she'd have to pay through the nose for a part of a 2002 Toyota Corolla. Back home, you could just put word out to your friends and kin that you needed a part for a 2002 Corolla and someone would know someone who had just such a thing in the barn, or sitting in the backyard, or *in* a 2002 Corolla that they were currently using as a chicken coop because the body was shot to hell but the part you needed was fine once you cleaned out the poo and feathers.

But the strawberries right this moment were perfection—an advantage of living in California was you could get excellent fruit even if you were cash-strapped—the sun was just warm enough to make her feel like a great lazy cat luxuriating in its beams, and thinking about Derek brought her from warm to hot in an entirely pleasurable way. Just thinking about him made her skin tingle. He even held hands sensually. That night at the movies hadn't involved anything she couldn't describe to her grandmothers. (Not that she imagined for a second Grand-mère would be shocked by anything for real, but she'd feel she'd have to pretend. Granny B. would be another story.) But she'd come home wet and just about to burst from pent-up feelings, emotional as well as physical.

He wasn't just hot. She clicked with him. The only off-note she could think of at all was that he'd gotten twitchy when she'd asked about the show. For a second, she'd wondered what was up there. But the creative process could be weird and fragile and once he explained he wasn't ready to say a lot, it made sense to her. She'd learned back in high school that she'd lose the spark of a design idea if she talked about it before it was clear in her head, and that she shouldn't show sketches to anyone except the client. Even Sandrine, who loved talking about herself (and her crazy-fabulous life did provide great story fodder, so why wouldn't she?), wouldn't get into details about her roles until filming wrapped, just focus on funny incidents that happened between takes or her co-stars' quirks.

So that was all right too. Just a further note of complexity in a smart guy with magic hands. And while Luanna knew she ought to be making a decision about the car part and seeing how much she could send the student loan company and still eat regularly, she'd just sit here and enjoy the morning and the sexy daydreams a bit longer...

Lost in sensuous thought, she jumped when the phone rang. Caller ID said it was the athletic-wear design firm.

Even if they were interrupting a damn good fantasy, work was work, and she was never going to take it for granted again. She swallowed her bite of yogurt, stored pleasant-Derek thoughts away for later, and answered.

Her good mood turned as fast as a storm coming in over the Gulf.

They'd clearly talked to Luscious. So obvious, by the way the HR lady expressed regrets without sounding regretful at all, and the bland, meaningless phrases she'd used. Nothing about Luanna not being qualified for the job, or even that they'd gone with another candidate. More along the lines of deciding to go in another bleeping direction.

Before she'd even gotten off the call, another came through: the people for her *other* student loan.

Lord, these people were getting as trigger-happy as Uncle Claude during hunting season. At least they couldn't repo her degree, and she'd worry about getting her wages garnished when she, you know, had wages. They could leave her another voice mail she wouldn't listen to anyway.

She politely thanked the design firm HR lady for her time, hung up, and leaned forward in her chair, her elbows on her knees and her thumbs pressed in the corners of her eyes.

Money was slipping away faster than a contact lens down a drain. She couldn't plug the hole—she'd cut her expenses down to the bare minimum—so she needed cash. Soon.

Think, Luanna.

She was almost done with Ray's dress, and he would pay immediately. In fact, he'd already commissioned her for another project: a bridesmaid type of dress (he already had a design in mind, even) for Chloe's wedding. Well, not *for* the wedding, but in honor of. Privately.

"I wanted you to have enough time to work on it before you had to make the actual bridesmaid's dresses," he said.

Obviously he'd figured out she needed money, and she knew that he knew, and she blessed his big ol' heart for not making a big deal out of it but giving her a way to save face.

She was half-tempted to ask for an advance on the dress…. No, not even half-tempted. Maybe one-half percent. She didn't like owing people money, and the fact was, she kept screwing up this current dress because she was rushing it so she could get paid sooner. She believed in artists getting paid for their art, but the minute the art started to be *about* money, it messed her up something fierce.

She'd already composed a carefully phrased email to her personal clients. Not wanting to sound too desperate (after all, it had been a couple of weeks ago, before she'd felt so desperate), so she'd simply noted that she was between jobs and had plenty of time for new projects, and thus if they had a project they'd been considering, this was an excellent time to book a slot. Didn't mention being broke at all, though she thought she implied she could use an infusion of cash if they had some to spend on new clothes.

She sent each email individually, both to personalize them and because bcc wasn't foolproof, and she had their anonymity to protect.

She wasn't going to ask her family or friends for money. Just no. Goodness knew Sandrine could afford to loan her some, but she was already living rent-free on the estate, so no.

Maybe she could ask Yancy if she needed any under-the-table assistance on her current job? Or would that look bad, and jeopardize things with *Magnolia Road*?

Before she had time to ponder the pros and cons of that, her phone vibrated yet again.

She opened one eye and looked sideways at the screen suspiciously.

Then felt a shiver of unexpected delight to see Derek's name.

Heard from the design firm yet? Fingers crossed for you!

She sighed, grabbed the phone, responded.

Big fat nope on the job. Hope your day's going like gangbusters, though.

It was a little too early in their relationship for her to be crying on his shoulder, but she felt better just knowing he'd been thinking about her and rooting for her and had taken a moment out of his no doubt busy day to say so.

Just thinking about him drained a little of the tension out of her body and a little of the frustration out of her soul. In fact, she felt better enough to go back in and tackle that sleeve once again.

When the phone rang, she almost ignored it, preferring to focus something she *could* control rather than whatever annoyance the outside world was trying to throw at her now.

On the other hand, the call might bring something positive. A client with a new commission. Chloe and Brand with an invitation over for cocktails and dinner. (She made a quick mental note to grab some dinner soon if the call *wasn't* an offer of Chloe's fabulous food.) Grand-mère with family gossip and supportive sayings, as comforting as gumbo and hugs through the phone.

The caller was better than all of those put together, though. It was Derek.

"I'm so sorry about the job, Luanna. That sucks."

"Could be worse, right? At least they called instead of leaving me dangling, so I can move on."

"I have to admit," Derek said, "I'm impressed with how quickly you're bouncing back."

Even though Derek couldn't see her, Luanna shrugged and tried to plaster on a smile. It was what you did when things got tough. No point in dragging your friends down with you. "If it had been the right job for me, it would have worked out. I'll be getting work before long, I know. Your movie's starting soon enough, and meanwhile I've pinged…"

She stopped herself before she could say *all my clients*, because Derek might ask more about her clients and then what would she do? She could misdirect like a champion, and had so far whenever she'd had to mention a private client, but she was terrible at actual lying, especially to someone she liked.

Speaking of misdirection, she'd better finish her sentence. "Pinged every temp agency in the greater Los Angeles area. But let's not talk about that anymore. I'm fine. Let's go on to something more cheerful." Which was on her list to do once she got off the phone with Derek, so it rolled off her tongue smoothly enough.

"I can't help much with the job hunt," Derek said, "but maybe I can help improve your mood." His voice dropped to a deep, intimate pitch. "Would you like that? And are you alone?"

Luanna clenched all over. It wasn't the first time today she'd clenched up, but definitely the first time it had been in the fun way. "I'm on the patio. Let me get into the house." Derek might be taking the scenic route to the ultimate destination of their prolonged tease, but the way the man talked, a guided tour of the scenic route was bound to improve her mood and release some of her tension.

As she headed inside, she added, "What exactly did you have in mind?"

A deep chuckle that reminded her of rum and sunshine. "I thought you might like to…get comfortable…and have me tell you a story. You'll have to give me some details to get me started, though. Set the scene for me."

Arousal skittered over Luanna's skin. Derek weaving a deliciously dirty story would definitely get her mind off her problems. Not to mention being hot as Tabasco peppers.

She took a deep breath, imagined Derek in the bedroom with her (which was less awkward, somehow, than spilling her fantasies into the phone), and said, "I have so many lovely, naughty ideas it's hard to pick just one."

She felt the tension fade, slowly being replaced by shivers of desire. She decided to ground herself by describing her (imaginary) outfit. It came as a surprise to no one, least of all herself, that she would think of clothing first.

"Picture me wearing an emerald green satin nightgown. It's floor length, and it has a deep V neck and it's snug over my bodice, then flares out a bit. And you're naked. No, you're dressed at the beginning, but I'll be getting you naked, very, very slowly." Her original fantasy had mostly involved what he was doing to her, but she'd also had ideas of fun stuff to do to him, and that part of the naughtiness felt more natural to spin out right now.

"I like where this is going."

"You'd be wearing a button-down shirt"—because if she was going this route, she might as well make it detailed. "A deep red one, because that color brings out the pirate in you. Makes you look all tanned and golden and fierce."

He laughed, low and husky, at that. "Pirate, hmm? Hmm…"

"Black jeans that have softened and faded so they're almost charcoal gray, ones that fit you well, cup your ass and thighs and…uh, accent your package." Her voice dropped to a whisper as she said that last bit and she felt herself flushing from her eyebrows right down to her cleavage.

She glanced down. Yeah, her cleavage actually was flushed, at least what she could see under a modest V-necked shirt.

"I'd start on the shirt," she continued, "unbuttoning each button carefully, then planting a kiss at the skin I'd exposed. I'd take my time, until you'd just want to rip the shirt off. But you wouldn't, because you understand what I'm doing. That though we're finally going to get naked and we're both looking forward to the end result, I'm taking my time getting there and making sure we both enjoy the process..."

"Even if it makes us crazy."

"Exactly." Sweet baby Jesus, how could he say six words that out of context weren't even sexy and jack her arousal even higher? She was turned on by the images in her mind, by her own daring and dirty talk, but he'd just ramped it up. "And once I'd unbuttoned your shirt, I'd run my hands over your chest and feel your skin, feel every inch of it. Then I'd stand back and just enjoy the view for a minute or two before I slipped that shirt off you. Only then would I start on your jeans."

"Would you kneel to open my jeans?" His voice was smoky, and she swore it caressed her skin. Not even intimate areas, but that sensitive spot on the inside of her arm he'd discovered at the movies.

Suddenly her panties felt warm and humid as the bayou on a summer day, because she knew exactly where kneeling in front of him would lead and it was a place she definitely wanted to go.

She brushed her hand over an aching nipple, taunting it through her shirt and bra but imagining silk satin, as she said, "I'd be tempted. But I wouldn't, not right away. First I'd cup your ass with both hands, just enjoy the feel of it. Then I'd trail the fingers of one hand around to the front and stroke around your cock without quite touching it. I'll wait until you start bucking your hips forward, seeking more contact, before I open the button at your waist and unzip you."

"I'm hard."

She could hear the tension—the sweet, erotic tension—in his voice even in just two words.

Two words that made her shiver again, knowing her words were what made him hard.

"And I'll trace the outline of your cock through your briefs before I finally do kneel down and kiss the head of your cock through the fabric."

"I'm stroking myself, but through my jeans, because I'm trying not to get too far ahead of what you're describing. It's not easy, though. I want to touch myself so badly. No, I want you to touch me."

Something exploded in Luanna's brain and something else exploded in her panties. All her skin felt sensitized, almost raw, but in a good way. She wasn't wearing much, just a light T-shirt and a pair of loose cotton-knit shorts, lavender and gray tartan, that were meant to be pajama bottoms. "Just a second," she said, surprised by how her voice slipped into a sultry whisper like something from an old movie. "I'm getting undressed."

Derek groaned as first the shirt, then the shorts, hit the floor. "I knew I should have made this a video call. Are you naked?"

"Except for panties." A devil—a cute one with a sprightly tail and some sexy lingerie—inspired her. "A very damp silk thong. I'm not sure I'll ever be able to get it clean again, and trust me, I know all about cleaning silk." She was actually wearing a very damp, bright blue polka-dot cotton hipster, but if she'd known this part of her day would involve phone sex as well as therapeutic sewing, she'd have gone for something sexier.

Another moan from Derek. "Imagine me pressing my face against that damp thong and just inhaling your fragrance. I bet you smell like spice and peaches."

The small part of Luanna's brain that could still think analytically wanted to protest that women simply didn't smell like peaches, though that was lovely poetic license.

The rest of her brain, along with her body, had melted too thoroughly to care about that, or to worry too much about the fact they'd gotten their erotic logistics all screwed up. But she did have to set the record straight, however feebly. "That's making me all fluttery, and it's a good thing I'm already sitting down or I'd be weak in the knees. But wasn't I about to go down on *you*?"

And she was rewarded by Derek saying, "If you described that now, I'd come in my pants like a teenager. Not that I think I'll necessarily be better off telling you about what I want to do to you, but at least that may buy me time to get undressed."

On top of the waves of desire, Luanna was hit by a feeling of unexpected power at Derek's words. Phone sex had been pretty new to her when she started seeing Derek—the occasional teasing conversation or salacious remark, but nothing like this. And while they'd had some seriously naughty conversations and some texting that skirted on sexting, Derek had usually taken the lead. She felt awkward, but based on Derek's responses, she was definitely getting the hang of it, and that was a heady feeling.

Especially since he was so good at both physical and verbal erotic games.

"So tell me a story," she said, opening her legs and settling back into a more comfortable position on the bed.

Chapter 11

*D*erek had called Luanna from his living room, but had wandered into the bedroom as they talked. And now that the conversation had somehow shifted from moral support to phone sex, he was glad he had. Yeah, no reason a person who lived alone couldn't jerk off in the living room, and he had on occasion. But he wanted to be in the right atmosphere because this was jerking off for and with Luanna, not purely for his own amusement. He wanted to be in his king-size bed with the cool burgundy cotton sheets so he could imagine Luanna spread on them. Wanted to be able to look into his mirror occasionally, not because he wanted to watch himself, but because he wanted to imagine the visual feast that Luanna paired with a reflection of Luanna would be.

When he finally got her in his bedroom.

Whose idea was this slow seduction crap anyway?

Oh, right. His. He couldn't blame anyone but himself for this.

And he didn't really blame himself, sexual frustration notwithstanding. He still believed in slow seduction. In addition to the obvious benefit of making the eventual sex truly mind-boggling—and oh, yes, it would be—it gave you time to get to know each other, see if there was anything more than initial hot attraction, and decide whether to just have some temporary fun if there wasn't. He was getting more certain with each interaction, even simple texts, that there was more than hot monkey lust between him and Luanna. And knowing there was the potential for something serious was good. Having a fling that didn't work out with Brand's future wife's BFF? Awkward, especially since they were Brand and Chloe's best man and maid of honor.

But damn, there was plenty of hot monkey lust, and he was definitely looking forward to a chance to exploring it in the flesh.

With that in mind, he said, "Think how much fun we're going to have when we can stop telling stories and start acting them out."

A throaty laugh teased at his cock, which he was desperately working to get out of jeans that currently seemed as confining and painful as one of those spiked cock rings. (He'd tried one once in the name of research. Definitely not his kink.)

"Yes, but don't ever stop telling me stories, Derek. Even when you're in me. I like the way you do it. It makes me hot."

My. Gawd. He'd been mostly joking when he said he might come in his pants, using it as an excuse to get a turn controlling the game because, much as he loved Luanna's sweet Southern voice describing what she wanted to do to his body, he was already downright addicted to her moans of pleasure. But now he was at definite risk.

He stood and fumbled with his jeans, thanking the tech gods for Bluetooth so he could keep talking.

The jeans were black, though not as faded as Luanna had imagined. His underwear was actually the wine-red she'd imagined his shirt might be, not the scarlet she'd envisioned, but close enough; she definitely had his favorite colors pegged. The shirt, which he was leaving on because he was way more concerned about getting naked from the waist down and fast, was a dark blue T-shirt. He wasn't going to mention that shirt to Luanna. He probably looked far more dashing in her mind than he actually had tonight.

That pirate thing she'd mentioned…he'd have to think of ways to capitalize on that, once he had blood back in his brain.

"It makes me hot to do it," he said. "I wish I didn't have to wait to actually taste you." There, he was free of both jeans and underwear. He stepped out of them, kicked them aside so they slid across the bare bamboo floor in the general direction of the laundry basket. "But it won't be much longer. Meanwhile, imagine me there, between your legs, breathing in your scent through silk."

"Oooh, yeah." He had a feeling she was doing more than imagining and her next words confirmed it. "I've cupped myself, just kind of hovering, you know. Not playing with myself yet, just feeling the heat pouring off me like you would be. I can smell how turned on I am. Wish you could."

Derek flopped down onto the bed, grabbed his cock. This had started as a slow tease, but for both their sakes, he was going to have to speed this session up. He glanced at the mirror for a second. Yeah, he'd be able to see Luanna and her reflection at the same time. Which was weird mirror placement when he wasn't having sex with another person because he wasn't into watching himself, let alone seeing himself all bleary-eyed staggering out of bed, but it was where the mirror fit.

Would definitely be fun in the future though.

"Now lie back. My head's between your legs, remember? And I'm pushing your thong out of the way."

The sound she made might have had words in it, but it was more like an animal growl, and it coaxed out a spurt of pre-come, slicking his cock as he worked it.

"It has bows on the side," she finally managed to say. "You can just untie those."

"I like that." Though at the moment, if he'd really been there, he'd be ham-handed with lust, unable to muster the coordination to deal with those tiny bows. "I slip the silk away. It's very wet, I bet, but still soft and it'll feel lovely against your clit and lips as I brush it over them."

Her answer was a moan.

God, he loved that sound! He'd never known how turned on he was by a woman's sounds. Maybe it was something about Luanna. Even her sexy noises had a bit of a Southern accent.

"Then I move down so I can taste you. One long, slow lick, savoring your juices. Then I start suckling at your clit." He should be more descriptive, but his cock was overriding his brain, and from the sounds Luanna was making, the mere idea of him going down on her was pushing her buttons. "You taste like…oh, I don't know how to describe it other than like everything I've been dreaming about lately."

"I want you. I'm going to come soon and I want you inside me when I do." A rueful chuckle. "For real, but your words and my fingers will do for tonight. Don't think I'll even need to fire up the vibrator."

Derek flashed to an impossibly vivid image of Luanna sprawled on her bed—he had no idea what her bed looked like, but he pictured a soft, spring-green duvet, the color of her eyes—hair adorably mussed, eyes half-closed in ecstasy, legs splayed open. And those hands, those clever hands of hers, one circling her clit, the other pumping…

"Oh, God. Too much. Too fucking much, Luanna. Yeah, I can't hang on much longer, beautiful. So use your fingers on yourself and imagine my cock instead. Just like I'm imagining I'm entering you…"

There was more he wanted to say, not just describing what decadent, delicious things he wanted to do to her, but telling her how she inspired him, how he smiled whenever he thought of her, how he was looking forward not just to finally doing what they'd been describing, but to the time before and after when they could just hang out and share time.

But the noises she was making, the images of her, the sensations pumping from his cock through his body pushed words away. As an orgasm ripped through him, all he could manage was a strangled, "Luanna!"

She echoed with a cry of "Yes, oh God, yes," and screams that degenerated quickly into happy burbling noises.

Those went on for a few minutes, after the moaning and screaming stopped, and Derek started to worry. They sounded happy, but still kind of…damp. Almost like sobs. That brought him back to his right mind so quickly he feared mental whiplash. "Are you all right?"

"Good tears," she assured, laughing through them. "Catharsis or something. I was wound up tighter than Grandpa's pocket watch and I didn't even know how bad it was until you helped me get rid of some of it."

"Glad I could help." He meant it. "Wish I was there holding you now." He meant that, too.

In fact, he was half-tempted to invite himself over, or invite her over, and do round two in the flesh, so to speak. But just then his phone vibrated, letting him know he had another call coming in.

He glanced at the screen, and a mélange of emotions swirled through him. It was his father.

It was an odd time of day for his father to be calling—he should be at work—and although his parents both insisted their split had been amicable, his father had privately, very briefly, mentioned that he'd been blindsided by the news that his fairly traditional, feminine wife of thirty-four years had morphed into a butch lesbian.

His life hadn't just been shaken up, it had been upended and shaken until the loose change fell out of its pockets.

Good grief. Derek was starting to metaphor like Luanna.

Although his parents had loved each other, and still did in their own way, he knew his father felt adrift, alone after expecting to spend the rest of his life with the woman he'd married. As his father had said, it made him examine their whole relationship.

Derek had gently suggested counseling—that it might help to talk to someone who could offer some perspective—and he hadn't been surprised at his father's frowning response. Professional counselors followed a strict code of silence, but it would still be sharing the family business with an outsider.

Derek didn't think his father needed serious professional help, but he wanted to be there in case his father did need something.

All the thoughts went through his head in a flash, but he also couldn't just hang up on a sobbing Luanna.

He let the call go to voice mail, but said, "I'm so sorry, Luanna, but my dad's calling. I don't want to stop talking to you, but I should call him back."

"Is everything okay?" she asked, and he heard the concern in her voice, and it touched him how quickly she could go from thinking about herself to being worried about someone else.

"I'm sure it's fine, but what with the divorce…he might need a shoulder to lean on." It wasn't a lie, even if it did omit a hell of a lot.

If their relationship progressed—and he seriously hoped it would— he'd tell her the details. There was a point where she might just be close enough to be considered family.

Right now, though, he felt the pinch of not telling her the whole truth.

"Sugar, you go right ahead and hang up on me and call him back," she said firmly, without a hint of the recent wobble of tears. "Family's important. I'll talk to you again soon." Her voice dropped. "Thank you for the story. I look forward to the sequel."

Despite how recently he'd come, and despite his concern over his father's call, Derek felt the stirrings of desire again. How did she do that to him?

"As long as you help me tell it. I'll talk to you soon. Bye."

"Bye, sugar."

As he hung up, he realized he was sorrier to no longer hear the sound of her voice than he was that they weren't going for round two.

And he kind of liked it.

*

The rest of Luanna's day didn't go too badly at all, probably because every time the stress got too bad, she thought back to the conversation with Derek. Phone sex with a delightful man might not solve her problems, but it certainly made them more manageable.

He texted her again that night, just to ask how she was doing, which melted her heart a little.

You put a spring in my step, she answered. *Everything ok w/your dad?*

Yep, he responded. *He was delivering custom table to client*—she remembered him telling her that his dad was a custom woodworker somewhere near Taos—*& saw a garden shop & wanted to know if Betsy would like a dinosaur sculpture for lobby of office.*

Betsy, his sister. A vet.

LOL! she texted. *Would probably frighten the dogs.*

Exactly what I said… Have an early meeting tomorrow, got to go. Sweet dreams. Mine will be of you.

His final words melted her heart a little. *Hope I don't keep you up all night. ;-) Sleep well.*

Chapter 12

The next day started out definitely promising, too. The first thing Luanna saw when she checked her phone was a good morning text from Derek that included some steamy suggestions about how he'd like to make her morning brighter. She responded in kind and the fun continued until Derek pinged back, *In meeting with a funder for MR and hoping I don't have to stand up soon. Better stop…*

Win!

Things continued to go well—if not quite as sexily—from there. Over the course of the day, a couple of clients got in touch regarding ordinary tailoring jobs that they were sending to her. Not much money—wouldn't cover her cell phone bill—but not much time, either, and she appreciated the work as well as the opportunity to help out, and show them she was reliable.

One client had even passed on her name to his sister, whose daughter wanted a special dress for her quinceañera, one that would work with the brace she needed to treat her scoliosis. (She made a firm mental note to herself to not bring up how Jorge knew she could make a party dress to die for unless his sister said something first.)

None of the temp agencies she checked with had anything immediate, but one said they were sending her résumé to be considered for a longer-term possibility that would open up in a few weeks. She even applied for a paid internship at the Fashion Institute of Design & Merchandising; the "paid" part was nominal, but more than her current income of zilch, zip, nada, and if she had to be broke, she might as well be broke, learning things, and bolstering her résumé.

Lance had stopped by with some lovely leftovers and had flirted just enough to be amusing without crossing the line into creepy. And now the satin of Ray's new "bridesmaid" dress was working its magic, letting her direct her energy into the pleasure of sewing.

It was fine until the phone rang at seven.

She snatched it up, hoping for either Derek or a potential employer/client. The number told her otherwise. Her parents. They each had a cell, but they'd clung to their landline as well, and when they called her, Mom took the kitchen extension while Dad grabbed the one in his office. They liked being able to talk to her—or lovingly lecture her—simultaneously, like they'd do if she were on the front porch sipping sweet tea with the two of them.

Dayum, she really needed to set a ringtone just for her parents. Not so she could duck their calls—they were her parents and she loved them and besides, that was a trick for bratty teens, not adults. But the right ringtone would give her a few more seconds to prepare herself.

She took a deep breath and answered.

"Luanna, what's this about a temporary job?" her father demanded. "This time if they want you to sign anything before you're hired, make sure to send to me first so I can be sure it's not so vague they interpret it any dayum-fool way they please, like the last company."

Her father claimed Luscious's use of the non-compete agreement was bogus in her case—but because of the loose wording, it wouldn't be worth suing them. And knowing her father, he'd tried six ways to Sunday to figure out a way he could get her job back or at least make life miserable for a few people at Luscious.

On the other hand, he'd been damned impressed with Zombie Iguana's contract, which had been a relief. Luanna herself had been especially impressed that a company in Hollywood—a town known as much for screwing people over as it was for silver screen entertainment—would be that fair and equitable.

She was sure Graham had had a hand in it, but in her mind, she was giving Derek almost all of the credit.

At the same time, Momma was chiming in with, "I'm so glad about this temporary job, honey! We've all been worryin' about you out there. Phil, did Momma Marie say it was sportswear or athletic wear?"

"I think was clothes for sports, which makes it athletic wear. But she doesn't have the job yet, darling. At least not as of Tuesday when she talked to Maman."

Oh hell. She should have known Grand-mère, aka Maman to her son and Momma Marie to her daughter-in-law, would say something eventually. The parents knew Luanna would sometimes confide in Grand-mère before she was ready to talk to them about something major, so they periodically plied Grand-mère with Sazeracs until she'd fill them on anything they'd missed in Luanna's life.

This time they may have supplemented the cocktails with Momma's famous fried chicken and a peach pie, because Grand-mère had sworn to secrecy until Luanna knew for certain. The timing suggested Grand-mère had been over for dinner.

"I'm still excited!" her mother proclaimed. "Even if it's athletic wear. Maybe Alice Lagrange can find less hideous tennis outfits if you're designing them. Can you picture her in lime green with a flounce, sugar? On the other hand, don't. It will just sour your digestion."

"She doesn't have your sense of style or Luanna's, honey, but let's not be cruel." Daddy was a kind soul unless a legal issue was involved, at which point he turned into a rabid badger on the side of justice and the American way. He even looked a bit like a badger with his stocky build and silver-streaked dark hair.

Momma laughed her just-for-Daddy laugh, the special, musical one that bubbled up when you really loved someone. "I'm not cruel. I'd never say it to her face. But bless her heart, Alice dresses like it's 1972."

"It's just that you always look so beautiful she fades in comparison."

Sweet baby Jesus, her folks could talk the bumper off a truck, and they'd obviously had a few Sazeracs themselves because they were flirting with each other like newlyweds. On the other hand, if they kept it up, maybe they'd forget to ask her directly whether she'd gotten the job. Maybe they'd do what they sometimes did in these moods and make an excuse to get off the phone. Which was cute in an embarrassing way, and tonight would be convenient.

No such luck. Her father's voice shifted from loving partner to loving papa—both affectionate tones, but entirely different. "So when should you get news about this fabled job? Maman thought you might hear soon."

Dayum. No way around it. She could have managed not to bring it up, but she couldn't avoid a direct question. She owed her parents the truth, even if they'd be more unhappy about it than she was.

She was unhappy, but she'd largely made her peace with it.

Deep breath. Brace yourself. "I didn't get the temp job." The words came out so quietly that her mother didn't catch them and asked her to repeat.

"Momma, Daddy, I didn't get it. I thought for sure this one would come through…but I didn't."

Immediately, all banter ceased on her parents' end. "Do you need money?" were the first words out of her father's mouth. "I can send it tomorrow. Hell, it's the 21st century; I can send some by PayPal tonight." She heard keys clicking. Her father was already at it.

"Daddy, stop!" Not that she couldn't use some cash, but she wasn't that desperate yet. She promised herself she'd never get that desperate. "You shouldn't."

Daddy chuckled. "Of course we should, honey. We're your parents. If we could pack you up right this instant and bring you back here safe and sound, we would. But we'll do what we can to help you out from a distance."

"I…" She wouldn't cry. She refused to cry.

Dammit, she was starting to cry.

Then it was Momma's turn. "You *could* come home, you know. There's always room for you here."

"Even less work there." They'd gone over this ad nauseam when she was home for the holidays. And now she had the movie gig, not to mention her clients.

"True." The word might have been an agreement, but Luanna knew her mother wasn't conceding. "You'd have to use this as your home base and expand. I know someone who makes Mardi Gras costumes and she's always flat out busy. I'm sure she could use some help."

"I'll think about it," she said, to placate them. "But I'm not ready to admit defeat yet. The movie job could open up a whole new world for me."

"That's my girl." She swore she could feel her father smile. "We'd welcome you home anytime. But I'm proud that you're continuing to chase your dream."

With that, she had to hang up.

It would freak her parents out to hear her cry.

She managed to pull herself together pretty quickly, though. Just a few sobs to get it out of her system, a few sobs because her parents cared so damn much, and as crazy as they might make her, she loved them and missed them.

Crying, though, wouldn't solve anything.

She didn't feel like she could concentrate on much of anything, so the best thing to do was find something silly on TV and chill. But just in case Derek had emailed—he did that sometimes instead of texting, especially if he either wanted to ask about fashion history or describe a really detailed fantasy—she checked Gmail.

Nothing juicy from Derek. A few cute pictures of a high school friend's new baby, which brought a smile. The usual spam you got when you were applying for jobs, and a couple of potentially decent leads. And an email from one of her clients, Viktor, although the From line of the email said Henry Warmoth, who had been governor of Louisiana during the Reconstruction and who'd died in 1931. She used the names of dead famous people from her home state for her clients, since their privacy was paramount.

Viktor was an older man who couldn't help looking a bit like Grandma Beauregard when he dressed up, with his round face and gray hair. He seemed to enjoy it so much, though, that it didn't matter. She'd done only a couple of commissions for him, but they'd both had fun planning them together.

This time, though, the Subject line of his email was "I can't."

I can't *what*? Can't get a new outfit right now, probably. Unlike most of her clients, Viktor wasn't wealthy; he had to budget for his custom clothes.

Once she opened the email, though, she found a different story:

I can't keep on doing this. My wife has liver cancer; she may not have long to live. I can't continue keeping secrets from her, not now, but how can I tell her when the doctors say she needs to avoid stress? I've never felt like I was doing anything wrong but in this time of crisis, I find myself turning to religion, and my church says this kind of thing is a sin. I love my pretty dresses, love being Georgina once in a while. But I love my wife more. Maybe it's irrational, but I feel like if I make a bargain with God and give up this indulgence, He may listen to my prayers and spare my wife.

That did it. "It's not fair," Luanna yelled to the universe at large. "Dayum you, it's not fair!" Not fair that Viktor's wife was so sick. Not fair that Viktor felt guilty and ashamed about something that had brought him such joy. Not fair that some churches preached that kind of narrow-minded nonsense. Not fair that no matter how hard Viktor bargained with his God, his wife wouldn't be spared. Not fair that so many of her clients were justifiably afraid to go public, and that included Ray, who was almost as brave and forthright as the characters he played. Not fair that gay people and transpeople and people who just liked to play dress-up got shit on by society.

For that matter, it wasn't fair that Sandrine and Brand's parents died so young, or that Jorge's niece would celebrate her 15th birthday in a brace, or that Baton Rouge almost washed away in a flood last summer while both California and the Northeast had a drought. And while it wasn't on the same scale of wrong as early death, injustice, bigotry, and global climate change, it was definitely not fair that she was twenty-seven and essentially back at square one after a promising start to her career.

"Face it," she said out loud to Evenrude, who'd sensed her distress and cuddled up next to her feet, "life just all-around sucks. Except for you.

You're okay. And my parents and Chloe and Derek too. Everything else, not so much." She got on the floor, wrapped her arms around the corgi, and burst into tears. Even though it wouldn't solve anything.

After she cried herself out, she'd considered a beer, but thought better of it and went straight for a shot of bourbon. All that did was make her tummy uneasy and her head woozy. She had the bright idea that food would help, but she'd eaten what Lance brought over for lunch, so she turned to some leftover Thai curry.

Which had gone from pleasant spicy to atomic-death-level overnight.

She ate it anyway. She was a tough Cajun woman, and besides, she couldn't afford to waste food.

Turned out bourbon did a good job cutting the heat. Or maybe made it so she didn't care anymore.

Goodness, her moods were hopping around like a man tryin' to put his pants on when his lover's husband was comin' up the stairs. She hadn't been *that* upset; she just hadn't had the benefit of a good orgasm after one of Derek's fine stories to jump start her catharsis.

She was overwhelmed, yes. She wasn't devastated.

She was just…maudlin might be the right word for it, she mused.

When you were in that kind of mood, it was best not to be alone. A friend to moan to and then laugh with was the prescription. She was reaching for her phone to text Chloe when the phone buzzed, indicating she'd received a text. A laugh startled out of her when she discovered Chloe was texting *her*. Chloe's ear's must've been burning.

Chloe's message was almost identical to what Luanna would've sent to her:

RU free after I get off work tonight? Need girl time. Luanna's response was swift and enthusiastic: *Yes!!!*

Chloe wouldn't get off work for a few hours yet, so Luanna decided to do something productive: clean her sewing studio. It wasn't large, so it got messy quickly, especially when she was working on multiple projects. Plus, having a clean slate showed the universe she was ready for new jobs.

Or so she liked to tell herself.

She put on a peppy music playlist, and as she swept fabric scraps into the trash, put scattered pins back in their magnetized holders, and folded extra fabric, she reviewed the reasons she was staying in California.

She'd made a commitment to Graham and his crew of movie-making maniacs, and it would be *wrong* to back out, especially since Brand had recommended her for the job. Not to mention she'd signed a contract, and she didn't weasel out of responsibilities like that. It might not be the type of thing she'd come out here to pursue, but it was a new, and exciting, possibility.

She had outstanding projects for her clients, too, some she'd committed to only today. Who else would make sure that Lucien had the perfect latex ball gown for that upcoming fetish event or that Beatrice would feel like a princess on her quinces, brace and all? Who else would guard Ray's secrets the way she would, since she was his friend as well as his seamstress?

She still had to make Chloe's wedding dress, too, and she couldn't possibly let her best friend down, and fittings would be a bitch if Luanna, say, ran off to explore getting a fashion job in Europe, where maybe the language barrier would mean the new design firm wouldn't understand Hernando from Luscious's accent.

And then—and then—there was Derek.

On one hand, it felt really premature to add that egg to her basket: a guy with whom she'd had only a couple of dates, and only one of those official. On the other hand, she'd never clicked so quickly and easily with someone before. Hearing his voice—hell, even thinking about him brightened her day.

The room tidied, and her head clear of the bourbon, she did a little work on Ray's bridesmaid's dress, pinning pieces on the dress form set to his measurements. The dress form looked like one of those fake people that football players practiced tackling, broad shouldered and solid.

That kept her occupied until a text from Chloe suggested they meet in the cactus garden. Luanna realized fresh air would do her a world of good, and Evenrude danced as Luanna clipped the leash to her collar.

She grabbed the bottle of bourbon on the way out. In truth, Luanna hadn't had more than that one drink with her leftover Thai. But she'd figured she and Chloe might indulge together. Luanna's recent budget hadn't allowed for alcohol purchasing; the bourbon had been a Christmas present from Grand-mère.

The cactus garden could probably more accurately be called a succulent garden, but Luanna's green thumb extended only to things that thrived in moist heat, like roses and hibiscus and magnolia, so she hadn't a clue what constituted cactus vs. succulent. There were a few stunted saguaros, which weren't even native to this part of California, but mostly there were fat, fleshy plants of various sizes and shapes, some already blooming with pretty red or yellow flowers.

Not her kind of pretty, but it was better than a cement freeway full of blown trash.

Evenrude might not be the sharpest tool in the toolshed, but thanks to her snoutful of spines at Christmastime, she now had a healthy respect for the cacti. She'd learned to pee cacti-adjacent, at least.

Now she whined, peering in all directions.

"I don't think the peacocks are here, darlin'," Luanna said. "But let's see if we can find them after we find Chloe."

Chloe was less hard to find than Evenrude's love interests; she was sitting on a gray stone bench, playing with her phone. She looked as drained as Luanna felt, which wasn't like Chloe, but she jumped up and took a step forward as if to give Luanna her customary hello hug.

She'd obviously stopped at the gatehouse before coming over, as she'd changed from chefs whites to yoga pants, an oversized T-shirt that was likely Brand's, and comfortable flat sandals.

"You look like you've had a day," Chloe said, eyeing the bottle of bourbon.

"Sugar, I have had several days all rolled into one," Luanna said, and held out the bottle. Chloe took a sip, handed it back, and Luanna took a swallow herself. "So what's going on?" she asked.

"You're alone, right?" Chloe asked, peering around Luanna much like Evenrude had just done.

"If you mean in the existential sense, then I'm not quite sure. But if you mean literally, it's just me and 'Rude. Why? Because now you're freaking me out a little bit here. And I'm not wearing a wire, if you're worried about that."

Chloe didn't snicker, which concerned Luanna more.

"I just don't want Sandrine or Olive to hear," Chloe said, sitting back down on the solid, carved bench. "Or Brand, actually, not yet. Not until I figure out what to do."

Chloe had an issue about solving her own problems (and everyone else's in the process), although Brand had been instrumental in showing her that it was okay to rely on friends. The fact that Chloe didn't want to talk to Brand about whatever problem she was having *really* alarmed Luanna. That and the fact that it was the middle of the night, Olive was no doubt at her own home, and Sandrine was in Romania.

"I take it you didn't call me here to talk about wedding dress designs?" Luanna asked.

Chloe brightened a little at that. "Actually, I did want to tell you that I'm leaning toward that design that looks like an evening gown from a '40s movie, with the low back? Although is it possible to lose the ruffles on the train and maybe add pearls on the bodice?"

Luanna let Evenrude off her leash, with a stern finger shake, while she and Chloe discussed dress options. She was looking forward to the challenge of making Chloe's dress, truth be told. It would be a labor of love for her best friend, and she'd never worked on anything quite that elaborate.

But the more they talked, oxymoronically, the quieter Chloe became, until Luanna made the mistake of bringing up shoes (and, more specifically, heels, because if Chloe would be walking down an aisle of grass or, Lord have mercy, sand next to an artificial wave pool, she'd have to rethink stilettos), and Chloe, without warning, burst into tears.

Luanna patted the pockets of her sundress, but she hadn't thought to carry supplies. No matter—Chloe was already fishing out a pack of tissues. Because Chloe, whether she liked it or not, was more prepared than a damn Boy Scout.

Or a Sherpa. Or a St. Bernard. Not that Luanna would ever, *ever* make those comparisons out loud.

"That's…that's what I wanted to talk to you about," Chloe gulped between sobs.

"Shoe heels?" Luanna asked, bewildered.

"No!" Chloe wailed. "The estate. Getting married here."

Luanna took a deep breath, accepted that Chloe wasn't likely to be talking sense for a few minutes, and put her energies into calming her best friend down. When Chloe was ready, she'd explain.

Which, eventually, she did.

Luanna had once gone to a Montiero family reunion. She was pretty sure most of the people at the reunion couldn't parse how exactly they were related to a good number of the others in attendance. The Montieros (and their side arm of Texeiras, bless them), were an enthusiastically fertile lot.

Chloe's "immediate family" included her parents, five brothers, two uncles, two aunts, and six cousins, not to mention in-laws. When you started talking second cousins and this-many-removeds, well, all bets were off.

The point was that all of them, right down to her brother Casey's six-month-old daughter, allegedly, were up in arms about Chloe getting married in California.

"They hate me," Chloe sobbed.

"Oh darlin', hating you is the farthest thing from their minds," Luanna soothed. "If they hated you, they wouldn't care where you got hitched. They love you—maybe more intensely than normal families—and they want to be a part of your celebration."

"Well, then, it's scary to have this level of guilt trip from people who love me."

"Point taken," Luanna said, knowing how strong the Montiero family ties were. "And you're right, they shouldn't be making you feel guilty for your wedding decisions."

Chloe sat up suddenly, out of Luanna's comforting embrace. "But they have a point, you know?" she said. She paused to blow her nose, then tucked the used tissue into a plastic baggie, because of course she had a spare baggie in her pocket. "I don't have any family here, and a very small group of friends—whereas I have an enormous family back east. Maybe I *am* being selfish by planning the wedding here."

Luanna shrugged. "The main pro to having it here is this amazing estate. Sandrine will pull out all the stops for you, you know. She likes you."

"But that's part of the problem," Chloe said. "Of course I appreciate everything Sandrine is willing to do, but it's becoming her wedding, not mine. *I* don't need a wave pool. She's making everything bigger and crazier. I've got a big family, sure, so I expected a big wedding, but not something so…elaborate."

She said *elaborate* like it was a dirty word, and Luanna understood. Chloe was many things, but she wasn't ostentatious (unless it came to food, and even there, she had her limits).

"And another main con to having it here, like you said, is that the bulk of the people you want to invite are back in Rhode Island, or East Coast, at least," Luanna pointed out.

"So do you think I should get married back there?" Chloe asked.

"I think it's something to consider," Luanna said. "It's going to cost a lot less for a few people to fly east than it is to fly half the population of Rhode Island west."

From the other side of the succulent garden came a woman's blood-curdling scream, but neither of them jumped, because they'd become immune to peacock shrieks.

"I think it's something you should discuss with Brand," Luanna added. "But I think he'll be on board with whatever makes sense and makes you happy. As much as he loves Sandrine, he's committing himself to you—and he's so not the type to want wave pools and giant ice sculptures."

"And a fountain shaped like a giant lobster shooting champagne out of its claws," Chloe said. "Sandrine apparently has been talking with some friend of hers who does fundraisers."

"The same one who suggested clowns?"

"I don't even know. Can you imagine?"

"As God is my witness, I cannot," Luanna said. "Talk to Brand," she repeated. "You two will make the right choice for the two of you."

Chloe hesitated. "I know the flight back will be expensive for you…"

"Don't you worry your pretty little head about it," Luanna said. "That's months and months away, and I'm sure I'll be back up to speed by then."

If she was afraid she wouldn't be, she was damned if she'd let that show to Chloe, who needed less stress in her life, not more. But then Chloe said, "So what's been going on with *you*? You've been crying, too."

Of course Chloe could see that, even though it had been several hours ago, Luanna had washed her face since, and there were only some dim solar lights to see by. It was Chloe's gift. She was going to make a terrifyingly astute mother someday.

Luanna sighed. Where to begin? "I guess things feel really up in the air for me right now, and I started to question everything, and my emotions have been all over the place. Today started out really well, you know? But then…"

She summarized the email from Viktor and her anger at the world over the unfairness of it all, and then her parents' call, sweet and loving and unintentionally laced with guilt.

"So then I got to thinking, what if one of them got cancer, or Grandmère or Granny B. up and died, and I'd been out here wasting my time. What if I fail and never make it as a designer, and that was time I could've spent with my family before they passed on?"

"Oh, honey!" Chloe hugged her so hard, she almost knocked over the now nearly empty bottle of bourbon sitting between them. "I'm so sorry that all hit you. First of all, you *will* succeed—you have talent and drive and you're absolutely going to make it. This is a decision we all make, leaving our families to follow our dreams. It's the American dream, practically." She was talking fast, almost tumbling over her words, probably a factor both of wanting to console Luanna and of how much bourbon she'd had. She laughed ruefully. "Look at us, both being all twisted up about wanting to make family happy. I'll bet they'd be horrified to see us this way."

"Because all they care about is wanting to see *us* happy, in the end," Luanna finished. She'd met Chloe's family; she knew it was true—and she knew it was true about her own family. Her parents wanting her to come home was only so they could take care of their baby girl. They hadn't said a peep when she moved to Boston for school, nor to LA for the Luscious job. Oh, they'd been sad to see her go, but they'd supported her one-hundred percent.

She whistled for Evenrude. "We should probably be getting back," she said. "It's late, and the bourbon's pretty much gone."

"You know," Chloe said, linking arms with her as they walked across the estate, "we make a pretty good problem-solving team. If our respective careers tank, maybe we can go into business as…as…shoot, I don't know where I was going with that."

"Advice columnists," Luanna said. "But we're not going to fail. Temporary setbacks happen—but we have each other's backs if they do."

Chapter 13

*D*ating Luanna was turning out to involve all sorts of experiences Derek hadn't expected to have. A Civil War reenactment (which, admittedly, he'd already been considering, but she'd spearheaded and organized it), and now this.

He could only imagine what unexpected things would happen when they finally started sleeping together…

He'd been pondering the idea that today would be the day they took their relationship to the next level because they'd realized they both had the entire day free, but before they'd made any plans, Brand had called and asked if he (and by extension, Luanna—Chloe was in charge of calling her) would be interested in something Derek hadn't even known existed until that very moment.

Glow-in-the-dark mini putt.

"A double date," Brand said. "But not really. You guys are officially dating, right? Then maybe it is sort of a double date, except I'm doing it for work research."

"You're researching a children's birthday venue?" Derek asked, wondering how that could possibly be related to Brand's job creating CGI special effects.

"It's not just for kids—they do adult parties, too. I mean, not *adult*-adult, but you can rent the place for an evening and BYO beer or wine."

Since Derek had been starting to mentally consider the romantic day he and Luanna could spend, he was about to bow out of the double not-a-date date when his phone buzzed and he saw Luanna was calling.

"Hang on," he said to Brand, and put his friend on hold so he could talk to his girlfriend.

Who, it turned out, was bubbling over with excitement about the prospect of glow-in-the-dark mini putt.

Well, that was that. How could he be strong in the face of such adorable enthusiasm? Of course he said yes, and found himself looking forward to it.

And now, here they were.

As the four of them exited the car, Derek scanned the other people coming and going from Friendly Monsters Glow-in-the-Dark mini-putt. It was a large crowd in the sense this seemed to be a popular spot—but a small one in terms in height, since about half of them appeared under twelve. Most of the other adults were riding herd on said children, except for a group of six who might be adults by courtesy in the sense of being old enough to drink or at least vote.

One of Brand's upcoming CGI projects involved creating a haunted mini-putt course for a movie. Or maybe it was a possessed mini-putt course—Derek wasn't entirely sure of that part. But the segment was supposed to be both startling and funny, so something called Friendly Monsters seemed like it could be a font of visual inspiration. Plus the place had comped Brand the tickets, so Derek knew Luanna didn't have to feel the pinch of paying her way.

"Mini-putt was great on family vacations when I was a little kid, but I don't think I've done it since I was eleven." He gestured around. "Which seems to be the target audience."

"You'll have a great time once you get playing," Luanna said. "Mini-golf is great. You'll see." She was actually bouncing in place with excitement. "It's just goofy. You can't take it seriously. Well," she demurred, "I guess Brand will have to take it a little seriously, since he needs ideas to make it silly-scary for his movie. But he'll still be laughing in no time." She poked Derek in the middle of his chest. "And so will you. I promise you'll have a good time."

After she poked him, she laid her hand flat on his chest and held it over his heart as she smiled at him.

"I guess I will." He pretended to sigh as she grabbed his hand and tugged, pulling him toward the entrance, Brand and Chloe following closely behind.

He wasn't fooling anyone. He wasn't even trying to. He knew he'd have a great time tonight.

This might not have been his first choice of date activities, but any chance to hang with his best friend and also spend more time with Luanna had merits. And seeing Luanna's genuine excitement, he remembered how much fun he'd had doing mini-putt as a kid. Those has been outdoor courses, and they'd mostly had goofy themes: pirates or cartoon characters or wild animals. Glowing friendly monsters sounded like they'd be worthy successors to those sun-faded, charming places of the past.

Luanna's hair was drawn up in a high ponytail, her blond waves bouncing around her shoulders as she bounced on her toes. She wore a white knit shirt with dark blue stripes, jeans that molded to her hips in a most appealing way while still looking comfortable (Derek had no doubt she'd be competitive on the links), and white tennis shoes that gave the whole outfit a somewhat retro feel even while it showed off her curves and made her look innocent and sexy in equal measure.

He liked a woman who could look casually sexy—it was less about going all-out on what she wore and more about her personality and energy.

She smelled like her familiar sunshine, with a note of something floral that wasn't one of the standards such as rose or jasmine or lavender.

As they got close to the entrance, he noticed a couple who managed to hold hands as they herded two small boys.

Bittersweet memories flooded him: his parents laughing together, pretending to "help" each other with shots as an excuse to touch. Looking at his memories with an adult perspective, he'd say they desired each other then. They'd definitely loved each other. Hell, they still loved each other—just not in a way that allowed them to be married anymore. Both his parents had changed over the years, his mother especially. Grown, she'd say, and maybe it was true, but shouldn't they have been honest with each other so they could grow apart with grace instead of waiting until everything exploded?

Before he lost himself in useless speculation and grieving—his inner little kid was still raw about the whole thing, even though his adult self could accept that people change and learn about themselves, and even once-healthy relationships can stop fitting the person you've become—he looked at Luanna's brightly smiling, open face.

Yes, even good people lied, sometimes because, like his mom, they were also lying to themselves. It was part of how humans got along. He'd be willing to bet, though, that Luanna didn't lie to herself and only lied to others in the most minor, of-course-you-look-great ways, or to pull off fun surprises. It wouldn't always be easy to deal with, because sometimes you'd rather hear a comfortable lie than an uncomfortable truth, but at least he'd always know where he stood and what was going on.

If he needed additional reasons to like her—and he had a long list already, only some of them related to her sexy curves and pretty face—that would be about five of them.

Then they entered the building and all such bittersweet musings fled, chased by loud music (the old Halloween standby "Monster Mash" at the moment), equally loud glow-in-the-dark colors that stood out against black walls, and distant noises he identified as old-school arcade games in a side room. The entrance area was semi-dark, using black light to garishly illuminate signage. An arched metal doorway past the cashiers' stations was flanked by black-lit mummies that reminded him of Scooby-Doo cartoons from the '70s—a little scary, but a little cockeyed and ridiculous. The sign over the archway read "Enter at Your Own Risk," but judging from the giggles and squeals he was hearing, the only thing people risked was snorting soda up the nose from laughing too hard. Many of the people making happy noises were obviously not kids.

The air smelled of popcorn and cotton candy. And a bit like too many people in an enclosed space, but he was willing to ignore that for the sake of popcorn and cotton candy.

"Okay, you were right," he conceded, squeezing Luanna close and breathing in her sunshine scent instead. "This should be a fun break from adulting."

She smiled up at him, her expression a heady cocktail of sweetness and mischief. "Of course I was right, sugar. I may be wrong about some things, but trust me: when a girl from Louisiana says something's fun, it's fun."

They grabbed their gratis sodas and popcorn from the snack bar (the two teenage workers were dressed like vampires) and entered at their own risk.

The black light illuminated red "bricks" that marked the edges of the path through the course. The first hole was in the form of a sarcophagus with a mummy rising from it. When you missed, which Derek, Brand, and Chloe all did the first time, it rose a little more. It looked more cartoony than menacing, but Luanna shrieked the first time, which was Derek's shot. Then laughed. "Someone had to, and it wasn't going to be you. And certainly not Brand, who could do a scarier mummy in his sleep."

"I think you could, back at UCLA."

Brand shook his head. "No way. I have never CGI'd a mummy in my sleep. I probably *should* have been asleep by the time I finished that assignment, but there was a lot of coffee involved, and some kind of sick smoothie with Red Bull, chocolate milk, and maté that a certain room-mate of mine invented."

Chloe made a face. "Derek, you didn't make that, and Brand, you did *not* drink that. Tell me it isn't so, even if you're lying."

Before either Brand or Derek could answer, Luanna lined up, wiggling her butt in a way that Derek found adorable and distracting, and took her shot. This time, the ball went exactly where it was supposed to go and popped out the mummy's mouth—which Derek thought was far scarier than the mummy itself.

"Nice shot!" Brand avoided answering the question.

Which was probably a good thing. Derek *had* made the smoothie and Brand had been so desperate to stay awake that he drank it. But what would really bother Chloe was that it hadn't been half-bad. At least not to their twenty-year-old palates at three in the morning.

Each hole that followed—there were eighteen in all, just like a real golf course—became more elaborate and sillier. A spooky glowing tree that appeared to have a face. A skeletal dragon, or maybe it was a dino-saur—some kind of huge glowing skeleton, anyway—where you had to get the ball in the mouth so it could come out the end of the tail. A haunted jalopy with eerie green headlights driven by a genuinely creepy clown. A ghost ship complete with ghost pirates. A "cage full of monsters" that tried to catch the ball if it got too close as you zigged and zagged it through the cage.

By Hole 4—a demented-looking jack-o'-lantern with sullen, fiery eyes—Derek dredged up childhood memories, not just of going to mini-putt courses but of how to actually play. He never did manage to catch up with Luanna, who kept getting through on the first stroke until Hole 13, the first two-level one, but he was beating the pants off Brand and Chloe.

Not that it was much of a contest. Brand was more interested in tak-ing pictures and making notes on his phone than he was in actually play-ing, and Chloe declared early on that since she had no clue what she was doing, she was going for maximum comedy. "Did she do that on pur-pose?" Derek whispered to Luanna as Chloe managed to bounce her ball so it skipped out of the area they were playing and into a gaggle of teenag-ers waiting their turn at the next hole, who howled with laughter.

Luanna thought for a second before shaking her head no. "Gotta be an accident. Who wants to be mocked by fifteen-year-olds? If you're doing on purpose, you'd aim at them"—she pointed toward two guys who appeared to be a couple, one with a cherry-red crew cut, the other with a Dr. Who scarf despite the warm day—"because they look like they'd play along."

Derek conceded she had a point.

The last hole was through a two-level Dracula's castle with shrieking bats on springs that popped out to distract you. "The bats look more like butterflies," Derek commented, since they looked orange and pale green thanks to the black light. "Only butterflies with fangs."

"Evil butterflies. Very scary. You better protect me." Luanna leaned against him and snuggled close.

He wrapped his arms around her, pulled her even closer. Partly Derek just wanted to hold her, but partly it was strategy. Only a couple of points separated their scores. A few caresses, a nibble or two on her neck, and maybe she'd screw up her shot and they could at least end in a tie.

He pressed his lips to the place where her neck flowed into her shoulder, meaning to nip playfully. Instead, he simply breathed in the flowers and sunny warmth. He inhaled again, let it out with a sigh, then remembered he was supposed to be distracting her as she set up her shot. He kissed where he was, then worked his way up toward her ear. She was letting out little breathy noises.

He might have been trying to distract her, but her reactions, her scent, her delicious sounds were doing a fine job of distracting him, not to mention the way she wriggled her ass against parts of him that were particularly sensitive even though his jeans.

Damn, this had better wrap up quickly. He wanted to get her alone and feel that round, lovely ass against him without clothes in the way....

And for tonight he'd have to keep on wanting, not doing. He had a meeting with some of the other team members for the show tonight—so many of them were freelancers that it was often easier to get together in the evening than at the Zombie Iguana office during the so-called standard workday.

As he was cursing his crazy schedule, Luanna took half a step away from him and took her shot.

It wasn't a hole in one. It wasn't clear, though, that you *could* get a hole in one on this last hole without actually warping the laws of physics. Instead, she made it in three.

And he was left trying to angle himself so the grandparents (or maybe great-grandparents) and small children in the party waiting their turn at Dracula's castle weren't getting a great view of the bulge in his crotch. Given how well Luanna had done, he couldn't have possibly caught up, but a three-stroke finish would have meant he'd wind up only a few points behind. Thanks to the combination of an awkward angle and the sensation he was being stared at by seventy-somethings, even Chloe did better than he did at the castle—and Chloe still wasn't really trying.

At the end, though, Luanna kissed him, and that made everything better.

Everyone agreed, as they headed back to the car, that Luanna had been right. Mini-putt was a hoot, and a great way to spend some silly time with friends.

"The only thing that would make it better would be cocktails." Derek sighed as he settled into the back seat of the car. Brand had driven, of course, since he had by far the biggest and nicest car. (Or, rather, cars plural. This time he'd chosen the turquoise-and-white 1958 Chevy that was the real-life version of the one Sandrine had driven in *Princess of Nowhere*.)

Luanna raised a fair eyebrow. "The mini-golf course at home had a bar. Not a great one, but a bar. They should do that here."

"Louisiana's special," Chloe said. "Derek's right, though. It would be better with cocktails. Most things are, except driving and knife-work."

"I bet Sandrine…" Then Luanna seemed to catch herself and rephrase what she'd almost said. "I bet Sandrine *would* love this, but it's a good thing we didn't bring her…"

Brand finished the sentence. "Or the next thing we knew, she'd be digging up the cactus garden to put in a mini-putt course with a bar at each hole. Not to mention the paparazzi problem."

"At least we'd have clubs for fending off the paparazzi," Luanna and Chloe said simultaneously.

"And Luanna wouldn't be afraid to use hers if she needed to. She's pretty fierce where her friends are concerned."

Derek felt a warm fuzzy that had nothing—well, not much—to do with the thoughts he'd had to squelch earlier.

*

Luanna had kept a journal since she was a bitty thing, inspired by an aunt who was a poet (with some minor success in literary journals, but far from a household name; it had been a passion for Aunt Ruby, not a vocation).

Luanna had never aspired to be a poet, but like many Southerners, she embraced history with a fiery passion; and even if her teenage-years' journals were full of angst and unrequited crushes and sappy song lyrics (not her own—it wasn't copyright infringement if you weren't publishing them, right?), she could look back on those journals with nostalgia and fondness.

Except for the lyrics. Thank the good Lord her taste in music had matured.

She still journaled, just for herself (she'd never seen the point of posting her innermost thoughts on the Internet for everyone and their mommas to see), usually in the morning, or right before she fell asleep at night. Often just what she'd done that day, or planned to do, and sometimes her thoughts and dreams and problems and to-do lists and sketches of fabulous clothing designs in the margins.

For a few days, her journal had been happy. Positive. Almost bubbly. She didn't give too much detail about the mind-blowing phone call with Derek (when she became a famous designer, after her death someone might want to publish the journal, and some things were just *too* private to share with the world), but her feelings about it were in there, oh yes they were. Including the thought that if they were that compatible sexually when they weren't even in the same room, it boded well for future romps with actual, glorious touching.

She noted that she'd had a fantastic time at mini putt. It also boded well for the future that she and Derek enjoyed doing a variety of things outside of the bedroom—canoodling on the last hole of the links notwithstanding. She'd been a bit disappointed that Derek had had a meeting that night, but there was still time. They were both a bit busy, that was all. It would sort itself out.

In other good news, dear journal, Chloe had finally decided on what style wedding dress she wanted and insisted on paying Luanna her regular deposit. That had allowed her to buy the part for her beater Toyota, and Brand had done the labor for free, since fixing up old cars was his hobby, and 2002 was old enough. Plus he was a nice guy, and she'd tipped him with a promissory for a custom vest for the wedding, complete with the lining of his choice. She suspected he'd choose spaceship fabric.

So she'd bought the yards and yards of satin and a vat of pearls, gotten a running start on Chloe's dress, and was making good headway on Ray's next dress, which meant she'd get paid well before the wedding, too.

Then, her journal turned chaotic. Everything landed on her at once, it seemed, after a period of hurry-up-and-wait. At least it included paid work…did they all have to come through at the same time?

Yancy's current movie project, *Belladonna*, had hit a snag: some studio executives had asked for reshoots, but the characters needed to be wearing costumes that had been water-damaged and shredded when they filmed the underwater base explosion scenes.

So all of the costumes had to be recreated, and of course the rest of the team had moved on to other projects. Could Luanna help?

Of course she could.

Then the active-wear design firm called. The original three-month position had been filled, but now another employee was out for emergency surgery, and would Luanna consider that job, which was really just cutting and assembling samples for their upcoming show, not working on their design team. Turned out someone who worked there was friends with someone who worked at Luscious, and the Luscious employee had raved about working with Luanna. It wasn't stated, but the subtext was that the athletic-wear firm still didn't trust Luanna in their design department, but they were desperate enough to ask her to fill in on a more menial position. Would she consider it?

Of course she would. Even if it galled her a little. Right now, income trumped pride.

And then her former client Viktor called, the one who'd found God in the face of his wife's cancer. Turned out his wife had known about his crossdressing all along, accepted it even if she didn't agree with it, and now wanted to see him happy in a beautiful dress before she died. Of course, Viktor had burned all of his women's clothing. Could Luanna do a rush job for him?

Luanna wept. Of course, of course.

So for the next three weeks and change, her journal looked something like this:

5 a.m. – get up and sew for client
7 a.m. – Starbucks, grab coffee and protein breakfast box, fight hell-
       ish LA traffic to get to temp job

8 a.m. to 5:30 p.m. – temp job; deliver costumes and/or run errands for movie on lunch break, racing back to temp job with seconds to spare

5:30 p.m. – remember that she hadn't had lunch, grab In-N-Out for dinner because protein; fight hellish LA traffic to get to the movie shoot; assist as needed

10 p.m. to midnightish or thereabouts – arrive home, grateful for adrenaline keeping her awake on the freeways; fall into bed, sometimes half-clothed.

Lather, rinse, repeat.

Luanna wasn't sure how she was surviving. She'd never liked the joking phrase "I'll sleep when I'm dead," because she knew the power and health benefit of getting a good night's sleep. In any other circumstance, she'd be horrified at herself.

She didn't have the energy to be horrified.

She barely had the energy to shower.

After the first week of shooting, they had Sunday off, and Luanna slept for fourteen hours. When she woke up, she stumbled blearily into the guest house's tiny kitchen to find homemade chicken soup, fresh bread, and a salad of arugula, pears, pumpkin seeds, goat cheese, and lemon dressing, all courtesy of Chloe.

She nearly fell to her knees in praise and thanks. She ate until she was beyond full, and went back to bed.

Monday morning, she was up at 4 a.m., somehow still not feeling rested, and the cycle repeated itself.

One more week, she promised herself.

One more week, and then she could sleep for days…

Chapter 14

*L*uanna finally got a break on the Tuesday of her final week at what she'd privately dubbed the Seven Dwarves period of her life, because it was turning her into at least three of them: Sneezy, Sleepy, and Grumpy. And probably Dopey, too, to be doing it at all.

The director of *Belladonna* wanted a couple of days to go over the dailies—or something like that; Luanna had tuned out after the phrase "time off"—so Luanna's Wednesday evening had opened up. She had time, blessed time, and she intended to use it wisely.

Finish up a small sewing project. Viktor was scheduled for a fitting on Saturday, and she still had a bit to do on his outfit.

Go to bed early enough to get more than four hours of sleep. It might only be five hours, but every little bit helped.

And the most important item on her to-do list: call Derek and actually have a conversation.

They'd texted, but because she was reading and answering when she had a spare thirty seconds (which was sometimes in the bathroom, not that she'd ever tell him that) and he was on a production deadline himself, it had been quick snippets like "Can't wait to see you again," "Miss you" and "Must sleep; thud," interspersed with the occasional naughty suggestion about what they'd like to do to each other when life calmed down.

At least half of her texts, even the simplest ones, contained typos and weird impromptu word choices thanks to being tired enough to trust auto-correct. And once she'd fallen asleep in the middle of writing one and hit send as she dozed off, leaving him mystified as to what she'd actually meant.

But he'd been so sweet, teasing her gently about the most egregious and funny mistakes, but obviously respecting how busy and exhausted she was.

She'd managed to hear his voice exactly five times in nearly three weeks.

And the two times they'd done anything other than light chatting, they'd set up the time to call by text.

Which would be enough to make a cat laugh back home, unless it was business or you were calling your cousin the missionary in some far-flung time zone. Folks in that old-dog-napping-in-the-middle-of-Main-Street town just weren't so busy they had to schedule chatting with friends. Part of the reason she'd been glad to leave and also part of the reason she missed it sometimes.

Tonight, though, the call took her by surprise.

Was it cute or pathetic that she grinned when she saw his number on her phone and her heart was beating a little faster by the time she said, "Hey there, handsome."

Cute, she told herself firmly. And overtired. That might have something to do with the touch of hyperventilation, right?

"Hey yourself, beautiful. Have you had dinner yet?"

"Not yet. I was just finishing up some alterations for a client. I guess I should shove something into my mouth and *then* finish up." It wasn't stupidly late, around eight, but late enough that she should have eaten.

"Is it bad that when you talk about shoving something into your mouth, I think of something much naughtier than a sandwich?"

"Not bad. Naughty, but not bad."

No naughtier than what she'd been imagining about him whenever she had spare brain cells: thoughts of finally getting to strip off his clothes and then carefully peel away what she envisioned as tight scarlet low-cut briefs. Peel them away ever so slowly, not touching the cock those briefs gloriously outlined, teasing him as he'd teased her all this time. She'd finally get to see him naked, and for a few minutes, that's all she'd do: See. Look her fill. Feast her eyes on what, to date, she'd only touched through clothing (and that had been enough to burn into her fingertips). And then, when she'd memorized his beauty, she'd begin to touch…

She realized with a start that she'd missed something Derek had said— she thought some silliness that had happened while filming *his* current work project, but it might have been more sexy teasing for all she knew. "I'm sorry," and she was, because it was foolish to be daydreaming so much about the man that she missed what he was saying, now that they actually had time to talk. "I was a little…" She paused significantly, because why not let him know she'd been thinking about him and wholesome naked adult activities, not about her work schedule for tomorrow or quarterly taxes or something else important but dull. Or dozing off, though she wouldn't want to swear that some of her flights of fancy hadn't actually been snippets of erotic dreams. "Preoccupied. Lost in thought. Thinking about you, as it happens."

"I hope they were good thoughts."

"Oh, yeah."

"I've been thinking about you too. Thinking that I'd really like to see you, even if it's just for a little while. How about I come over with takeout, we'll eat—I got lost in writing and I haven't had anything but a banana since lunch."

Luanna's stomach growled at the prospect of food. The last thing she'd eaten was some canned peaches, and that had been…long enough ago that she wasn't sure.

The idea of seeing Derek made other parts of her growl.

"That's sounds perfect on all fronts," she said.

"Great! Any requests for food?"

"Whatever's fast and on your way."

He suggested the Thai place up the street from his house, and after a quick discussion of dishes, they agreed that they were ordering far too much food, but who cared?

Luanna's face cracked into a yawn as soon as Derek hung up. Well, she'd have time to make some coffee before he arrived. And, she decided, to slip into a pretty pair of matching bra and panties—she was thinking the black-and-cream lace set with little ties on the side of the panties. She figured it would probably be too late after they finished eating to toss out their notion of waiting and finally have mind-altering sex, but being prepared meant the difference between making it to shore or going down with the damn boat.

A few minutes later, she was back in her sewing chair, Evenrude curled at her feet, ready to tackle Viktor's gift to his wife.

Viktor had been a teenager in the '60s, and he'd been dreaming about the fashions of the time ever since. Luanna had found some wonderful white gauzy fabric, heavily embroidered with flowers, to make a yoke-fronted, breezy peasant dress. As a special gift for Viktor, she'd picked up an olive-green-colored shawl that matched one of the hues in the embroidery and a flower crown she was sure he'd love. He deserved it.

Because this would be a looser piece, Viktor's masculine shape didn't affect the design much. An easy job. She could practically do this stuff in her sleep—or could do it while imagining Derek teasing her nipples through her shirt and the lace of her bra until she was half crazed, then easing open the buttons of her green-and-blue striped shirt and slipping it off her shoulders. Once in a while, she took a break and ran her hands over her body, pretending the hands were Derek's.

By sheer luck, she made the last stitches when Derek knocked on her door. Evenrude woke instantly, scrambled to her stubby legs, and headed for the door, bouncing and barking. Not defensive barks, exuberant ones; Evenrude figured every stranger was a chance to make a friend.

She stifled another yawn as she went to open the door. Maybe she should have asked him to get one of those potent Thai iced coffees laced with condensed milk.

Once she saw him, though, she perked up considerably—or at least her nipples did. He wore a simple T-shirt in his favorite deep red and those khaki cargo shorts that guys always wore even though they made most people look lumpy. He managed to look good, although that was probably because she was finally getting a chance to see his legs and they were (as she'd suspected) excellent. Runner's legs, tanned and lean and strong, but not so lean the muscles looked stringy.

He closed the door behind him, set the takeout bags on the floor, and took Luanna into his arms. The kiss went on for a long time, re-expressing everything they'd been saying to each other in their phone calls, both the raunchy ones and the sweeter. Maybe a few things they weren't ready to put into words yet, too. It was easier to talk about lust than about tenderness and deeper feelings—that was hard to do when you weren't yet at the point of declaring love—but the way he kissed her suggested that Derek, like her, might be eager for connection beyond the physical.

Although her wet pussy and the hard cock grinding at her mons through their respective shorts made it clear that the physical was a huge factor.

The phone sex had been wonderful, but being actually, physically touched by him was glorious.

His hands caressed her body. He lingered at her nipples long enough that she gasped, but then moved down. She held her breath, hoping he'd slip a hand inside her shorts and explore how wet and wanton she was already. Instead, he brushed his fingers lightly over her mound, just barely teased at her clit. She bucked her hips forward, canting toward his hand, but he'd already moved away to stroke her belly.

Which choose that moment to produce a sound similar to a bull alligator's mating bellow.

Momma's ladylike influence warred with that of her Devenaux cousins, who were technically grown men but still took pride in really gross digestive noises. In the end, she settled for the unavoidable blush and a shrug before saying, "Well, butter my biscuits, that was special. Guess I was more hungry than I realized."

Derek smiled. "Me too. And not just for your body. In an ideal world, that would be the first course and the actual food would be dessert. But in the real world, shrimp green curry and pad Thai are sounding excellent. Besides, your dog's sniffing at the bag. She's been polite so far, but I don't know how long that'll last."

"Evenrude!" The dog didn't have the grace to look even a smidge guilty, but she slunk away from the food and Luanna rewarded her with scritches and a "Good girl!"

Luanna, admitting to herself that she was half-past starving, sprang into hostess mode, though in a more casual way than either of her grandmothers would approve. The coffee table was covered with the detritus of a busy life: keys, purse, and a Hawaiian-print messenger bag with a coral background and turquoise flowers she used for her temp jobs (it held, along with protein bars, tissues, the latest weekly print-compilation issue of *Women's Wear Daily*, and the thoroughly Post-It-studded script for *Magnolia Road*); junk mail that hadn't made it to recycling; a menu for a Mexican place she'd kept, but never ordered from because delivery got complicated when you lived on a gated estate; and to her embarrassment, a coffee cup she should have washed three days ago. Or maybe three weeks. She cleared the mess by pushing everything else onto the floor and palming the cup as best she could. "Make yourself comfy," she said as she puttered. "I'll grab some plates and napkins," she said.

"Can I help?"

Luanna was about to say yes to Derek's offer—not that she needed a hand with the simple task, but because she wanted to enjoy his company as much as possible.

But she'd left the sewing room door open, a bad habit from living on an estate where everyone knew Ray's proclivities and her side work (although not her other clients). If Derek followed her, he'd get a clear line of sight to see Ray's dress and Viktor's hippie outfit on dress forms. Ray's dress in particular was clearly not for a woman, and that would be bad.

She headed out, suspiciously green-crusted coffee cup in hand. Evenrude trotted along in her wake.

Derek started to take Evenrude's cue. "I'll just…"

"No!" She realized she sounded a little too firm, maybe even snappish, so she turned back the few steps she'd gone—Evenrude continued toward the kitchen because that was where approved food lived and her quest for unapproved food had been thwarted. The necessary steps later, she wrapped her arms around Derek and kissed him soundly. "It's just a few things. Besides, I have this silly Southern girl thing," she bluffed when they came up for air. "I know it's old-fashioned, but when I have a gentleman call for the first time"—she simpered in an exaggerated fashion—"I simply have to pamper him."

Which was a little bit true—Momma and Grandma Beauregard had trained her in charming and spoiling boys for fun and manipulation since she was tiny, though that training was countered by Grand-mère's more down-to-earth and quietly feminist approach to life.

"Since you brought the food, I can at least get plates and napkins," she said. "And drinks, though the choices are pretty much down to water and sweet tea." She'd finished the bourbon the night she and Chloe had had their impromptu girls' night, and deemed it safer for both her budget and her liver not to restock.

"I'll have water. No offense, but sweet tea kind of scares me."

"More for me, then!" She was used to people who weren't from the South dissing her favorite non-alcoholic beverage. To be fair, you probably did have to grow up with it.

She headed toward the kitchen, making sure to shut the sewing room door as she passed it, and scooped out a serving of kibble for Evenrude before grabbing the items she needed. Which, with two glasses (one water, one sweet tea) added to the mix, were more unwieldy than she'd imagined. Thank goodness for Chloe, who'd bought a set of cute serving trays decorated with cocktail-sipping corgis and left a couple for Luanna.

Bonus: not only did the tray make things easier, she actually looked like Super-Hostess even if she was doing nothing more complicated than grabbing plates, forks, and serving spoons and filling two glasses.

Before long, she and Derek were snuggled on the couch, a spread of Thai food on the coffee table (and Evenrude under the table in case of dropped tidbits), drinks handy. Distracting as Derek's thigh was, pressing against hers, Luanna fell on the food with gusto that would please her Cajun relatives and appall the Beauregards. "Perfect," she exclaimed after a couple of bites of the spicy curry. "Thanks for not holding back on the heat. I'm glad you like it three-star spicy too."

"It's a nice contrast to pad Thai."

She took a swig of sweet tea before answering, savoring its cold, sugary flavor. "Chloe could probably explain why it works so well with the noodles. I bet there's a fancy foodie-type explanation for it. I'll stick with *yum*."

Derek was looking at her, not the food, when he echoed her last word. His version of *yum*, though, made her senses sing in anticipation of what would happen after dinner.

She figured they'd eat quickly, but the food was just too good to rush. Besides, after the initial gobble, they had fun feeding each other shrimp and bits of vegetable by hand. Not as elegant as prosciutto-wrapped melon or grilled asparagus spears, but the end result was the same: an excuse to clean your partner's fingers as slowly, sensually, and suggestively as possible.

No wonder that, by the time the food was dwindling, they were licking and nibbling on each other's exposed skin—and quite a bit more of Luanna's skin was exposed than before.

Derek finished the job by unbuttoning her shirt the rest of the way, slowly, his gaze locked with hers. She could see the lust in his eyes, and knew they reflected her own. There was something damn fine and sexy about a man thinking impure thoughts about you but still watching your reactions rather than getting all googly-eyed over your breasts.

Until, that was, he looked down and she heard his breath catch.

She slipped her shirt off the rest of the way and let it hit the floor. He kissed his way down her body, paying special attention to her nipples. Lips and tongue sent tremors of pleasure through her, and she couldn't keep herself from arching her back, pressing herself closer to the source of the erotic sensations.

Everything felt swirly and vaguely unreal, as if the startlingly intense sensations were at the same time distant, dreamlike. Lust and pleasure, sure, but she thought fatigue factored in—she *was* the Queen of the Underslept right now. The fatigue wasn't stopping her nipples from springing to attention under Derek's ministrations, though, or keeping her hands from appreciating the various textures of Derek's body, both the clothed bits and the bare skin. Somewhere along the line he'd lost his shirt. It was a damn shame she'd missed the moment of stripping. The first time you got naked with someone, you revealed more than skin. Had he taken it off slowly, a dance of sorts? No, he must have gotten impatient and ripped it off. Otherwise…

She'd been thinking something, hadn't she? Only Derek's lips had just crossed her body's Mason-Dixon line and were heading south, following the path revealed as he unfastened her shorts. In their wake, they left a devastation on the scale of Sherman's, but in a purely pleasurable way.

Then, just above the blond fluff on her mound, Derek stopped and moaned in frustration.

"Wha…?" She was pretty sure there'd been a complete sentence in her head, but that was all she could manage. With luck he'd take it as the compliment it was.

"Three-star spicy," was all he said, a groan in his voice. He made it sound like a tragedy.

Having come of sexual age in a land of where Tabasco constituted a food group, Luanna understood immediately. It almost *was* a tragedy, at least when you were worked up and inches from your oral goal. "We should both brush teeth and wash our hands," she conceded, "or we'll be sorry."

He grinned wryly as he stood. "Mind if I go first? Might as well pee while I'm at it."

"I've got a spare toothbrush in one of the bathroom cupboards…." She got as far as sitting up straight, but Derek gently pushed her backward against the soft cushions of the couch.

"Stay." He patted his back pocket. "I got this covered."

"You brought a travel toothbrush?" She snorted. "You are such a Boy Scout. Between you and Chloe, Brand could forget his head and one of you would have a spare for him. Just in case."

"Brand's on his own for his cranium challenges. But I knew we'd be having Thai. And that's not all I grabbed at the drug store on the way here." He patted his other pocket, and now that Luanna was looking closely, she saw the outline of condoms. Plural.

"Second door on the left," she directed. She really ought to go with him. Ought at least to go to the kitchen and clean up as best she could so they'd both be ready and there'd be no further interruptions. Ought to make sure he didn't go to the wrong door.

But Derek's magic hands and tongue—and maybe thirty-six hours of little food and almost no sleep—had rendered her boneless. And the couch was so comfortable. "Second door, not the first," she shouted as an afterthought. "Don't open the first. I'm…working on something and it's a surprise." The shawl and flower crown were surprises for Viktor, at least, so it wasn't a lie. Quite.

A laugh came from down the hall. "Your secret is safe from intruders. The bathroom door's open anyway."

Well hurray. That meant she could sit back and relax guilt-free. How come she'd never appreciated before just how cushy this couch was?

*

"And then he says he came out of the bathroom and found me snoring," Luanna told Chloe during her lunch break the next day, as they Skyped on their phones. She was sitting in the small courtyard created by a circle of buildings, one of which housed the athletic-wear firm. The sun dappled through the palm tree fronds, warming the waffle-weave black metal bench she sat on. She stuck her fork into the incredibly good grilled salmon salad Lance had dropped off for her, because Sandrine had decided she couldn't eat salmon for reasons that Luanna didn't quite understand, because Lance spluttered indignantly every time he tried to explain.

"He got me as far as the bedroom," she continued to Chloe, "kissed me on the forehead, said he'd call—I kind of woke up for the kiss and the talking, but I don't remember the walking at all—and went home. After putting the leftovers into the fridge. I'm never going to live this down. We've been teasing each other forever—and by teasing I mean explicit phone sex—but when we finally have a chance to do the deed, I pass out on him. I don't know whether to laugh or cry."

Chloe didn't have any problem making up her mind about the laughing versus crying quandary. She was cracking up in a way Luanna hadn't seen her friend do since wedding madness had started eating her brain. "I can't believe it!"

Luanna sputtered. "I was really tired, but I can't believe it either. How could I pass out on such a hottie?"

"Remember the night I met Brand? I did the same damn thing to him. Embarrassing, but it worked out all right in the long run." Chloe wasn't usually one to flash her engagement ring, but the gesture fit the conversation and definitely made her point: the right guy will laugh off a little disappointment.

How could she have forgotten? Luanna hadn't been there, obviously—well, she'd been in the guest house, but in her own bedroom, with earplugs in because she was a light sleeper—but she'd heard all about it later. Chloe and Brand had attempted to hook up after the first (nightmarish but ultimately successful) party Chloe cooked for Sandrine. Only poor Chloe, exhausted and more than a little tipsy on celebratory champagne, had passed out while Brand was using the bathroom. Scary parallel.

Luanna shook her head. "Girl, you know I love you, but this has to stop. Synchronized periods are normal. Coordinating our meltdowns is odd, but useful. But having the same awkward thing mess up the first time we end up in bed with our boyfriends is just too much!"

"The curse of the modern young professional woman," Chloe said. "We're running ourselves ragged. Of course, Brand's gotten super-busy again as well; I think our honeymoon will end up being more about sleep than frisky times."

"I'm just hoping I get to stay awake long enough to *have* frisky times with Derek," Luanna said. But she was smiling, albeit a bit ruefully. Her life wouldn't be this crazy forever, and when she was working for Zombie Iguana, surely she and Derek would have chances to sneak off…

But right now, her lunch break was over, and her life still *was* crazy. Dammit.

Chapter 15

*I*t was over. Hell month (okay, three and a half weeks, but that counted) was over.

Luanna had enough in her bank account to survive, at least for a little while. It was Friday night, the temp job was over, *Belladonna* had wrapped, Viktor's dress was done, Ray's dress just needed the hem, and the body of Chloe's wedding dress was ready for the first fitting.

But Luanna still had a major conflict.

She wanted to sleep the sleep of the damned.

She wanted to fuck Derek until both their eyes rolled back in their heads.

And Sandrine was just back in town, and *she* wanted an intimate get-together to celebrate wrapping her latest film. Since Luanna technically was squatting on Sandrine's estate (and daily she prayed that Sandrine wouldn't figure that out), she couldn't say no.

She could, however, invite her boyfriend, which would make for a quicker start to the sexy times afterward. Given that Derek was Brand's friend, too, inviting him wasn't too weird.

She blinked gritty eyes as she crossed the estate to the main house. Spring rain softened the air, bringing the fresh scent of eucalyptus and ocean into the evening. Not the glorious Louisiana thunderstorms she was used to, but better than nothing in the desert of Los Angeles.

It woke her up, put a spring in her stride. She had a plan. She figured she'd have one celebratory drink, then drag Derek back to the cottage for a long, long overdue roll in the proverbial hay.

Jump each other's bones. Make the beast with two backs. Knock boots. *Finally.*

She didn't care how exhausted she was—this time, she was going to stay awake. She wanted to touch every last inch of him, feel him touching every last inch of her. Wanted to explode around him as he exploded into her.

And then she wanted to sleep for days, and wake up with him, and somehow convince Chloe, or even Lance, to bring them a sumptuous breakfast in bed, so they had the strength for another go-round.

That was a mighty fine plan, although she hadn't yet consulted with Chloe, or even Lance, about it.

On the way home, she'd picked up coffee, eggs, cheese, bread, Greek yogurt, granola, grapes, and bananas. If they had to cook for themselves, they wouldn't exactly starve.

Luanna tilted her head to feel the misty rain on her face, and didn't even care that she stumbled a little on the gravel pathway. Evenrude paused at the end of her leash and turned her doggy head back at Luanna. *Okay, lady?*

"It's all good, Evenrude. Maybe the peacocks will be there."

The plan had been to have drinks and nibblies by the pool, but the tiny bit of weather drove things inside.

The pathway, lit by solar lights, led to the front walkway. Technically Luanna could have let herself in the side door, but she didn't want to tromp over the wet grass.

"Hey, stranger!"

Footsteps crunched on the gravel behind her, and she turned to see Chloe and Brand. Chloe ran ahead to envelop her in a fierce hug. For a tiny thing, Chloe was unexpectedly strong. Must be all that chopping and kneading.

Brand caught up with them. "How's the shoot going?" he asked.

"Wrapped today, thank the sweet baby Jesus and all the apostles," Luanna said. "And the temp job finished yesterday. I am free and clear to sleep until the cows come home and go out to pasture and come back in again, and *then* we'll do the fitting for your wedding dress, Chloe."

Plus, even though she didn't have another temp job lined up, another one of her crossdressing clients had contacted her about some new pieces, which would help fill in the money gaps for a little while longer.

Chloe nodded as they started walking again. Her dark curls, fluffed up by the sudden and unexpected moisture in the air, bounced around her shoulders. "We have months," she said. "No stress."

"Darlin', I never get stressed—you know that." Luanna grinned. Except most of the time since last fall, but at this point she was used to it. Zen stress. You just accepted it as a natural state of being.

As they came around to the front of the massive Mediterranean mansion, big enough to house a small country, headlights came up the drive.

"That'll be Derek," Brand said. "I keep telling him one of his headlights needs adjusting."

At the mention of Derek's name, Luanna felt the breath go out of her in a *whoosh*. She was only vaguely aware of Chloe tugging Evenrude's leash out of her suddenly nerveless fingers, vaguely had a sense that Chloe and Brand headed into the house, leaving her alone to greet Derek.

The headlights went off, and in the glow of the lamps on either side of the wide steps leading up to the mansion, she saw him lean over and grab something from the passenger seat.

He slid out of the car, smiled, and said, "Hey, you."

The sound of his voice, right in front of her instead of over the magic of Bluetooth, skimmed over her body like her silk robe when he slid it off her (soon…*soon*). He'd make sure it slithered over her hard nipples before it hit the floor. He might even catch it, wrap his hands in it, caress her with silk-covered fingers, frustratingly light and teasing, until she begged him for more.

"Hey," she managed to say.

Boots. Tight jeans. Blue button-down shirt, possibly silk, that matched his eyes. Even from here, she saw the glitter of that tiny hoop in his ear. Her pirate, come to ravish her.

All she could do was stand, somewhat helplessly, her bones melted into pure lust, as he slammed the car door and walked over to her.

He shifted the flowers he clutched into the hand holding the bottle so he could put his free arm around her, which he did, pulling her gently toward him until their bodies molded together. Only then did he bend his head to brush his lips across hers, sensitive flesh rubbing lightly against flesh.

"Missed you," he whispered.

Screw it, Luanna thought. She grabbed his head with both hands, tangling her fingers into his silky hair, and yanked him in closer for a searing kiss that probably would have set the decorative shrubbery nearby on fire if it hadn't been for the misty rain.

She finally let him go, and they both gulped for air. "Missed you, too," she said.

"I can tell," he said. He glanced at the house. "Do we have to?"

Every tingling, horny inch of her body said *Oh, for fuck's sake no, we do not.*

"We do," she said reluctantly. "Just one drink to welcome Sandrine home."

"Okay," he said. "Give me a minute to…not be an impolite houseguest."

He glanced down, and Luanna made the mistake of following his gaze. Her mouth went dry, because all of the moisture in her body went to dampen her panties.

She cleared her throat. "Oh, my. Well. It's a big house, and we can walk slowly. Are those flowers for me?" The arrangement of orange birds-of-paradise, with spikes of white orchid and chartreuse anthuriums, which she always thought of as "flowers with dicks," was striking, but she wasn't sure she liked it. On second glance, she was sure she didn't—she preferred something simple and bright, like tulips, or soft-looking, fragrant flowers that might have come from some grandmother's garden—but she'd never admit it to Derek if he'd gotten her this elegant but weird bouquet.

The question distracted him. "What? Oh, actually, they're for Sandrine. I didn't want to visit empty-handed."

Thank the sweet baby Jesus for that. Sandrine would probably love that exotic sculptural thing they have going.

He held up the bottle. "Ron Zapatera rum from Nicaragua. I know Ray's a fan."

"How piratical of you."

"In that case, I should have brought Sandrine gold or jewels," he said. "But I don't think I can afford her taste." Suddenly his blue eyes widened. "You're not mad I didn't bring you flowers, too, are you?"

She snorted. "Don't be silly. I know my present is the saber you're hiding in your pocket."

"Wicked woman."

She caught his earlobe in her teeth, gently licked the hoop that glittered there.

"Keep that up, and I'm never going in the house," he said, his voice faint.

"I'd say I'm sorry, but I'm not, not really," she admitted. "I'm just thankful my reaction to you isn't as noticeable. Now, we should probably go in before they send out the cavalry—or Evenrude."

As they reached the top of the steps, the door opened. "Hello, you two," Olive said.

Luanna wondered how the hell Olive had known when to open the door. Olive was the sweetest dayum person she'd ever met, but was a little spooky, too, like her Aunt May, who always knew when "Are You Lonesome Tonight" was about to come on the radio.

"Everyone's in the atrium," Olive said.

"There's an atrium?" Luanna asked. She knew she'd seen only a fraction of the house, so she wasn't sure why this surprised her.

"Of course there's an atrium," Olive said.

No, Olive was right. Of course there was.

Derek held the flowers down low as they followed Olive through the house, and Luanna was a good girl and didn't tease him.

She was saving that for later, anyway.

Once again, she was glad she wasn't a guy.

A few moments later, she discovered the Mediterranean-styled ginormous house's secret atrium.

In the middle of the house was an open-air courtyard ringed on all four sides by a covered porch-like area, wider than a walkway to accommodate groups of seating. The interior was gently lit by muted lights tucked into lush greenery the likes of which she couldn't quite identify. Rain pattered on the leaves.

Sandrine, Ray, Chloe, and Brand were already in wicker furniture with deeply cushioned seats near a glowing fire pit. The fire pit had a wide mosaic rim, which was currently decorated with plates and bowls full of nibblies. Luanna wondered when Lance had been informed he should be making hors d'oeuvres for seven. Knowing Sandrine, he'd found out half an hour ago and done Chloe's kind of kitchen magic: grab all these random things and somehow create amazing dishes out of them.

"Darlings!" Sandrine rose from her seat—there was no other way to describe it; she didn't so much "get up" as "levitate"—to give them air kisses. "It's so wonderful to be home among friends!" She wore tailored linen pants and a body-skimming silk tee that highlighted how tiny she was, and she smelled like violets. Luanna never understood how terrorized Chloe had been by Sandrine in the beginning. Sandrine could be a little eccentric, sure, but she always meant well.

"For you," Derek said, holding out the flowers. He looked like a little kid seeking approval, and Luanna was charmed by it. The fact that he'd brought a hostess gift had gone a long way to melting her panties already.

"Oh, how sweet," Sandrine said, accepting them and burying her face in them. "I'm probably allergic," she added, handing them to Olive, who was already standing there with a vase in hand, "but I don't care because they're lovely."

Brand got out of his seat like normal people did. "Drinks?"

Luanna blinked at Chloe in surprise. Her friend was insane about taking care of everyone and not being taken care of. But Chloe lifted a shoulder. "He's the hunky bartender/pool boy, remember?" she said, referring to their first crazy night on the estate, before they knew Brand was Sandrine's brother, not just the shirtless hot guy mixing drinks at a party.

Impressive. He'd actually mellowed Chloe out.

"Wine for me," Luanna said. "Red or white, whatever's open."

Brand nodded, reaching for a bottle.

Derek handed Ray the bottle of rum.

"Ooh," Ray said in his bass rumble. "Thank you. Should I crack this open now?"

Derek shook his head. "I'll stick to wine as well. Plans later."

He said it casually, but Luanna was pretty sure everyone knew what he meant. Especially Olive, who missed *nothing*.

She sipped her wine—a delicate, citrusy Pinot Grigio—and listened to Sandrine tell stories about Romania. The oversized chairs meant that she and Derek couldn't do more than hold hands, but even that was excruciatingly sexy. The warmth of his fingers, the way they squeezed hers a little when he laughed, the way he traced every line on her sensitive flesh like a blind palm reader, just one finger casually setting fire to every nerve in her body.

So she almost missed the change of subject.

"So tell me," Sandrine said, clapping her hands together like a little girl, "how is the wedding planning going?"

Brand blew out a long breath and took a sudden interest in the flora of the atrium.

Chloe froze like a bunny rabbit about to be eaten by a crocodile.

Uh oh. Did Sandrine even know about the change of venue from Brentwood to Galilee, Rhode Island?

Apparently she did, because Chloe opened with "My family." And then she stopped.

Luanna sympathized. Chloe's family was large, loud, and they loved their baby girl to the point of smothering, which was partly why Chloe had moved across the country with Luanna when Luanna had gotten the job with Luscious.

"Your *precious* family!" Sandrine burbled. "Oh, I adore them. Tell me, how are Adelina and dear, sweet Mário? I can't wait to see them again."

Sandrine and Brand's parents had died when Sandrine was fifteen and they were pretty much all the family each other had. When Chloe's family had unexpectedly descended on the estate just in time for Sandrine's extravagant birthday bash, which Chloe had been catering, everyone had pitched in to keep them occupied so Chloe could do what she was best at. Sandrine had been one of the pitcher-inners, even.

"They're fine," Chloe said. "They're really excited about the wedding, especially my mother, because I'm the only girl. It's just…" She stopped again. Luanna knew her friend would happily vent to her in private, but in front of the group, she didn't want to say anything negative; she really did love her crazy mob of relatives.

And, Luanna knew, Chloe especially didn't want to say anything in front of Sandrine.

But the question hung in the air like a pregnant spider looking for a place to start weaving her web.

"I'm sorry, Sandrine," Chloe said at last. "I love my family, you know that, but…but they're just driving me crazy about the wedding!"

Luanna bit her lip. She and Brand were probably the only ones who heard the words Chloe thought but didn't speak—that her family was driving her as crazy as Sandrine had. Luanna gulped her wine and braced for the worst.

But Sandrine did the unexpected: she burst into peals of delicate laughter that tinkled like bells.

Luanna leaned over to Derek and murmured, "This is random. Hold on to your hat."

"I'd rather hold on to you," he murmured back, squeezing her hand. "Preferably naked."

Dammit. She squirmed in her seat. They couldn't leave now, not unless everybody bolted simultaneously.

"Oh, darling," Sandrine said finally, "of *course* your family is driving you crazy. That's what families *do*."

They all stared at her, and she waved a pale, fine-boned hand. "In the film I just wrapped, I played a family therapist."

"I thought it was a spy movie," Brand said.

"Well, yes, but before I went on the run, I was a family therapist, so I did lots of reading," she went on. "So I totally understand what Chloe's going through."

If playing a family therapist made Sandrine an expert, Luanna wondered, then what did it mean that she'd played a deadly assassin in *Silk and Suede*? She decided she didn't want to know. Ray, however, beamed proudly at his girlfriend as if she'd just cured cancer or given birth to a litter of puppies.

Brand wisely got up, went to the bar, and refreshed everyone's drinks.

Luanna hadn't planned to have a second glass, and she hoped it wouldn't put her to sleep. She glanced at Derek, and he smiled his dashing piratical smile. Nope, there were parts of her that were wiiiiide awake.

"So what exactly are they doing?" she asked Chloe.

Chloe blew out a breath. "What *aren't* they doing? They're trying to take over every aspect of the wedding—I'm surprised my mother hasn't bought me a dress, even though I've told her you're making mine. Right now they're insisting on Uncle Carmine's clam shack doing the catering and holding the reception at the town hall.

"If I hold the wedding here, it would be too much of a strain on all of them to come. But if I hold the wedding there, I'll be butting heads with them over every detail—plus I didn't realize how hard it would be to plan a wedding on the other side of the country.

"I'm not even sure what I want—what we want," she amended, rubbing Brand's shoulder, "anymore."

Everyone murmured their sympathies, but it was, of all people, Derek who finally spoke up.

"I know I'm pretty far on the outside of this," he said, "other than being Brand's best man. I mean, other than putting together the bachelor party and talking him down if he starts to panic, I figure my job is to put on the monkey suit and show up when he tells me to. But it sounds to me like you'd be better off running off to Vegas and eloping."

Silence all around. Even Luanna cocked her head, unable to get a handle on the idea. It was...well, it was elegant in its simplicity, like a navy blue linen sheath dress.

Chloe blinked. "We can—we could actually *do* that?" This confused Luanna for a second, because hadn't they had a conversation that touched on that idea? But that had been a flash of frustration at wedding craziness. This, now, must sound almost like permission to give in to temptation.

Brand turned in his chair to face her, taking her hands in his. "Would that be something you'd consider? You have more ideas on how you want the wedding to go than I do—I just want you to be happy, and see your beautiful face coming down the aisle to marry me. Or next to me as we jump out of a plane, or whatever."

"Stop, man," Ray said. "You're making us all look bad."

Chloe closed her eyes for a moment, and when she opened them, there was resolution in her dark gaze. "You know what?" she said. "Yes. You're right—all I really want, too, is to marry you. So let's do it! Let's go to Vegas. As long as we don't get married by Elvis, though. I'm going to put my foot down when it comes to Elvis."

Aunt May would be so disappointed, Luanna thought. But then, Aunt May wouldn't have been invited anyway, given that she was Luanna's aunt and had never met Chloe.

"Right," said Olive briskly, the first time she'd spoken since they'd all sat down. She had her tablet out. "When?"

"Next weekend?" Brand asked. "Or is that too soon?"

"Yes," Chloe said. "Perfect. Let's do it. Of course you're all invited."

"Fly out Friday, then," Olive said. "Let me check flights."

"Don't be ridiculous," Sandrine said. "We'll charter a plane for all of us." She held up an imperious hand to forestall objections. "Ray and I will pay for everything. I insist. It's not every day my only brother gets married. Olive, book the top floor of the Botany Bay casino—all the suites. And Chloe, don't worry about Gerard—I'll make sure he gives you the time off."

Chloe twitched, both at Sandrine organizing her life and Sandrine calling the ferocious M. DesJardins "Gerard," but she nodded and said thank you. Luanna felt her heart swell. Love had done so much for Chloe's insane need to take care of everyone and not be taken care of.

"We'll pick up bridesmaids dresses there, and rent tuxes," Sandrine said, and Olive took note.

Something pierced Luanna's exhausted, slightly tipsy, and distracted-by-Derek brain. "Dresses!" she yelped, even before her brain actually processed the problem.

Everyone's looked at her.

"Your dress," she said to Chloe. "This means I have to finish your wedding dress *right now*."

Chapter 16

Derek walked Luanna back to the guest house. The rain had stopped, and in the glow of the solar lights sunk into the ground at the side of the path, the grass glistened. If it didn't start raining again, by tomorrow afternoon all the moisture would be sucked into the arid earth as if the rain had never happened.

He'd lived his entire life in the desert; it was just a given.

They reached the guest house, and Luanna let Evenrude inside, then turned to Derek. The light by the front door sent the dark circles under her eyes into sharp relief. He'd known she was exhausted; had made a decision on the walk over.

He pulled her close, his hands on her upper arms. A friendly gesture rather than a sexual one, but even gently rubbing the cotton of her shirt, feeling the definition of her triceps beneath it, turned him on.

He'd wanted to touch her—really touch her, explore her, every damn fine inch of her—for so long that something as simple as holding hands was driving him nuts.

"I'm not coming in," he said.

Her eyes widened, and she sucked in a disappointed breath. He chased after it by kissing her, a brush against those luscious lips that he really wanted to devour. She tasted of Pinot Grigio, and she was just as intoxicating.

More so.

"You're beyond exhausted," he said, "and instead of having some time off coming up, you're headed right back onto the roller coaster. Don't get me wrong, Luanna: I want you, and I want you *bad*. This isn't about the teasing, about taking it slow and easy so the end result is off the charts. This is about taking care of you."

"But we had a date. I don't go back on my promises."

"Circumstances change," he said. "Am I disappointed? Sure. But this is my decision. I have a new plan. Want to hear it?"

She pursed her lips, considering, then nodded.

"Go to bed," he said. "Take a long, hot, luxurious shower—if you can stay awake that long—and then go to bed and get a good night's sleep. Sleep as long as you need to. When you wake up, you'll feel a million times better, and then finishing Chloe's dress won't seem like as monumental a project."

She sighed, and he guessed that the concept of a full eight-plus hours of hard sleep was pretty damn enticing.

He tugged her up against him, molded his body to hers. His lips near her ear, he added, "We're going to Sin City, baby. Once that dress is done, and we're in some crazy over-the-top luxury hotel suite, we're going to have that phenomenal sex we've been promising each other. We are going to blow the top of the hotel off. I'm going to make you come so hard, you won't be able to sew a straight line for weeks."

He thrust his hips so his erection—which he'd managed to keep in check until now—pressed against her sensitive mound. She made a strangled noise somewhere between a gasp and a moan, and that erotic, spontaneous sound shot straight to his groin, making him even harder.

"And you know what?" he whispered, his voice rough. "I'm not going to touch myself again, no matter how badly I'm fantasizing about you. That way, you're going to make me come as hard as I'm going to make you come. And *that* is a date neither of us is going to miss."

*

Luanna had mostly—*mostly*—become used to the excesses of the Moss estate. She didn't take it for granted, oh no, but the grounds and her guest cottage had become familiar (and the guest cottage was "normal" enough that she could pretend it was simply a small house on its own). Some details of the main mansion monstrosity still startled her at times, but her brain compartmentalized it into "that's so Sandrine."

This trip was now pushing at all her boundaries about what constituted "normal."

First there was the limo ride to the airport, then the fact that the limo went straight to the runway and dropped them off planeside. No waiting in line for security for the fabulously rich, oh no, darlin'. No security at all when you'd chartered a *private plane*.

By that point, the lack of sleep had been making her a little woozy anyway, so she sort of accepted the plane, with its enormous cushy seats (seatbelts, schmeatbelts) and a flight attendant who was more of a personal assistant/cocktail waitress.

Using your personal electronic devices the whole damn time? Pfft, whatever.

If she'd been more awake, she might've worried about safety.

Pfft, whatever. This level of exhaustion made her feel drunk. She accepted a glass of champagne, took one sip of the chilled, bubbly perfection, and put it down. Oh, that single swallow was heaven on her tongue, but a second swallow would have made her fall face-first into Chloe's wedding dress.

The dress was done—Chloe had come over for a final fitting that morning, and thank the baby Jesus, the dress *fit*, and Chloe looked so beautiful and perfect that the two of them had burst into tears. (That Luanna's tears had been partly relief was not something she shared with the bride, who was having enough stress issues of her own. She and Brand might have chosen elopement to have control over the situation, but the truth was, Chloe didn't have very much control over the details. "Details" was Olive's middle name.)

Yes, the dress was done, insofar as it fit. But speaking of details...

Luanna spent the flight with the silken concoction on her lap, hand-beading the bodice with tiny seed pearls. Olive loaned her reading glasses. Luanna was too young for reading glasses, dammit, but Lord, those pearls were tinier than baby ticks on a baby hound dog. The limo, the flight, then a limo to the hotel, where they were whisked through a private entrance and up to a suite of suites that took up the entire top floor. It had its own elevator.

Check-in? Pfft, whatever. We'll just usher you on up.

The four private sets of rooms—one for each couple and one for Olive to organize in solitary splendor—surrounded a common area complete with a fountain on one wall. A fountain in the Nevada desert. Luanna shook her head. About as useful as a pockets on a dead man's coat.

"This is…incomprehensible," she said, flopping back on the mega-king-sized bed in the suite she'd share with Chloe tonight and Derek tomorrow night. She slurred "incomprehensible," just a wee tiny bit.

Derek grasped her wrist and pulled her back into a sitting position. "If you lie down, you'll fall asleep."

His touch made her shiver, a delicate, whole-body spasm. *Oh, Momma, he is indeed a dangerous one.* She chalked it up to the fact that really, they hadn't spent much time in each other's physical company yet. Half of the time they'd known each other had been phone calls, texts, Skype.

It could turn out they weren't compatible at all. (Pfft, right.) They'd get the chance to find out tomorrow night, after the ceremony and celebration.

Chloe and Brand had surprised them all by going for the traditional "don't see each other the night before the wedding" thing. "We already live together," Chloe had explained. "Of course I'd rather sleep together than apart. But a night apart means the wedding night is a little more special—we'll have missed each other."

Which meant, of course, that Chloe would be spending tonight in Luanna's suite, and Derek would be in Brand's.

Logically, Luanna knew it made sense for her and Derek, too. She needed sleep. She needed to be one-hundred-percent alert for their first evening of sexual fireworks: she was *not* going to fall asleep again. She kind of understood Chloe and Brand's decision, although she and Derek had been waiting a lot longer…

She blinked, looking around the enormous set of rooms. Their suite had a massive bedroom, a bathroom you could host a party in, a sitting area with a small kitchen and a baby grand piano (she hadn't played in years, but you bet your bippy she was going to pound out a rousing round of "Chopsticks" before they left), and a balcony complete with hot tub.

Everything was beyond plush, in shades of plum and wine red and a brown that was somehow pretty. The bed had enough pillows for Chloe's entire extended Portuguese family, and the sitting room sofas were gushy enough to disappear into. Greeting them had been an enormous fruit basket, a gigantic, sweet-smelling floral arrangement, a box of European chocolates, and more champagne in a silver ice bucket. And not itty bottles of minibar sparkling wine, either, but the pricy, actually-from-France kind.

And that didn't even begin to cover it. The baby grand piano. The patio garden and outdoor hot tub. The TV in the bathroom—in the *bathroom*—which, despite being the smallest of the three in the suite, was still bigger than Luanna's.

Apparently, off the common area was a workout room and a spa room for massages and other treatments. Oh, and an award-winning bartender was on call to come on up and mix them award-winning drinks.

The bathroom soap smelled like sunshine and heaven, and the sheets on the bed were approximately eighteen-million count. Luanna had checked.

She fantasized about sliding between them...

"Chloe's dress is done and put up," she said to Derek. She glanced at the closet. In fact, there were two garment bags in there—the other being the dress Ray had commissioned. Sweet mercy, she could *not* get the two mixed up.

To help keep them straight in her mind, she'd put Ray's dress in the pink garment bag.

"I have almost three hours before we have to go shopping for bridesmaid's dresses," she continued. "That's enough time for..." She tried to tug him down onto the bed.

He made a soft, rueful laugh, and didn't waver. Dayum, he was stronger than she'd realized.

"Our date is for tomorrow night," he said, "and I have to get to my interview. I'll see you tonight at dinner, gorgeous." He leaned down to kiss her and her entire body perked up again, but then he pulled away. "Get some rest," he murmured, and left.

Luanna clambered to the head of the bed, fumbled with her phone to set an alarm, and lay down. There was no way she was going to sleep, not with her body all a-tingle from…

…she jolted awake to the sound of Arcade Fire's "Wake Up" coming from her phone. Chloe and the rest of the dress-shopping crew were ready for her.

The nap insanely made her feel rested, at least for now. Or maybe it was the knowledge that if she got through this evening, she could have a proper sleep, and tomorrow would be normal, as opposed to blurry around the edges like most recent days had been. (If she turned her head too quickly, she got dizzy. Not recommended.)

Lord have mercy.

She washed her face, reapplied her makeup, dressed. A simple sundress, a convertible bra (she had no idea what style of bridesmaid dress Chloe would choose), slip-on wedges. If she had to be trying dresses on, she wanted to get out of her clothes easily enough.

She met Chloe, Sandrine, and Olive in the common area, where the Roman-inspired fountain burbled merrily.

Sandrine clapped her delicate, fine-boned hands together and trilled, "Shopping! Fun!" as they entered the private elevator.

For the most part, Luanna agreed with her wholeheartedly. After all, this was *fashion* Sandrine was talking about, and Luanna loved fashion like hogs loved mud: she could pretty much roll around in it.

But, well, bridesmaids dresses. In the South, that didn't necessarily mean…fashionable. Much less tasteful.

Luanna had made pin money in high school making bridesmaids dresses. Fact was, few brides took into consideration the size, shape, and coloring of their dearest friends who'd been roped into this shindig.

But Chloe wasn't most brides, wasn't from the South, and loved her friends.

Luanna felt hopeful.

And, it turned out, a bit out of her league.

The boutique they entered had a pretty, hand-lettered sign in the doorway that proclaimed this a fragrance-free shopping experience in respect of their customers with allergies. They were immediately offered chilled champagne (Luanna, feeling more alert thanks to her nap, happily accepted) and chocolate-covered strawberries (who could turn down chocolate-covered strawberries?).

The shop was also closed to other customers, thanks to Sandrine's influence and Olive's organizational abilities.

Every time Luanna tried to peruse the merchandise, she was gently escorted back to her comfortable wing chair so that the staff could bring out dresses for them to consider. The wing chairs were quite comfortable, in truth, and rather pretty, off-white with French phrases in black, looping handwriting on them. Luanna noticed that the phrases made no sense.

The main saleslady—a woman on the cusp of middle age who was doing everything she could to avoid it, including obvious Botox—pursed her lips (well, a reasonable approximation thereof) and looked Luanna up and down. Then she made a huffing noise through her nose.

Sandrine, tiny in the wingback but yet somehow taking up the whole thing with her presence, raised an eyebrow whose manicure had cost more than Luanna's bra and said, "Is there a problem?"

It wasn't so much what she said, but how she said it. Luanna heard a slight Southern accent, and was impressed at the authenticity of it. Southern accents could be used to disarm, and Sandrine was absolutely doing that. Her tone was light, her question innocent, and yet Luanna, Chloe, and Olive all tensed immediately.

The saleslady, oblivious, said, "Of *course* not, Ms. Moss. We're just not used to accommodating a…woman of her size."

"Her size," in fashion parlance, meant anyone larger than a size 6. Luanna wasn't offended by the saleswoman's assessment of her. Yes, she was tall, and she had boobs and hips—but she was more than happy with her figure. Biology said she couldn't ever be Sandrine-waifish, and she didn't want to be. She was fit and healthy and strong.

She wasn't even all that offended by the saleswoman herself, who clearly judged Luanna on her shape. Luanna had gotten used to that, working in the fashion industry, especially in Los Angeles. She'd learned to choose her battles.

This wasn't one of them.

But apparently it was one of Sandrine's.

Sandrine levitated gracefully out of her seat before the saleslady had the last word out of her mouth.

"I'm sorry," Sandrine said, and her honey-sweet tone was so cold that everyone, including Olive, shivered as the temperature in the boutique dropped a good ten degrees. Luanna was amazed, because Olive was the one person who normally didn't seem at all fazed by Sandrine. "I was under the impression that this was a *full-service* shop. If you can't accommodate us with what we need, we won't take up any more of your time."

And there goes your mind-boggling commission was left unspoken.

The saleswoman, who was already pale as death (smart woman for avoiding the Vegas sun), with dark hair and red lips and a flawless expression, didn't quite cringe, although something akin to fear flickered across her gaze. Like a wounded, formerly oblivious muskrat suddenly realizing that there was a soulless gator with pure hunger in its cold, black gaze. Spots of red bloomed on her cheeks.

"Of course not, Ms. Moss," she said. "We offer full alteration services, including rush jobs. I understand this is for tomorrow afternoon? Not a problem, of course."

"Wonderful." Sandrine drifted back down into her seat. The smile on her face spoke of warmth and agreeability, but there was still an undertone of *Do not cross me.*

"Chloe," Luanna said, desperate to break the icicles dripping off everyone's foreheads, "did you have a thought on the style of bridesmaids' dresses? Because your dress has that kind of late forties evening gown line, did you want the bridesmaids' dresses to echo that? Or are you thinking cocktail length since it's Vegas and an afternoon wedding and we can be a scootch less formal?" Chloe nodded at the latter. To the saleswoman, Luanna added, "I see you have some Luscious Couture's Fierce Fifties Flirts line, which I helped design. Do you have any of the fit and flare dresses with the sweetheart necklines? Preferably in Blue Suede Blue."

It was the teeniest of fibs: she'd been on the Luscious Couture staff when the FFF line came out; she just hadn't really done more than assemble some samples.

But it got the saleslady's attention, that was for sure. Her snootiness clicked down a couple more notches.

The Luscious dresses Luanna had in mind were sold out in blue, turquoise, and almost every color except Trixie Tangerine, which Sandrine vetoed on the grounds it clashed with her hair. Not that it was really her decision, but it *would* clash with her hair and Chloe had too much sense to argue with that. So Luanna, enjoying a moment of power, proclaimed, "Bring us your beach colors. All of them."

Mere moments later, they were swimming in a blue and teal sea of beautiful dresses, with a couple of "Bermuda sand" pinky beige ones thrown in for good measure. Let the mad trying on begin!

Ray would have loved being here, Luanna mused. He got most of his fix of pretty clothes from looking at Sandrine's—goodness knew, that was a *lot* of clothes—or from looking at pictures. He never really got to have the shopping experience.

She wondered if there were some way to pull something like that off. With Sandrine's access to not only money, but security, could they rent a place? Have a private fashion show? Now wasn't the time or place to mention it, so she filed the idea away to discuss with Sandrine later.

Of course, thoughts of Ray led to thoughts of Derek. He'd said something about an interview, but she'd been too distracted and tired to really process it. Then again, he probably hadn't said a lot lest he jinx it or lose the spark or whatever.

He'd have enjoyed this, too—he'd probably have homed in on the high-end lingerie, murmured in her ear about how she'd look in various outfits before he peeled it off with his teeth. He could talk the good talk, Derek could. Luanna shifted in the cushy wingback, feeling flushed and restless and, yes, horny. Based on their steamy necking session—and even on the less-lengthy but no-less-intense kisses they'd shared—she was pretty sure he could walk the walk.

Or whatever the crazy kids were calling it these days.

Bottom line, she believed him when he said they were going to blow the roof of the hotel off. She wondered if she should warn the rest of the party to stay away, although she couldn't exactly hang a sock on the elevator door.

She wished she had the funds to pick up some of the high-end lingerie, except that one of her small suitcases was nothing *but* lingerie. She hadn't been able to decide, so she'd brought pretty much all of it.

Maybe she'd have to give Derek a private fashion show….

"Are you okay?" Chloe asked quietly. "You're looking kind of warm."

"Thinking about Derek," Luanna admitted.

She and Sandrine tried on the first batch of dresses. None of them was quite right, and the pinky sand proved to be the one color in the world that washed Sandrine out. They sat back down while another batch was assembled. Luanna took the opportunity to enjoy another strawberry. Olive wandered off to look at the lingerie, which surprised Luanna for a second. She spent so much time with Sandrine that one tended to forget she had a private life—was in fact married.

"I'm kind of sorry Joannie's not here," Chloe commented. "She would've gotten a kick out of this. She's always been a good friend."

Chloe's cousin Joannie was one of the few female members of Chloe's extended family in her own generation. It was hard to imagine Joannie—a quiet, intense person who divided her time between running the development office at a Catholic college (and scaring the nuns) and taking care of her mentally ill father—in Vegas. Then again, one of the last times Luanna had seen her, she'd been flirting with Lance.

It was the quiet ones you had to watch out for, or something. Not that they'd have to watch out for Joannie. Like Olive, she could kick back and have fun, but not if there was something that might need organizing or managing.

Luanna gave Chloe a quick, one-armed hug. "I know, sweetie. But the minute you open the door to more bridesmaids, you start down that slippery slope to an enormous wedding with a million relatives and no control."

Chloe nodded, smiled. "You're right. I know you're right. I'll have to find something really special for Joannie while we're here, to let her know I was thinking of her."

A few more dresses, and they hit on the right one: an off-the-shoulder silk fit-and-flare dress, similar to the Luscious Couture one Luanna had thought of before (but, she had to admit, even prettier). The style suited both Sandrine's petite form and Luanna's taller, lusher figure. And miracle of miracles, it was available in a lovely marine blue in Luanna's size and a pale but vibrant aqua that brought out the unusual color of Sandrine's eyes in *her* size, or close enough in both cases that Luanna didn't feel too sorry for the person who'd be doing the rush alterations. Sandrine handed over her super-platinum-no-doubt-diamond-encrusted credit card. The dresses would be altered and sent up to their suite.

"Oh, my God," Chloe said, looking kind of stunned. "It's really happening, isn't it?"

Luanna gently took the flute out of her friend's hand. "No more champagne until you get some dinner in you."

"Speaking of which," Olive said, glancing at her tablet, "our reservations are in less than an hour. Time to join the boys before we part ways again for the bachelor and bachelorette parties."

All Luanna heard was "join the boys." Her pulse quickened. Dinner with Derek, even surrounded by all their friends, sounded like nothing short of heaven.

Chapter 17

Despite all the years Derek had known Brand, he'd never quite adjusted to the fact that his down-to-earth friend's sister was *the* Sandrine Moss.

Going to college in LA and now working in TV, Derek was blasé about occasional brushes with celebrity. But Sandrine lived her life large even by celebrity standards, and she was delighted to share her wealth and over-the-top luxury with…well, not anyone, but if you happened to be an old college friend of her brother's, you might find yourself in slightly surreal situations on occasion, just because Sandrine had no reason not to indulge her most grandiose whims and invite others along for the ride.

This whole weekend fit into that category, what with private planes and booking an entire floor of posh suites at a casino. Now he sat in Lorelei, an upscale restaurant that resembled a futuristic warehouse (in a future where people cared a lot about aesthetics, not one of the gritty ones like Brand's most recent movie), a restaurant where he normally couldn't afford more than a beer or a cup of coffee. The room was three stories tall, but two balcony bars looked down on the dining floor. They looked like modern versions of something from one of those BBC period dramas, lighter wood and paler upholstery but still quiet places to enjoy some serious conversation and equally serious drinks.

The main dining area was elegant simplicity: brick walls (ones that bore no resemblance to the actual construction of the building), white tablecloths, and warm, almost gold leather chairs that looked austere but practically embraced you when you sat down. The china was white but about as far from basic as you could get, with squared edges where you'd expect round ones and curves where you'd normally see straight lines.

The cavernous space should have echoed with chatter and the sounds of dining and drinking, but somehow the ordinary background noises seemed muted. Maybe Brand could explain it—he'd taken a number of science and engineering classes on his way to becoming one of the best CGI specialists in Hollywood—but Derek was inclined to write it off as magic.

A "wine siren" in a scarlet catsuit was rappelling down a forty-foot-tall glass wine tower to fetch their second magnum of a rare champagne that supposedly made Dom Pérignon and Cristal hang their corks in shame, because when Sandrine Moss wanted to toast her big brother and his bride-to-be, it wasn't going to be in any ordinary setting, with any ordinary bubbly. (No ordinary dinner either, based on what the bride-to-be had raved after her first few bites—and Chloe ought to know.)

And as far as Derek was concerned, it could have been dinner at some half-decent chain restaurant—say Olive Garden or TGI Fridays—and any old cheap-and-cheerful sparkling wine, because ninety percent of his attention was on Luanna. On her bright eyes and rosy cheeks, on her laughter and her sweet accent and the way her pink-slicked lips shaped words. Okay, okay, and on her cleavage, artfully displayed by what he thought was called a sweetheart neckline that showed off her assets without flaunting them. Her dress was deep rose, a style that reminded him of a sexy dame in an old movie without actually being vintage, and it clung to some of the places he wanted to caress and brushed like a whisper over others. Every once in a while a delicious morsel of food or the crisp bubbles of the champagne would recapture his attention, or he'd heed something someone else was saying. But mostly it was her, sensory impressions of her, memories of their earlier play, and dreams of what he hoped to do to, for, and with her after Chloe and Brand finally said "I do."

As a result, he jumped (he hoped in an non-obvious way) when Sandrine tapped her glass so it rang like a bell and announced, in that lovely voice honed by years of delivering lines, "To Adelina and Mário, Chloe's wonderful parents, who can't be with us tonight."

"And who finally decided they'd forgive me, someday, as long as we throw a party in Rhode Island," Chloe followed up. She sounded both ecstatic and wistful, which, Derek supposed, made sense. Also a little tipsy, which also made sense. Being a professional foodie, she could prob-ably appreciate the fine champagne even while distracted by her beloved and pre-nuptial jitters.

Derek started paying closer attention. Chloe had opted to tell her par-ents about the elopement after they got to Vegas so she didn't get talked out of it. He knew Chloe had talked to her parents—a lot, he suspected—about the decision to elope, but she hadn't been ready to talk to anyone but Brand about their reaction until now and he wanted to know how it went. "Weren't you trying to avoid the party in Rhode Island?"

Chloe laughed. "It was getting crazy trying to plan a wedding long dis-tance, but I definitely want to celebrate with my family and Rhode Island friends. And it's an olive branch to my mother; she loves organizing parties even more than I do. Besides, Brand still needs to meet a bunch of them."

"Yeah, I've only met a fraction of the seven million or so," Brand chimed in.

"Even Mom finally admitted that getting married was the important part, not the details of the wedding. In fact—" Chloe laughed as she said it "—we're going with the town hall for the venue and Uncle Carmine cater-ing. Everyone can stuff themselves silly on clam cakes and lobster rolls and as long as they aren't wearing fancy wedding clothes, I'm thrilled. It's great food, just simple and really messy. I did draw the line at Narragansett beer, though. I don't care if it's a local tradition; it sucks."

Luanna, sitting next to Chloe, rubbed a comforting hand on her friend's back. "I'm amazed your momma's taking it so well."

"Oh, there was plenty of shouting, and a few tears from my dad. Mom's way too tough for crying; she's more the ranting type. But they came around. I think it helped that Carl just popped the question to his boyfriend, so, as she put it, she'll get to do the mother of the bride thing anyway. To be clear, I'm pretty sure neither of the guys plans to wear a bridal gown, but they want a big blowout wedding in Newport, so Mom will still get to do her thing with people who *want* all the fuss and feathers."

"Hey, if Carl did opt for a gown," Ray said, "I'd have a drink in his honor. And probably demand pictures, because it takes a special kind of macho to do that when you're a commercial fisherman." Ray sounded surprisingly thoughtful on the subject, as if he really did think Chloe's brother would deserve props for wearing a dress.

Since completing his interview this afternoon with a drag king Elvis who'd offered another thought-provoking take on fashion and masculine and feminine presentation, Derek had been thinking about everything except work—okay, mostly he'd been thinking about Luanna, and by extension, about sex—but he couldn't help making a mental note about the fact that Ray Stark, whose public image was the definition of big manly hunk, not only didn't have a problem with homosexuality and crossdressing, but could see a cool side to it, at least in the right context. Might be an interesting angle to cover: unlikely allies. Not that Ray was really all that unlikely. His characters were the big, silent type, more about action than thought, but Ray himself seemed like a smart guy, quiet because he was thinking, not because he had nothing to say.

"I'd demand the commission to make that mythical gown. Talk about engineering. Hell—" Luanna looked adorably eager at Chloe "—I want the commission to make his tux. He's going to have a hard time finding something off the rack with those shoulders of his, and since he's practically family, I'd give him a much better rate than anyone else will." Luanna took another sip of champagne and ran pale-pink-nailed fingers through her wavy hair. "That is, as long as the wedding's months and months and *months* away. No more last-minute jobs for a while if I can help it." She giggled decorously.

"I'll let him know, sweetie," Chloe said. "And I know you'll like this part: Nick's going to wear a kilt."

"Which is nothing like a dress. Not at all," Luanna proclaimed in a way that let Derek realize just how much of that lovely champagne she'd been enjoying, or maybe how little sleep she'd had lately. Not even tipsy yet, but she was starting to relax after a few long, stressful weeks and the champagne was definitely helping. It was kind of adorable. He liked to think that wasn't just because he thought she was adorable anyway.

Luanna took a few bites of her food, chewing slowly and thoughtfully. Swallowed. Sipped more champagne, and let the hovering wine siren refill her glass.

Then Luanna stood, swaying slightly and holding her glass high. "I'd like to propose another toast to Adelina and Mário, because they really are great." Everyone obligingly raised their glasses, though, Derek reflected, it was getting toward the point in the party where someone could toast Bozo the clown and everyone would go along with it, just for an excuse to sip more champagne—which really was exquisite, now that he was paying attention.

"Yeah, I know. My parents rock!" Chloe said.

So did his, Derek thought. So did his. Sure, he'd been a little rattled by his mom coming out, but the new, short-haired, sledgehammer-wielding version of his mom was still the wonderful woman who'd raised him.

Only, he had to admit, now radiating a new confidence and happiness.

And he respected both his parents so much for working so hard to establish a new relationship with each other, one born from years of affection and friendship.

Luanna sat down, a little abruptly. "Seriously, your mom is so understanding," she said to Chloe. "I mean, she gets that this is your wedding and Brand's, not hers. My momma…I mean, I love Momma, she's awesome. But if we were getting married, I'd be lucky to get a word in edgewise, because she'd want to make everything what she thought was right. I'd have to fight to pick out my own dress because she'd have her own vision and bless her heart, it would be all over ruffles, and a white lace picture hat might just be involved."

"A picture hat might be nice," Sandrine mused. "Unusual, yet striking."

"For you, darlin', but you're a classic beauty," Luanna said quickly. "I have a round face and it just wouldn't work for me. But Momma wore one for her wedding so she'd want me to do it too. And Derek—" she shot him a heated look "—you wouldn't get consulted at all."

Everyone fell silent for a second, even Sandrine, who'd been chatting with Ray about something, maybe picture hats.

The silence was broken by Olive. "Have I missed something? Do I need to add *another* date to Sandrine and Ray's calendar?" Ray gently took her iPad away and muttered something along the lines of "not yet."

Luanna turned even pinker, and she'd been a bit rosy to start with thanks to excitement and champagne. "Oh dear. Oh wow. That's what I get for openin' my big mouth when I've been putting too much fine champagne into it. I feel about as awkward as a skunk with its head stuck in a mayonnaise jar. I…we… That is, I meant Derek *for example*. Derek or whoever I might be marrying when the time comes. Which isn't now. Even though I suppose we could get married tonight if we wanted to, because Las Vegas is like that, but we've only just started dating so it's too soon. I think you're supposed to meet each other's families before you jump to getting hitched. Right?"

Derek's heart lurched in a funny way. He felt like he should say something, but it took a while to agree. "Right," he said finally. "I think we'd need a few more official dates before that step." He squeezed her hand as he said it, because he kind of felt like he was letting her down, letting them both down, by agreeing.

Damn, it had been hard to say that. It was true, though, right? They were *so* far from being at the getting-hitched point. People had gotten married for centuries without having sex first, but this was the twenty-first century in the U.S. He and Luanna should at the very least make sure they were as sexually compatible as they seemed to be before they asked themselves, let alone each other, about a commitment of the ideally permanent type.

If he had his way, they'd be taking care of the sexual compatibility test right now, in that big, glorious bed in their suite. She'd have started out in that pink silk robe she'd described in such loving detail during one of their phone sex sessions, but it would be tossed over a chair by now. After all the waiting and all the flirting and dirty talk and all accidental postponements and still more sweet teasing, naked this time, as they explored each other's bodies thoroughly at last, he'd be surrounded by something pink and soft but much warmer than that pretty robe…

And he'd better get off that train of thought before his dick actually lifted the table.

But he wanted more than that lovely erotic interlude. He couldn't wait for them to spend more time in each other's company.

Yeah, too soon to ponder marriage to the woman beside him. Before that kind of momentous decision they'd need, among other things, to spend some serious time together out of bed as well as in it, and without someone else's wedding to both distract them and fill their brains with romantic notions.

And they'd probably need to take the big step of meeting each other's families.

He'd heard enough about Luanna's wacky and wonderful clan to know they'd welcome him with open arms, ply him with cocktails, and probably make some legit-sounding threats to his person should he ever hurt their little Luanna. (He suspected the men would talk a tough game, but her grandmothers would be the ones he'd have to worry about if he was ever stupid enough to hurt her.)

But Luanna knew almost nothing about his family. Given how open she was herself, she might even imagine he was covering up a hideous secret or at least an awkward, distant relationship with his mom. The habit of keeping family business in the family was a good one in a small, conservative town. But he wasn't there anymore. It was high time he told Luanna about his unusual but seriously cool family. Even about Beatrice, who wasn't officially a stepmother, but might be soon if he'd been reading the signals right at Christmas.

He wouldn't be breaking the code, he realized. Because when you're at the point that running off with your girlfriend to find the nearest

Elvis-impersonating JP sounded almost reasonable, she was close enough that she deserved to be included in the family umbrella. He didn't just lust after Luanna. He liked her. He trusted her.

He wasn't ready to say the words out loud yet—it seemed dangerous when surrounded by wedding fever—but he might just love her.

He'd tell her the whole odd but (now that he had some perspective on it) kind of heartwarming story about his mom's journey of self-discovery before they left Vegas.

Once that was out of the way, some treacherous part of his brain suggested, they could find themselves that JP. Maybe the drag king Elvis he'd interviewed would give them a discount.

Chapter 18

Other than visiting some of the high-end restaurants Chloe had worked at, Luanna had never really experienced the finer end of fine dining. The really pricy, fancy places.

Lorelei was one of those places.

And yet, she was surprised at how understated most of it was.

Crisp white table linens. Comfortably padded straight-backed dining chairs covered in butter-soft, umber-colored leather. Unornamented silver, but real silver, with weight and a meticulously designed curve to fit comfortably in one's hand. The only pops of color were the large spray of flowers on the host desk—but yet, they were all yellows and creams with dark greenery, fitting with the white and brown—and the single, canary-yellow tulip in a plain glass vase at each table.

But then there was the forty-foot-tall glass-and-steel cage looming in the middle of the room, filled with wines that cost more than her last car, and those cat-suited women flipping and rappelling their way up and down. Maybe the simple décor was to make the spectacle more striking.

In the end, though, Luanna knew it was about the food. Even though her palate wasn't sophisticated enough to appreciate it at some higher level, she had to admit it was excellent. The look on Chloe's face—Chloe being the one with the sophisticated palate—spoke volumes, however.

Luanna had gone for the filet mignon with peppercorn sauce, and the beef practically did melt in her mouth, leaving behind a trail of spicy pepper like the fading, but still breathtaking flutters of a firework display. It was all she could do not to lick the plate.

Finally, after the excellent food and possibly more of the exquisite champagne than they probably should have enjoyed before going out on the town, Chloe finally said, "So, what *are* we doing after dinner, anyway? This all came together so fast we didn't really have a plan other than the fact that because it's such a small group of us, it makes sense to have a combined bachelor/bachelorette party."

Luanna gulped, waiting for everyone to stare at her. If the wedding had gone according to a the original plan, bachelorette festivities would have been on her shoulders as the maid of honor, but she'd been way too busy finishing the wedding dress (and Ray's dress) to look into fun things to do in Vegas. She'd managed to pick up a few toys—a silly bachelorette veil with attached plastic tiara for Chloe and so-tacky-they-were-fun rhinestone-and-lace bedazzled buttons that said, "I'm with the bride" for her and Sandrine and Olive. But that was as far as she'd gotten, and then only because there had a party store near one of her temp jobs and she'd snatched them up on clearance long before plans came together.

Luckily, with the change of plans, they got Olive.

And Olive was a checklist-packing goddess who, thanks to Sandrine's impulsive nature, didn't bat an eye at throwing together a wedding in a few days. (It wasn't, after all, a formal bash for one-hundred-plus people. Although no doubt she could handle that, too, without breaking a sweat.) She glanced at her iPad briefly as if solidifying details, then said, "First off, I'm sorry, but Cirque du Soleil is almost sold out for all its shows. There are enough tickets for everyone at the Beatles one, but they're not together and they're in nosebleed seats."

Brand and Chloe quickly agreed that this wasn't a great idea. Sandrine's grimace might have had something to do with the speed of the response.

Besides, who needed Cirque du Soleil when you had acrobatic wine sirens who delivered booze?

"There's a magic show at the Excalibur, which looks cheesy but fun, and Nate Fox is in concert at the Pearl." Olive frowned and swiped on her tablet.

Chloe, who might just be Nate Fox's biggest fan, was the one who was shaking her head. "If this was a girls' night only, I'd so be there. But we decided to stick together for the first part of the night and my otherwise-perfect sweetie isn't a Nate Fox fan."

Brand shrugged. "He doesn't suck. He's just not my favorite. If you really want…"

After going over a few more options, none of which seemed quite right to the guests of honor, they finally decided on a classic Vegas night out: a little gambling, a little dancing, and probably more than a little drinking. Chloe and Brand were all set to head downstairs and join the scrum in the casino, but Olive got on her phone and pulled rank, because that was what Olive did, and they found themselves on the list for the VIP room.

Luanna would never get used to this secondhand lifestyles of the rich and famous. But she was definitely getting to like it now and then. VIP room indeed! She'd better take a few minutes and touch up her makeup. Momma would never forgive her otherwise…

And Evenrude would never forgive her if she didn't take the corgi for a walk soon. She was a well-behaved dog unless her beloved peacocks were around to provoke her, but Luanna definitely didn't want to push it in an expensive hotel room. Luanna stood. "I need to take the dog out. I'll meet you downstairs."

"*We* need to take the dog out," Derek insisted, standing too.

Brand snorted. "Don't wear Chloe's maid of honor out too much. We need her for tomorrow. For that matter, you've got the rings, so you're pretty important too."

Luanna felt herself turning pink and wanted to protest they really were just relieving Evenrude. But it wasn't like anyone would believe they wouldn't get in some naughty business before they hooked up with the party again—not even Luanna. And while she'd confessed to Chloe that they hadn't done the deed yet, no one else knew and it really wasn't their business. "We'll be back in two shakes of a coonhound's tail," she insisted. "I have the props for tonight so I can't be too late."

*

After the refined quiet of Lorelei, the noise and lights of the casino seemed almost overwhelming at first. But Derek had twined his fingers with hers, and Luanna savored that simple touch as they weaved their way around people heading intently toward slot machines, clutching drinks, chatting loudly, or all three at once.

"I feel just awful that I didn't plan anything for Chloe's bachelorette party," she confessed to Derek. "I feel like I let her down."

He gave her hand a squeeze. "I don't think you let her down," he said. "Chloe herself said this came together really quickly—so quickly you've been sewing her dress day and night. Besides, Chloe doesn't seem like the type of person to want to be fussed over."

The laugh that burst out of Luanna caused people to glance their way, but most smiled at the infectious sound (and if they didn't, she didn't care). "My stars! You figured that out a lot faster than poor Brand did!"

Derek chuckled. "Comes from being a writer, I guess. I'm always watching people, trying to figure out what makes them tick."

She tossed a flirty glance at him. "Is that so? Tell me, what do you figure makes me tick?"

"Hm. You're creative both visually and tactile-y. That's not a word, but you know what I mean. Color, shape, and how things feel are important to you. You're outgoing and can talk to just about anybody, and you put people at ease. But you don't get close to just anybody—you don't let just anybody in. People have to earn your trust and your devotion."

"And do you think you've earned it?"

She meant it as a joke, a continuation of the flirtation, but as the words left her mouth, she realized how serious the question was. Because he was right—once she let someone in, they got the benefit of her fierce loyalty, and that meant she had to trust them to do the same.

Derek stopped walking, tugged on her hand, gently spun her around and pulled her to him, taking her other hand in his and holding both hands close. Her breath caught and she felt as though they were in a bubble, just the two of them, and everyone else flowed around them, a stream diving and reforming around a rock.

"I'm working on it," he said, his voice low and earnest, "but I'm not there yet. We're still learning each other, Luanna, and as with everything else, I'm willing to take it slow and do it right. Because I'm the same way—once I commit, I'm all in. And I can tell you this: I believe it's worth going for. You captivate me, Luanna Devenaux. I want in, and I'm going to work to be worthy of your trust and your devotion."

Her heart stuttered, and for a moment all she could do was gaze up at him, seeing the truth of his words mirrored in his dark eyes.

"Goodness," she said finally, with a shaky little laugh. "That was some speech. And for the record, Derek Acosta, you captivate me just as surely. I believe this is worth going for, too, and I'm looking forward to having the rest of the weekend to learn more about you."

Against her fingers, twined with his, she felt his chest move as he took in a breath. Then his lips were on hers, a soft kiss, a brush that held and shared a world of promises.

When he pulled away, he said, "Now that that's settled, let's get upstairs and get Evenrude outside, so we can get back to the evening's festivities."

Once they entered the private elevator, they had a moment of time on their hands, and Luanna knew just what she wanted to do with that time. And, it seemed, Derek had the same idea.

After weeks of being subtly seductive and slow, he grabbed her now her like the pirate he'd always looked like to her: fast, hard, decisive. Almost commanding, the way he gripped her ass and pressed her forward against his hardening cock. As his lips took control of hers, she decided she liked this aspect of Derek as much as the sensual, slow-smolder one and the sweet, funny guy who'd send silly texts to help her stay awake when she was crazy busy.

As Chloe would say, he made her panties happy.

She fisted his steel-gray silk shirt in her hands, feeling the hard muscles of his back beneath the soft fabric. They were pinned too tightly together for her to do what she wanted to, which was curl her fingers beneath the vee in front to toy at his crisp chest hair. Instead, she ran her tongue along the hard column of his throat down as far as she could, tasting salty flesh and savoring the low, impassioned noise that rose out of him.

She was vaguely aware that the elevator pinged, announcing their arrival at the penthouse. It took them so long to disengage that Derek had to shoot one hand out to keep the elevator doors from closing again.

Laughing, they tripped through the lounge to Luanna's room. Then she was in his arms again. Even though one of his hands rested on the small of her back and the other cupped her ass in an only slightly naughty way, the touch made her feel like they were naked and doing things that were illegal in Arkansas. Evenrude was doing her short-legged version of the pee-pee dance around their ankles, but for the moment, they refused to pay attention.

"If tonight wasn't for Brand and Chloe," Derek whispered, his voice husky, "I'd have you out of this dress so fast they'd want to get me into that magic show Olive was talking about. I'd lay you down on the big bed and kiss every inch of your skin. Lick and nibble until you begged me. Then I'd kiss my way to your sweet pussy and stay there for about an hour."

Her knees felt like rubber and it wasn't the champagne. She was a little sozzled—sleep-deprived as she was, the bubbly was definitely tickling her brain—but nowhere near the knee-buckling point. That was purely Derek's smoky voice and those intense blue eyes, bright against his dark skin. "Oh. My. God. Derek, I wish… I want…" She wasn't as good at the dirty talk as Derek, but she'd gotten better thanks to their extended courtship. This time, though, she couldn't think of anything poetically nasty to say. So she went for the direct approach. "I want your mouth on my body. Then I want your cock in my mouth, nice and slow and teasing until you're slick and hard and can't stand it anymore. And then I want you on top of me fucking me senseless until we blow the roof off this penthouse."

Derek grinned a slow, sensual grin. "I'll be on top for the first time, sure. But the second time I want you riding me. And after that…"

Evenrude head-butted Luanna and let out pathetic little woof, clearly too weak from hunger to be loud and too desperate to pee to dance anymore. (Never mind that she'd been fed and taken outside before they'd headed to dinner. That had been earlier than her usual dinnertime. Now it was later than her usual time and she was perfectly ready to scam a second helping and a second trip outside.)

"Just a second, baby," Luanna cooed. Then she stood on her tiptoes and kissed Derek with all the passion stoked by dirty talk and the warmth of his body on hers.

By the time they broke apart, Luanna's breath was coming in quick pants, Derek's cock strained his fly in a tempting way, and Evenrude was going nuts. Derek had rose lipstick smeared all over his shit-eating grin, and his eyes were cloudy with lust. The bed was so close. She knew they'd decided to wait until after the wedding, but they could…

No, they really couldn't. Not without Evenrude potentially exploding all over the carpet or the pretty parquet floor.

She could tell from Derek's expression that his train of thought was on the same track as hers, both the desire and the practicality that interrupted it. "Let's get this over with and join the party."

Derek sighed. "Yeah. Otherwise we'll have a really unhappy dog. Though we'd be happy ourselves."

"Not when I got the bill for cleaning the carpet. Give me two seconds."

Along with grabbing Evenrude's leash, Luanna quickly wiped the lipstick smears off her face and made sure her dress was covering everything it was supposed to. This might be Vegas, where anything goes, but there was no point in running around looking like a whore staggering into church on Sunday morning. She grabbed the leash from the nightstand, along with a few treats and a plastic bag for cleaning up after Evenrude, then shoved the silly props for the night into her bag.

She took two steps, turned back, and palmed a few more tissues to clean the lipstick off Derek. Rose just *wasn't* his color.

Chapter 19

*E*verything went smoothly at first. It was a beautiful night, warm but not blazing hot, and the bustle of Vegas seemed far away in the well-manicured "pet garden" on the hotel's grounds. The pet area was plainer than the regular courtyard, and nothing compared to the amazing grounds at Sandrine's mansion, but it looked fine when seen through a blur of champagne and desire. Derek's fingers were interlaced with hers, and Evenrude could have been an obedience-school advertisement, she was behaving so well.

Having done her business, the corgi was trotting around the garden determined to sniff every last scent before heading back inside, but she was largely ignoring the other dogs. A sign at the entrance said that "canine guests" could be off leash in the dog area as long as they were under human control, and since Evenrude was being so good, Luanna allowed her a bit of freedom. Evenrude wasn't given to darting anyway—she knew where her treats were.

Luanna heard the problem before she could see anything. First came the high-pitched yipping from over by the door. Then the shrieks started. "Bruiser! Bruiser! Come back here!" repeated over and over in a rising tone of desperation.

"Bruiser?" Derek said. "I'd be nervous, but based on the bark, if it's a dog that deserves a name like that, it's still a puppy."

Then Bruiser came into view, darting under a hedge, between a few ankles, provoking laughter from the other people as she went. Luanna knew it was Bruiser because the brown-faced white ball of fluff with adorably oversized bat-wing brown ears—a papillon, Luanna thought—sported a pink sweater with its name incorporated into the design in black. Luanna had a bad feeling the dog's owner didn't appreciate the irony.

The little dog, showing no fear and not much sense (or maybe a sixth sense that the corgi was no threat), trotted up to Evenrude to say hello. Corgis weren't a large breed, but Evenrude dwarfed the tiny creature, and Luanna swore she drew herself up taller and puffed herself to look even bigger in comparison.

"Behave!" Luanna hissed, mostly as a precaution. Evenrude always got along fine with other dogs, even Uncle Claude's hunting dogs, which normally didn't like any dog that wasn't part of their little pack.

Bruiser wasn't cowed by Evenrude. Bruiser's ridiculous ears perked up and her fluffy tail wagged. She gazed up at the corgi adoringly.

And Evenrude evidently decided that while Bruiser wasn't her beloved peacocks, maybe they could have their own doggy party while the humans were busy. She sniffed gently at the feathered ears, ruffling the fine fur, and Bruiser shivered in evident delight. Then they circled each other until they could indulge in the time-honored canine ritual of smelling each other's butts to get to know each other better.

"Cutest. Thing. Ever. We'd better keep an eye on her until her owner catches up."

Derek nodded in agreement and squeezed her hand.

Evenrude pressed her nose into the smaller dog's butt, then opened her mouth and licked as dogs were wont to do.

And that was when a young woman in an extremely short, extremely expensive-looking cobalt-blue dress tottered over on exceedingly high sequined silver heels. "Bruiser! There you are… Oh my God! Your monster is going to eat my baby!" She bent down and snatched up Bruiser.

In doing so, she put her face within snapping distance of Evenrude. Not that Evenrude ever snapped, even at idiots with ear-damaging voices, but Luanna still winced. She'd known since she was knee-high to a grass-hopper not to provoke a strange canine that way. Especially not one you thought, however incorrectly, was dangerous.

She thought of telling the girl how foolish she was in terms heated enough to scorch the bristles off a boar, but opted for sweetness instead. "Is this little cutie yours? Thank goodness you found her so quickly."

"Before she was *eaten*." The young woman cuddled the papillon so violently it yipped in discomfort, then more or less shoved it into her huge pink purse. Bruiser didn't seem exactly thrilled to be there, but in proper canine fashion, she looked up at her owner adoringly.

Poor pup. Bruiser might be all of six pounds and that mostly fur and ears, but it seemed like a sweet little critter and deserved a smarter human.

Luanna made herself laugh, even though the few other people in the dog garden were staring and she was sure people could hear the girl's shrieks inside. "Butt-sniffin' and lickin' is how dogs say hi." She turned her accent up, as most people seemed to find it soothing. "My Evenrude was just bein' friendly."

"Friendly?" The girl—and she really was a girl, Luanna realized, nine-teen or twenty at most, maybe still in high school despite her dressed-to-party look—let her voice reach an appalling shriek. "So your disgusting dog wasn't trying to eat my baby…he was trying to rape her! And she's a *purebred*!" The thought of canine miscegenation seemed to upset her even more than the possibility her dog was being attacked. "I'm calling security. And if she's pregnant, I'll…I'll sue you."

This, Luanna decided, would make a great story to tell later. Much later. But if the girl did call security, it could mess up Chloe and Brand's evening and have repercussions for Sandrine. She was still trying to come up with mollifying words when Derek stepped in.

Derek smiled a version of the pirate smile that was clearly intended to disarm without seduction. It seemed to work, because a little of the angry tension left the girl's body. "Your dog's virtue is safe. Evenrude's a girl, too."

The girl's eyes narrowed. "Are you sure? Or are you just saying that so I don't sue you?"

"Well, she squats to pee," Luanna said thoughtfully, "and she doesn't have dangly bits. Besides, the vet says she's female and he ought to know."

At that, the girl laughed. It was a laugh loud and abrasive enough to make an alligator whimper, but it was still a laugh. She studied Evenrude, who was now thoroughly bored since her new friend was out of reach and had flopped against Luanna's calf, tongue lolling. Luckily, she'd flopped in a way that made her sex obvious. "Yeah, no boy bits. All I noticed was teeth. But I'm still not happy that you let her come over to my dog when she's so much bigger than poor Bruiser." She giggled a bit. "Though now that she's not next to Bruiser I can see she's pretty small, just pudgy. And toothy."

Derek leaned a little closer and said in a conspiratorial whisper, "Evenrude was doing the good big-sister thing. I think Bruiser was on her way to check out that big guy." He pointed toward a large, energetic lab mix—definitely a boy—being half-dragged back into the hotel by a small boy accompanied by a bored-looking father. "Evenrude knew a pretty girl like yours could get herself in trouble that way and decided to intervene."

She shuddered dramatically. "Eww! He could split her in half!" She shook her finger at the dog. "Bruiser, you are a nasty girl!" Looking up at Derek, she then asked, "Do you think I should get her fixed? I wanted her to have puppies because papillon puppies are the cutest thing ever, but she's so tiny. I mean seriously, some dogs' things have to be as big as she is. If she gets away again, who knows what might happen?"

"I think that's a good idea," Derek said, his voice solemn. "Did you know that dogs that have been spayed or neutered live longer?"

Her face lit up. "Really?"

"One to three years. My sister is a veterinarian, so I get to hear about this a *lot*."

She looked almost thoughtful. "I want Bruiser with me as long as possible. But I don't want her to miss out on being a mom."

Luanna had an answer for that one. "Sweetie, dogs live in the now, so if Bruiser never has puppies, she won't miss it. And she'll always be able to give all her love to you like she does now if she's not distracted by being a momma."

"I hadn't thought about that." The girl nuzzled the papillion's fluffy ears, which the dog seemed to enjoy. "Think you can handle staying a single lady, Bruiser? Just you and me?" The dog woofed softly and the purse shook as if Bruiser was wagging her feather-duster tail. The girl might be clueless, but she sincerely loved her dog (even if she hadn't done all her dog-owner homework), and it was clear the dog loved her back.

Derek touched Luanna's arm, a soft, casual brush that made her shiver. Damn and bless the man. She might not survive the pleasure when they finally had sex if she reacted this way to an innocent touch. But hell, everyone had to go sometime, and if her brain exploded from too many orgasms, she'd die a happy woman. "We should get back. The bride and groom won't notice because they're being cute at each other, but Sandrine just might get upset."

Their young friend let out a squee of joy that made both dogs jump. "You're here with a wedding party? Go, go, go! Don't keep the bride waiting!" She made little shooing gestures. Luanna noticed for the first time that her nails with bright blue, ornamented with cheery yellow suns, and each index finger sported a crystal mid-sun. Not Luanna's style, but cute as the spots on a ladybug.

Then the girl paused, one hand frozen mid-shoo. "Is that Sandrine as in Sandrine *Moss*? I heard a rumor she was staying here. Is that her dog? Who's getting married?" The hand dipped into a front pocket of the huge bag and came out with a crystal-encrusted phone, obviously ready to post the gossip or text it to her friends.

Thinking fast—for all Sandrine loved the limelight, she might get twitchy about some random girl spreading inaccuracies on her Twitter feed—Luanna laughed. "Sandrine Moss is here? I had no idea. Our friend's really Sandy." (Which, in some senses of the word *really*, was true. No one else dared to use Sandrine's inelegant birth name, but Brand would call her that when she was being too over-the-top even for him.) "But she's just a teensy bit of a diva so we started calling her Sandrine."

God, Sandrine would slay her if she heard that story, but she'd also slay her if somehow Sandrine Moss and Luanna's chubby corgi ended up conflated online. Well, by *slay* Luanna meant *threaten to slay*, loudly and pretty hilariously, because Sands really was sweet as sorghum syrup. Her moods blew over quickly, but why risk even a hint of drama on Chloe and Brand's big weekend?

Derek shrugged casually. "Shows you what I know. I thought it was her real name, but I don't know her as well as you do. Let's go."

As she bent to clip Evenrude's leash back on, Luanna finally dared to ask, "So, why did you name that sweet little dog Bruiser?"

The girl let out an exasperated sigh. "I didn't. The stupid breeder did. Talk about a dumb-ass name. But she won't answer to Princess."

Somehow, Luanna and Derek both managed to suppress their laughter until they were back in the elevator with Evenrude.

Then they cracked up. Even Evenrude flashed a bigger version of her normal corgi smile.

"I think we handled that well," Derek said, drawing her close. "We make a pretty good team in a crisis, at least a ridiculous crisis."

Luanna's laughter changed to a warm smile as she realized how right he was. She was in no hurry to test their working-together skills on a problem more serious than an overwrought young woman and her fluffy pooch, but it boded well. "We sure do."

Derek pulled her close. Luanna closed her eyes, assuming he was going in for a kiss.

He did kiss her, a light brush of his lips that hinted at things to come. It didn't seem like it should be a panty-melter, but she was so on edge the gentle smooch reverberated in what her Grandma Beauregard would refer to as her nether regions.

Then he pulled back. "Do you mind if we take a few minutes before heading back to the party?"

"I thought you'd never ask." The elevator wasn't the best place for serious canoodling but they shouldn't stay away too long… On the other hand, what was the worst that could happen if they lingered to make out? They'd get teased.

Derek laid one hand on Luanna's cheek. He smiled, but he didn't look particularly piratical, even though the lights in the elevator happened to glint off his earring in an alluring way. No, he looked thoughtful, serious. "That's not what I meant, even if it's what I wish I meant. There's something I need to tell you."

*

The lights dimmed in the elevator. No, that was just the joy dimming on Luanna's face, and Derek's heart sank. Wow, that came out all wrong. One of the reasons he liked writing was you could edit when you realized that what you meant to say wasn't what you actually said. He'd have to do his best without the backspace key or delete function.

"It's nothing bad," he assured her, caressing her face. "It's good, even. I want to tell you because I think we're getting serious and this is kind of important to me. And I don't want to wait much longer to tell you."

She looked up at him with those big green eyes and smiled, kind of a pale echo of her usual vibrant grin. But something about that smile said *I trust you; I was just startled*, and that gave him all the more reason to spill his not-so-dark secrets. "Let me guess," she said. "You left the rings in LA."

"I said it wasn't bad," he protested. "Forgetting the rings would be bad. But if I had, I trust that between the two of us, we'd figure out a solution, even if it involved commandeering Sandrine's plane or something equally nutty. Knowing that is part of why I need to have this conversation with you."

Luanna raised one eyebrow. "Color me intrigued, sugar. Nervous as a cat in a room full of rocking chairs, but intrigued."

The elevator dinged its arrival on their floor. As soon as they exited the elevator, Derek slipped his arm around Luanna's waist. "There are two cats in that room full of rocking chairs," he whispered as they headed into the posh seclusion of their suite. "I suspect I'm the jumpier one."

Evenrude, turned loose in what she obviously considered her territory now, trotted over to her doggie bed and promptly flopped. Without any plan, Derek sat on the love seat in the living room. Without any prompting, Luanna sat next to him and put her hand on his knee. He covered it with one of his. He hadn't had much chance to think through how he was going to say what he needed to say. He figured he'd need some buildup, some background to the heart of the story, maybe going back several generations in his family history to explain how taciturn German-Americans on one side and proud recent immigrants on the other had created a family tradition of not sharing anything controversial with outsiders.

Instead he opened his mouth and blurted, "My mom's a lesbian."

For a moment, Luanna was terrifyingly silent. Then she laughed. "That's not at all what I expected to hear. But it's not a big deal." She shrugged eloquently. "Not to me, that is. I don't care who she dates, just that she's your mother and I hope I get to meet her someday. But I imagine some people give you a ration of horse-hockey about it, and I imagine *that's* not been easy for you and your family."

Derek struggled for words. No one had said anything unkind or homophobic to anyone in the family, but that might be because so few people who knew them as a family had any idea. "It's just…she came out in the middle of last year. That's why my parents got divorced. And it takes getting used to. All the time I was growing up, she was all cute dresses and lipstick, but it turns out she's way more comfortable being butch. And that's just the surface stuff. She's still Mom, still loving and supportive and wonderful, but she's changed. Still changing, I think, growing into herself. She's a lot more confident, which is great, but I'd never realized she *wasn't* confident before. We're all still shell-shocked, even Mom."

"*Especially* your mom, I'd imagine," Luanna said thoughtfully. "When you've been married long enough to have grown kids, it can't be easy to wrap your head around realizing something so important about yourself and changing your life to align with it. For what it's worth, changing the way she dresses is probably a big part of creating a new life. And maybe the way she dressed before was a way of thinking herself into *that* life that wasn't such a great fit." She squeezed his hand and he realized that while they'd been talking, she'd shifted so her fingers were entwined with his.

It felt right. Comfortable. Like their hands should always tangle together like that, if they weren't touching in more intimate ways. It felt even more right that she was so accepting and that without knowing his mother, she more-or-less paraphrased what Mom had told him about her new look.

"It feels good to tell you," he said. "It was starting to weigh on me that I hadn't said anything, but I wasn't sure how."

" 'My mom's a lesbian' works. No need to beat around the bush. But I wish I'd known you last year," she went on. "I get the feeling you haven't felt comfortable talking to too many people about it."

Might as go on with the cue. "You're the first. Graham and Brand know about the divorce, but not why. I don't think anyone in my home town knows the whole story, which is pretty impressive considering there are about six hundred people in town, and I think the census may have included a few pets to come up with that number. It's gossip central. Some of them must realize my parents split up and my mom moved away, simply because she isn't *there* anymore, but Dad only told a few people who really needed to know. The postmistress may have said something to her husband and girlfriends that she was forwarding Mom's mail to Albuquerque. But as far as I know, they're still in the dark that she left Dad for another woman. Who's pretty cool," he added hastily. "Beatrice and Mom are very happy. We just don't talk about it."

Luanna's eyes had been getting wider and wider as he went on. Finally she had to ask, "Why ever not? You can't keep it a secret forever, not in a place like that. I'm from a teeny-tiny town myself, so I know how they work. If people aren't spilling the beans about a divorce or something, people will make up stories that are way worse than what's really going on."

He smiled. "You may be right. But my family's always been big on keeping our business private." He'd always wondered if there'd been something back in the family history that had made being closed-mouthed a matter of life or death: bootleggers on his mother's side, maybe, or revolutionaries on his father's. He'd never asked because he'd rather keep that dashing illusion than admit that both sides of his family were a bit uptight. Besides, if there were interesting stories several generations back, they were probably lost because no one would have talked about something potentially scandalous once it had blown over. "I felt like I'd be violating my parents' privacy if I talked about it too much. But I've gotten so close to you it feels wrong not to tell you. Even if it's kind of hard to explain that my mom's queer, my parents split up because of it, and they really *are* still friends."

"Sounds normal to me. Remind me when we have more time and some bourbon to tell you about Uncle Claude, his ex-boyfriend, the ex-boyfriend's ex-wife, and amicably shared custody of a one-eyed cat and a pack of Catahoula hounds. In that case, everyone in the parish knows about it. But I respect your family's not like mine. I won't go telling the world about your parents because it's none of the world's business. Thank you for trusting me. It means so much to me."

Derek's heart swelled. At least that seemed as good a way as any to explain why he was swallowing a lump in his throat.

Damn, Luanna was special.

"Thank you for being you."

She leaned forward and kissed his cheek, then said, "Can't exactly be anyone else. Not with my upbringing. I'm the least eccentric person in my extended family."

And if he were lucky, she might end up being one more eccentric person in his family. It would do them all good.

He wasn't sure where that thought came from. He liked it. But if he focused on it too much, they'd never get back to the pre-wedding party. Speaking of which…

"We should head downstairs before they call for search-and-rescue."

Luanna's pretty lips pouted a little. "I suppose you're right." Derek pondered for maybe two seconds. "They can wait a little while longer. After all this seriousness, I need some sugar." He pulled her close.

"That sounds like one of my lines," Luanna said as she straddled his lap.

And that was the last thing either of them said for a few delightful minutes.

·

Chapter 20

Thankfully, Olive didn't start singing until they were all on the private elevator heading up to their suite of rooms.

Not that she had a bad voice—far from it, in fact. She could've had a career belting out the blues—and Luanna had heard some mighty fine blues singers in her day, thanks to growing up in Louisiana. Olive wasn't singing the blues now, though; she was giving Annie Lennox a run for her money.

It was a good thing that she'd waited until the elevator doors closed, or else the rest of the casino would've been paying far too close attention to the celebrities in their midst.

The elevator hummed upward. No one in their party looked at the rich carpet at their feet, because it had a lovely pattern that, when you'd had a generous helping of alcohol, became way too squiggly for comfort.

Luanna hadn't even realized Olive was drunk; the older woman had walked and talked as if she were just fine until now.

Somehow, in her blurry mental state, Luanna felt like that was a metaphor for the evening, but she wasn't quite sure why.

The doors parted at the entrance to their massive foyer. Olive abruptly stopped singing. They all waited, slightly stunned, in the silence. Then Olive started giggling. She giggled her way out of the elevator and over to the door of her room with nary a stagger. She opened the door, paused, turned.

"Do you need anything before I retire?" she asked Sandrine.

"I've got her," Ray said. "You're off the clock."

"Toodles," Olive said, with a wave of her hand and without a hint of slur, and closed her door. She started singing again, but the sound faded as she no doubt moved deeper into her suite.

Sandrine gazed adoringly up at Ray. "Aww," she said.

Ray swept her up into his arms as if she weighed no more than a baby bird—which was probably fairly accurate—and headed into their room as she gave a tiny shriek of delight.

"Let's get you to bed, darlin'," Luanna said to Chloe, who was a little unsteady, but wasn't wasted. The remaining four had switched between alcohol and water all evening, so they wouldn't be too messed up by tomorrow (today?) afternoon's wedding. "I'll be right back," she added to Derek.

Brand gave Chloe a sound kiss and said, "Good night, soon-to-be Mrs. Mossiman."

"Still not changing my name," Chloe said. "Sweet dreams, soon-to-be Mr. Montiero."

"What *are* you going to do about names?" Luanna asked as she ushered her through the sitting room into the bedroom of the suite they'd share tonight. Chloe's pajamas—red cotton shorts and a white T-shirt top printed with bright cherries—were on the bed.

"Oh, I'm changing mine legally for when we have kids, but keeping Montiero professionally," Chloe said. Most of the words were even clear, or clear enough that Luanna understood them. "It's just a running joke, you know? You're a good friend," Chloe added as Luanna filled a glass of water and put it on the nightstand on Chloe's side of the bed.

"Goes without saying," Luanna said, making sure Chloe's toothbrush and toothpaste were out on the bathroom counter. The counter was a gray marble shot through with gold, and the sink was one of those bowl things that sat above the counter, with a waterfall spigot. It was almost more than Luanna could face. She found her own toothbrush and facial wash, set them within reach.

Chloe abruptly sat down on the end of the bed. "I'm getting married tomorrow," she said, wonderment and a hint of something akin to panic in her voice.

Luanna sat beside her. Dayum, the bedspread was luxurious. It was more of a duvet cover, purple embroidered with burgundy and gold, and stuffed with the gushiest filling. She was really, really going to enjoy sleeping beneath it. She was also probably going to fall asleep before she actually had time to enjoy it. "Yes, you are," she said to Chloe. "To an incredible man who loves you beyond reason."

Chloe's face split into a goofy grin. "Yeah," she said. "And I love him to pieces."

Luanna patted her on the back. "So get yourself ready for bed, and get a good night's sleep, because tomorrow is going to be epic, and by epic, I mean so good it'll make you want to slap your grandma."

Chloe stood up, a little unsteadily, and frowned. "What does that even *mean*?"

"I have no idea," Luanna said. "I've had some very good days, and I've never wanted to slap either of my grandmothers."

Chloe took a few careful steps toward the bathroom. "You're having some good days with Derek," she noted.

Luanna was pretty sure her grin was as goofy as Chloe's had been. "Why yes, yes I am. And I'm going to go see if he's still around so I can say goodnight. I'll be back in a few minutes."

"No rush," Chloe said, concentrating very hard on squeezing the toothpaste. "I'll probably be ashleep—aspleep—asleep before you get back."

Luanna closed the door between the bedroom and sitting room and leaned against it for a moment, both to steady herself because the room was the tiniest bit spinny, but also to bask in the knowledge that Chloe's words had been very true.

Sometime that evening during the second (but larger-than-average) margarita, it had dawned on Luanna that this weekend was going to be the longest time she'd spent with Derek since they'd started dating. Physically speaking, that was—they'd talked on the phone and texted and emailed and Skyped, but as of tonight, she'd spent more in-the-same-breathing-space time as him in one day than any other.

By the time she was licking the salt off the third margarita (seductively, because Derek was watching, and her inhibitions were melting like a distracted toddler's ice cream cone), she realized that she'd been a little worried that they wouldn't get along once they spent copious amounts of time together. That they'd find some tics, some little thing that the other did that was going to be incredibly annoying after a few months.

The only reason she realized that she'd been worried was because that worry had melted away, too.

She knew their relationship had taken a turn when he told her about his mother. His family valued privacy, something she understood from her work for her clients, even if her own family tended to be an enthusiastically open book. In both situations, loyalty was paramount.

By telling her, Derek had trusted her enough to bring her into an inner circle.

On top of that, she'd learned that she genuinely, sincerely *liked* spending time with Derek.

Which boded well for when they weren't having sex.

Not that she expected the sex to taper off once they got going, or that the sex wasn't going to be better than an eighty-percent sale on silk charmeuse. It was just that she liked to be able to have a good time with her sexual partners when they weren't actively having sex. There was nothing worse than having nothing to talk about outside of the bedroom.

Plus she liked the way they'd worked together during the Evenrude Vegas Incident #1 (as opposed to the Evenrude Cactus Incident #1 or the Evenrude Peacock Incident #82 But Who's Counting Anymore?). Grand-mère had always told her that how a man handles a crisis—and how you handle a crisis together—told you more about him than a million sweet kisses.

Luanna had always thought that was a wise sentiment.

She kicked off her heels and went back out into the foyer of their suite. Derek was alone—Brand had clearly made it back into their room safely—sitting on one of the gushy love seats arranged to make a conversation area.

She skirted a fern, one of several that were either real or so close to real it would take a botanist to confirm or deny, and settled down next to him.

He handed her a cold bottle of water and slid his arm around her. "Oh, bless you," she breathed, twisting off the cap and guzzling. She dribbled a little on her rose-colored dress, but she didn't care. Soooo good.

She propped her feet on the table and wiggled her toes. Sandrine—well, Olive, but it was Sandrine's treat—had booked them for the full spa treatment tomorrow: manis, pedis, massages, and of course hair and makeup for the wedding.

"I'm feeling a little overwhelmed by how much Sandrine's shelling out for this," she commented.

"Brand's her beloved brother, and she wants him to be happy. Doing all this makes *her* feel happy." Derek raised one shoulder in a lazy shrug. "It's a way for her to pay him back for everything he's done for her over the years. Well, that and the cars. I'm kinda jealous about the cars."

"I was terrified every time I drove the Mustang," Luanna admitted. "Speaking of which, those player cards Ray handed us tonight were worth a car." Whether it was the booze or the newfound comfortableness she was feeling around him, she added a confession. "I stood there thinking about how I could've just cashed my card in and bought a car made in this decade."

"I know," Derek said. "I nearly shat myself when I realized how much it was worth." She felt his chest move as he laughed. "I did the same thing—thought about what I could do with the money."

"Then I realized I was missing the spirit of the thing," she said. "It was for us to gamble with and have fun—so we could all have fun together."

"Well, except for Olive."

Luanna started giggling, almost couldn't stop. "I didn't think we could actually *lose* her."

Partway through the evening, they'd all slowly realized that Olive was nowhere to be found. They'd eventually found her in the high stakes poker room, and from the looks of it, she was cleaning up.

It was only after that that she'd started drinking. Wise woman.

"I didn't gamble it all away," Derek said. "I wasn't sure if we'd all go out again. But I was thinking, maybe you and I could do something nice when we get back? Go to Catalina or Cambria for a weekend?"

"I have a little left, too," Luanna said, a warm feeling spreading through her at the thought of them planning future things together. "Let's pool that money and continue having fun."

He quirked his rakish pirate's grin at her, and her body flared with need. If she'd been standing, she might have melted into a puddle of lust (whether or not alcohol had been involved). Before she could protest, he'd scooped her onto his lap.

"'Continue' having fun?" he said. "We're just getting started."

She put a hand on his chest to steady herself, felt the rapid beating of his heart through the steel-gray silk of his shirt.

Against her thigh, she felt the throb of his arousal.

The room spun a little, desire and margaritas combining in a deadly, heady brew.

Luanna lifted her hand to cup his jaw. His five o'clock shadow rasped against her palm, and her brain made the dizzying plummet to wonder what that would feel like against her breast, against the sensitive flesh between her thighs. She dragged a thumb across his lower lip, watching his pupils dilate, aware of how the motion harkened back to that first night of necking in the car.

When he'd driven her mad just with kisses.

When he'd told her how good it was going to be.

She didn't want to wait until tomorrow night.

She knew they would, though. It would be better than a drunken fumble out here in the sitting room, where any of their friends could stumble upon them. She wasn't averse to a little hint of exhibitionism (see, again, necking in the car) but as much as her body ached for more, privacy in the bedroom, with a proper bed, and clear heads (well, as clear as they could be) would be better than a quickie bent over the loveseat. At least for their first time.

Still, it was crazy that she was this aroused and hadn't even kissed him yet.

She fixed that part by leaning in the few more inches needed.

The kiss was slow, seductive. She tasted a hint of hops, smelled a perfect combination of aftershave and maleness. The clothes that separated them felt like more of a barrier than a suit of armor, yet focused her in on the touch of their lips, his jaw cradled in her hand, the way his hand came up to tangle in her hair.

The room dipped, twisted.

Luanna slid her hand down to find Derek's nipple beneath his shirt, but her hand kind of skidded against the silk.

"Hey," Derek said against her lips, "Chloe's passed out, right? Do you thing she would notice if…"

Luanna sputtered. "She's not drunk, and the bed's not *that* big—she'll notice."

"Damn," he murmured, and his hand found her breast, only slightly less fumbly than she'd been.

As aroused as she was, the spell was broken. It was crazy, but she wanted their first time to be phenomenal, not the result of drunken groping. Taking it slow might have been his idea, but she agreed with him.

Reluctantly.

She ached for Derek's touch. She wanted more.

She was also halfway drunk, exhausted, and technically in charge of her best friend's wedding tomorrow. And she had a date with a hot, hot, hot guy tomorrow night.

She reached for her water bottle on the table, took a swig. Still blissfully cold as it hit her system.

Luanna took a deep, shuddering breath.

Derek did the same.

She managed to haul herself to her feet, offer him her hand.

He stood and raised her hand to his lips, just as he'd done the night they'd met.

She shuddered with desire.

"Tomorrow night," he said.

"Will be phenomenal," she said.

Chapter 21

*D*erek woke annoyingly early on Saturday.

He was a morning person, sure, but he hadn't quite planned for this.

He also woke up knowing it was going to be a good day.

No, a *great* day.

Thankfully, a liberal application of water and Advil before bed meant that he was muzzy, but not headachy-hung-over. Before he headed into the suite's private gym, he took a grateful Evenrude out for her morning constitutional and left a note to that effect for Luanna and Chloe.

A brisk run on the treadmill, followed by a relaxing twenty minutes in the sauna, and finally a hot, pounding shower, and he was practically whistling.

Today, his best friend was getting married to the woman he loved, and Derek was thrilled to be a part of it.

And tonight, he was finally going to spend the night with a gorgeous, vibrant, funny woman who made his heart sing every time he saw her, every time he heard her laugh.

He hoped he'd planned everything right. Dinner in the room, with champagne. Candles. Rose petals on the bed—please, let that not be too cheesy. He'd pondered bringing a few fun little toys, but decided against it in the end. They'd be busy enough exploring each other; the possibilities were endless even before props could be introduced.

Although if Luanna had something on hand, he wouldn't be averse. No, not at all.

When he got back to his rooms after his workout, he discovered Brand was up and in the shower. Good. Derek knew his friend hadn't imbibed much more than he had, but he hadn't been looking forward to nudging him out of bed. Although Brand was singing loudly and off-key.

Well, that would be Chloe's problem after today.

All he had to do was get Brand to the church on time.

*

Derek looked around the casino chapel's dressing room for the groom and his party. Check, and check.

Despite the fact that the room was upscale and immaculate, there still lingered in the air a hint of expensive cologne from previous occupants. Derek rather liked the space; its dark wood-paneled walls and plush carpet, tan with a plum-colored swirl-and-leaf pattern, was reminiscent of an old-world gentlemen's club.

The comfortable chairs, crystal tumblers, and snifter of brandy didn't hurt. He wondered briefly if the alcohol was standard or whether they were getting a VIP treatment, but he didn't much care—especially after he tasted the brandy.

Their tuxedos had been delivered before they arrived, hanging neatly on a wooden rack, spit-polished, shiny black shoes lined up beneath.

The only hitch had been some fans of Ray's outside, who'd noticed him and yelled to get his attention, snapping some cell phone photos. Ray, ever the polite Midwestern boy (albeit in a beefy, action-hero body), had waved, calling out an apology for having an appointment.

Ray was changing in the lavatory, which struck Derek as a little odd, but hey, to each his own. He'd spent time in Scandinavia during his misspent post-college years, when he thought he'd be a high-falutin' documentary auteur, and a few sessions in a Finnish sauna had stripped away any issues he might have had about being naked around other men.

"How're you holding up?" he asked Brand.

"As God is my witness, I'll never learn how to tie one of these damn things," Brand said, struggling with his bow tie. "I really can't use a clip-on? Really?"

"Look," Derek said, taking the strip of black fabric from him, "I know Chloe's a great lady, but trust me, I think she'll notice if you're wearing a clip-on."

"Really?" Brand spun around, nearly strangling himself on the tie Derek had started to put around his neck. "See, that's what I'm afraid of here. She's... Chloe is someone who knows what she wants. I love that about her. But all this—this is a compromise. This isn't her dream wedding. The details aren't—"

Derek took Brand by the shoulders and spun him back to face the mirror. He reached around to make the knot in the bow tie. "Chloe loves you, too. This is kind of a compromise, sure, but it's a compromise that makes things better; it takes away everybody else's ideas and choices, and lets her—and you—have the wedding *you* want."

"Are you sure?" Brand asked.

"I'm sure," Derek said. "There." He stepped back. The tie was perfect.

"When did you get to be so smart?" Brand asked. He adjusted the tie one millimeter to the right. Derek smiled.

"I started dating a really smart woman," he said. "Who happens to be Chloe's best friend."

Ray came out of the bathroom. His bow tie was perfect. But then, of the three of them, he was the only one to have walked a red carpet. And won major awards.

"Check us out," Brand said. "We clean up nice."

"Gotta keep the ladies on their toes," Ray said. "By the way," he added to Derek, "would you mind telling Luanna that it would be really great if she could let Sandrine catch the bouquet?"

Derek's eyebrows shot up. "You have something you want to tell us?"

Ray shrugged one mountainous shoulder. "Nah. It's just that Sandrine likes to be the center of attention, you know? And I know you and Luanna are falling pretty hard for each other—it's obvious, man—but you two haven't been together as long, so if Luanna catches the bouquet, Sandrine might feel…well, you know."

Derek hadn't spent that much time around Sandrine, but he kind of knew.

He glanced at his watch. "One last toast for the road," he said, and poured them each a finger of brandy.

"To the women in our lives," Brand said. "May they always inspire us to be our best selves."

"I'll drink to that," Derek said, and smiled, because he knew in a few minutes, he'd see Luanna again.

*

Spring in Vegas. Not a hint of a cloud in the sky. That was the only reason they'd decided to have the wedding outside, on a covered dock overlooking a small manmade lake on the casino grounds. The blue water sparkled, and a low fountain at its center sent diamond-sparkle droplets into the air.

The water and the high, peaked canvas ceiling counteracted the fact that it was unseasonably warm for spring, even spring in Vegas. Derek suspected discreet air conditioning. Yes, outside. Because Vegas was not known for its subtlety.

The men took their place under the fragrant bower of mauve and white roses at the end of the dock.

The officiant stood at the end of the dock along with Olive, who apparently was licensed to perform wedding ceremonies in both the states of California and Nevada. Derek had long decided that nothing Olive did surprised him anymore.

When the bridesmaids appeared, Derek's mouth went a little dry. Because Luanna looked *stunning*.

It was the only word to describe her. Sure, Sandrine was a gorgeous, waifish model of perfection. But Luanna…Luanna shone.

Her sleeveless blue dress was off the shoulder and dipped low in the front, enough to show a hint of cleavage without being tacky or taking attention away from the bride. The fabric caressed her luscious curves, and for a fleeting moment, Derek envied it, envied the way it got to skim her hips, drape over her breasts.

Her thick blond hair was caught up in a loose coif, with tendrils framing her face. He wanted to toy with those tendrils as he kissed her, feel them tickling his skin.

Tonight, he promised himself, tamping down his lust. Right now he was here for Brand and Chloe. Later, he'd get the chance to shimmy that dress off Luanna's shoulders, down her hips…

She and Sandrine came down the dock in measured steps to the strains of the love theme from *Jane Austin in Space*, the movie Brand had been working on when he and Chloe met, and took their places across from Derek and Ray.

Luanna caught Derek's eye and smiled, then looked back down the dock. Derek understood: this was Chloe's show. Luanna, her best friend, didn't want to miss a moment of it.

Fierce loyalty was what Luanna was all about. He got that. He respected that.

He kinda loved that.

Chloe appeared, and she looked stunning, too. Derek didn't have a clue what kind of dress she wore, just that it looked perfect on her short, curvy figure. She'd left her curly dark hair down and loose, with a sparkly tiara affixing a filmy veil to her head. She was clearly trying stay composed, but as she got closer, her face broke out in a joyous smile. Derek glanced at Brand, and saw his friend's expression mirroring Chloe's joy.

They'd written their own ceremony, and it was short and heartfelt. Derek had thought, during the rehearsal, about pitching an episode about wedding traditions throughout Western culture. (He'd always been amused by couples who insisted on "The Bridal Chorus" from *Lohengrin* without knowing what it was really about. Of course, Mendelssohn's "Wedding March" recessional was probably worse, and he knew they weren't using that, either.)

Right now, in the moment, he celebrated his friends' union.

Until things went wrong.

Olive asked for the rings. Luanna handed Chloe's bouquet to Sandrine and headed back down the dock to the room just inside where Evenrude would be waiting. As per the rehearsal, she'd lead Evenrude down the dock with Evenrude carrying the pillow with the rings on her back.

It had worked fine during the rehearsal. Evenrude loved Chloe and Brand, and had trotted toward them with her tail wagging almost as hard as it did for her beloved peacocks.

Now, Luanna disappeared through the arched opening and turned right. A moment later, she passed the doorway in the other direction.

Chloe and Brand were gazing at each other and didn't seem to notice yet.

Derek murmured to Ray, "I'm going to go help," and hightailed it back down the dock.

When he got to the antechamber, he found Luanna wide-eyed with panic, although she wasn't actively panicking, which Derek respected. *He* was feeling a little panicky.

"Evenrude's gone," she whispered frantically, even though nobody at the far end of the dock would be able to hear them. She pointed. The pillow with the rings was on the floor, next to the wall with the hook where 'Rude's leash had been hooked. So, it wasn't about stealing a pair of white-gold wedding bands. Who would dognap an innocent corgi?

Luanna picked up the pillow. "Where would she go?"

They stared at each other for a moment. Derek had a flash of insight, and apparently great minds thought alike, because when he voiced his thought, Luanna spoke at the same time.

"The pet garden!"

The pet garden was practically next door, although it involved going into the casino, dodging patrons who weren't looking where they were going (which was ninety-three percent of them), and back out another door.

And there was Evenrude, on the grass beneath a palm tree. Peeing.

Because, apparently, when you gotta go, you gotta go. Derek had gotten Brand to the church on time, but nobody had explained the plan to the dog.

Evenrude spotted them in mid-pee, finished, and trotted up to them, tongue lolling and tail wagging. Luanna sighed and crouched to give her a scritch between the ears, heedless of her pretty dress pooling on the cement walkway.

"I want to yell at her, but I know she won't understand," she said, looking up at Derek. She grabbed the end of Evenrude's leash and rose. "Let's go," she said.

As they were double-timing it through the casino, someone said, "Hey! You can't bring a dog in here," but Luanna waved the pillow and Derek said "Ring bearer dog!" and the person apparently didn't bother to call security as they left him in their wake.

Luanna quickly fastened the pillow straps around Evenrude's torso and unhooked her leash. Then Evenrude headed up the dock ahead of Luanna and Derek with an air of "We have somewhere to be; keep up, now, won't you?"

Derek didn't even realize they were holding hands until they got up to the rest of the party and had to go to their respective sides. He gave Luanna's fingers a little squeeze and took his place next to Ray.

But he couldn't stop looking at Luanna.

Even when, after the ceremony, Chloe skipped through the casino in her wedding dress.

Chapter 22

"Oh, land," Luanna whispered to Derek after Chloe and Brand had excused themselves from the low-key after-party (low-key in a very "the groom is Sandrine Moss's brother" way—simple but perfect passed hors d'oeuvres, still more champagne, and held in a posh VIP private room with charcoal gray leather couches just as buttery as the chairs at Lorelei) and more or less floated toward the elevator on a cloud of bubbly and bliss. "I am happy as a ladybug on a lily for those two, but I kept hoping they'd hurry up and start their honeymoon already."

"Glad I wasn't the only one. Didn't they realize we have a honeymoon of our own to start?" Derek laughed. "Except we're not married, so I guess we have to call it something else."

Luanna pondered that for a second or two. Many of her brain cells, drunk on anticipation, seemed to be inhabiting her panties, but being giddy with lust, in this instance, was helpful. "Bunnymoon," she said. "Because we'll be going at it like bunnies."

"Until the next full moon, if we could get away with it. That works for me. But I have one question for you."

Luanna squeezed his hand. "Fire away, sugar."

"Why are we still sitting at the party instead of on our way to the room, and why are we talking instead of kissing?"

They necked in the elevator. Okay, maybe they did a little more than necking, but no clothing was removed. Not completely, anyway.

Luanna unbuttoned Derek's shirt to the waist. He looked rakish and piratical with it hanging open, especially since she'd left the bow tie in place. "Good enough to eat," she purred, and maybe she would have except the dayum elevator moved too fast. And in the short time the elevator took to reach its destination, he'd removed most of the pins from her updo. She shook out the rest, glad that she'd talked the hairdresser out of using more than a minimal spritz of hairspray. Sure, she had about a million pins to contend with, but her hair didn't feel gluey and wasn't sticking out like she'd had a run-in with a light socket. A few pins fell to the floor between the elevator and their suite but she couldn't be bothered to pick them up, instead making a mental note to tip housekeeping a smidge more. The stray hairpins were only the start of what might be a grand, decadent mess.

They stumbled into a hotel room full of delicious scents: garlicky shrimp, she thought, and some other wonderful food smells, and roses from a big, fresh bouquet on the piano. A bottle of champagne chilled in a silver ice bucket on a stand. In any other hotel, Luanna would have figured it was stainless, but in this crazy place, it might actually be silver, or at least silver plate.

But all those lovely details paled compared to the fact she was alone with Derek, neither of them had any responsibilities tugging at them, Evenrude was in the capable care of Olive, and this time, there was no reason to wait.

One of the reasons Luanna was happy to end up with this particular dress was that it was so easy to get out of. No tiny, fussy hooks, no awkward side, no belts that fastened in odd ways. Teasing was one thing, fumbling was another, and this dress made it easy to be suave. All Derek had to do was unzip one simple zipper and ease the dress off her. He took his time, obviously having fun moving the silk over her skin, but any fussing was his choice, not because he was fighting with a stubborn fastener. It took a while for the dress to reach the floor despite its simplicity, but every silky millimeter of its journey added to both Luanna's and Derek's pleasure.

Luanna had chosen pale blue lace bra and panties. The bra was functional, though lacy and silky enough that it didn't look like it should be. The panties were purely for matching color; if she'd somehow slipped and upended herself, they'd have been more revealing than going bare because they called attention to the bits they accented rather than hid. Derek's eyes widened and he sucked in his breath in a gratifying way. "Wow." Then he blinked a few times and repeated, "Wow. You are so gorgeous."

"And you are so overdressed for this party," she purred. "Let me help you with that."

A tuxedo wasn't as easy to dispose of as her dress—and because it was rented, she couldn't just rip it off him. Luckily, Luanna's line of work meant she'd had practice getting people into and out of complicated clothes, often with pins involved. Usually those people weren't helping out quite as eagerly as Derek was.

Plus, as much as she wanted to shred it from his body, she understood, at a primal level, what he'd meant all along by taking it slow, building up to what was going to be a phenomenal finale. Like a fine meal to be savored, rather than bolted down, barely tasted. She wanted to remember this later—but more importantly, she wanted to experience it now, every moment of it.

She was keenly aware of how her body yearned for him. Her nipples were already hard against the lace and silk of the bra, taut and needy. Her groin felt heavy, her sex slick, her clit trembling with a heartbeat of its own. Yet she wanted his hands, his lips, on every part of her: caressing the skin at the nape of her neck, tasting the sensitive flesh on the underside of her wrist, sliding across the quivering planes of her stomach….

So she took her time. Time for both of them to enjoy.

She deftly undid the impeccably knotted bowtie and slipped it from under his collar with a whisper against the starched shirt. She stepped close to him, pressed against him, her softer body against his harder one, as she reached around him to unfasten his cummerbund. She was still wearing her heels, making them almost the same height, and his hard cock pressed against her pelvis. She couldn't resist a little wiggle against it as she gazed into his deep blue eyes, and she watched them widen, accompanying the catch of his breath.

Cufflinks. One, two, in her palm, then clinking into a little silver dish on the coffee table. Then, finally, his shirt. She popped the final buttons, stepping back a little for access. She tried to keep eye contact, but finally she couldn't take it anymore, had to look and savor.

Yum.

She ran her hand down his caramel-colored chest, enjoying the texture of his skin, the little bit of crisp hair, the play of his muscles under her hand. Enjoying the sounds he made low in his throat as she touched him.

Oh, God, he looked every bit as good as she'd imagined. Better, even; a little more cut. Not crazy Ray Stark cut, but not many people had Ray's combination of fortunate genes, athletic ability, the best trainers money could buy, and multimillion-dollar incentives to spend hours a day working out. Derek looked like a guy who took good care of himself and wasn't a couch potato and that was plenty fine.

After tugging the shirt out of his waistband, she dragged it down his arms. Before she pulled it off his wrists, though, she stepped forward again, arms around him, gently trapping him. She kissed him, teasing him further by not letting the kiss deepen, by nipping at his lower lip, then swiping her tongue there to soothe the sting. Toying, playing, teasing.

He'd teased her for so long. No—they'd teased each other.

Enough. Her nipples ached, her clit pounded, and she wanted more.

She tossed his shirt atop the growing pile of tuxedo parts on the gold brocade settee by the door. With fingers trembling from lust, she unfastened his black pants and yanked. He stepped out of them, toeing off his socks in the process.

Still squatting, she ran her hands up his legs, marveling at the strength of his thighs. She slid her hands around to his firm ass, squeezed indulgently. His husky laugh floated down.

Now she was face-to-face with his briefs, which were her favorite red just as she'd fantasized, and stained glossy dark at the spot where the tip of his straining cock met the fabric. She didn't take a lot of time to appreciate the way the color looked against his skin, though, just tugged them down. Long before they hit the floor, his cock sprang out proud. Dusky like the rest of him, shading to red at the head, which glistened with clear moisture.

"Even better than I imagined," she whispered, not sure why she was whispering other than it felt right to do it. "Just makes me want to…"

Oh hell, she didn't need to talk about what she wanted anymore. She could do it. *Finally.*

With delight, she took his cock into her mouth. He started to protest, or at least she thought it was going to be a protest. She swirled her tongue around his shaft while taking him deeper and instead of arguing, he buried his fingers in her hair.

He was hot and hard and just the right size and he tasted like male musk and some fancy soap with undertones of cedar. His balls settled into her hand perfectly, crinkling up with pleasure. And the noises…oh, sweet Lord, the sounds coming out of that man's mouth as she swirled her tongue around the swollen head of his cock, then sucked him in deep.

So right. So very right.

She knew they'd talked in great detail about what they wanted to do together their first time, how they wanted to explore each other in slow, tantalizing detail.

And lordy, she still wanted that. Wanted to caress and taste every sepia inch of his skin, wanted him to stroke and kiss and lick her. Wanted him on top of her, underneath her, behind her doggy-style, and possibly bending her over the piano.

But that was going to happen in later rounds. She didn't want to rush, per se, but lengthy foreplay, however exquisite, seemed unnecessary at this time. So, for that matter, did a bed. She was wet as the Delta in springtime already, her whole body on fire. And the room they were in had a plush sofa and several armchairs big enough for a small family. Not to mention the piano.

She was—she knew, a rush of pleasure surging through her—enjoying every moment, every touch, every taste, every reaction.

Derek eased away from her. "Too much," he said, his voice husky with need and strain as he grasped her wrists, pulled her to her feet. "Want you too much. I have so many plans for you. So many things I want to do to you. Or with you. Or for you. Don't know where to start."

But obviously he did know: with a kiss that sucked her breath away. Cradling her face in his long-fingered hands, gentle and yet commanding, he plundered her mouth. It was a different sensation from the first time he'd kissed her, in the car in front of his house, when she didn't want it to end. And as then, she wanted to experience every last lingering sensation that came with this kiss.

He'd gotten her so fired up that night. She was so fired up tonight she could hardly stand it.

"How about in the blue chair? You know, the one that's right behind you." She gave him a playful little shove. It wouldn't be enough to budge Evenrude, let alone a grown man, but he took the hint and sat down.

"Wallet," Derek said. She raised an eyebrow and he elaborated. "There's a bowl full of condoms on the bedside table, but I foolishly didn't stash any out here. Luckily there's a condom in my wallet, which is in my pants. Been there since we had the date that ended up…well, you know. I have a feeling that we're not going to make it much longer without needing one."

She found the requested item and put it in easy reach. Then she straddled his lap—the enormous overstuffed chair was big enough she could do that. Oh, sweet mother of pearl, his cock and her clit and pussy were perfectly positioned that way. Perfect for riding him when the time came, and right now, perfect for mutual teasing. She rubbed herself against him, letting him feel her moist heat while she enjoyed his hardness. "So good," she moaned. "If having you against me feels this great, having you inside me is going to be amazing."

Derek smiled and pushed up, letting her feel his strength and how he'd be able to move inside her even if she stayed on top. His cock slid along her clit, and the exquisiteness of it made her jerk and gasp.

Then Derek captured one of her nipples between his lips and added another layer of sensation. She cried out softly and clenched, not quite coming, but as close as Biloxi was to the Gulf.

"That's right," he murmured, more or less around her nipple. His hand went to work on the other side, teasing that nipple, too, to a hard, aching peak.

Then his mouth and hand switched places. Not too hard, but not too gently either, a nice firm pressure with his long fingers, suction and an occasional nip of his teeth.

Fire. She was on fire. She writhed against his cock, teasing herself, but not quite letting herself come, determined to hold off until Derek was inside her. Wasn't going to be easy, though. She wanted to wait, wanted to let the pleasure build, but my God, it was like the Mississippi in flood and the levee wasn't up to its task. She couldn't remember when she'd ever felt this much sexual need and greed, and the great thing was that Derek was right there with her, encouraging her.

She unwrapped the condom, placed it at the head of his beautiful, perfect cock. Derek freed her nipple long enough to say, "Oh, God, yes."

Her hands were shaking with lust, and she fumbled like an inexperienced teen trying to get the condom on, but then his hands came down with hers, and although she swore they shook with lust, too, they worked together. Then he gripped her hips and eased her down onto that perfect cock, just the tip. And again she remembered that first night, that first kiss…

…and so did he, because he said, in a voice catching on desire, "I told you, that first night, that when we took each other, it was going to be because we couldn't not, because if I didn't slide my cock into you, we'd both die from the need. I promised you, Luanna…when we had sex, it would be *phenomenal*."

As he spoke, he slid up into her, and she took him in, inch by glorious, phenomenal inch, and she knew what he meant so exquisitely that she thought she might pass out, a first for her. She'd waited so long for this. So long. Her fingernails dug into the arms of the chair, and her back arched, her hips grinding forward, down. To finally feel him inside her, filling her…it was a completion, a *rightness* that almost made her want to sob.

She choked out, "You feel…even better than I imagined, and what I imagined was…pretty dayum amazing."

Derek cupped her breasts in his big hands and teased at the nipples, a sensation that rippled out from her breasts to meet those coming from her clit and pussy. "I know. It was. The real thing's a million times better, just like I knew it would be. You're so beautiful, and you're so tight, and I love the way you're riding me." He flashed the pirate smile she loved so much. "Can you imagine being like this in some tropical lagoon, the water lapping us as you rode me? My mouth on your breasts, my hands free to move your hips or cup your ass." He moved one hand down to do exactly that. "We'd be all alone, but under the open sky. Anyone could see us, but no one actually will…not unless you want them to."

Luanna had been puzzled when he began to spin the fantasy while they were very busy fulfilling one, but then remembered that she'd said once she hoped he'd still tell stories when he was inside her. Heat blossomed in her, not just from the words and the image they painted (though it was an enticing one) but that he'd remembered. That heat, combined with the story and the pleasure that was already building, made her post faster, buck her clit harder against him. He pinched her nipples, not roughly, but more intensely than he had been.

"Stories later," she managed to say. "Can't talk now." Sensation reached a boiling point and she exploded, crying out Derek's name.

She expected Derek to follow shortly. Instead, he gritted his teeth, screwed his eyes closed, and kept going. After a few ecstatic minutes, he managed to choke out. "Can you come once more? Just one more for now, Luanna."

She did, as much from the words, and the banked heat and control and grit in them, as what his body and hers were doing to each other. As she began to convulse, he grabbed her hips and thrust wildly up into her.

She couldn't be bothered to analyze whether the result counted as a third orgasm or a delicious continuation of the second. Because really, who cared.

*

Eventually they got around to eating the dinner. They ignored the silverware and fed each other delicious morsels with their fingers while drinking the champagne straight from the bottle because glasses seemed like too much trouble in their post-sex bliss. Luckily, Derek had ordered some finger-appropriate food like prosciutto-wrapped melon and grilled aspar-agus spears and shrimp skewers (because, he admitted, he figured there was bound to be some feeding each other), but they managed to treat even the risotto as finger food.

That got a little messy, but since they were naked, they just licked and nibbled the stray bits of delicious cheesy rice off each other. That, inev-itably led to Luanna sprawled, one leg flung over the arm of the couch and the other resting on the coffee table perilously close to the remains of dinner, with Derek crouched on the floor between her open thighs.

For about a year—probably more like a minute or so but it felt like years to Luanna—he just hovered there as if drinking in her scent. His breath was hot on her wet sex. Still sensitive from their earlier adventures and tantalized by the fact she and Derek had nibbled on each other more than on their food, she rolled her hips, spread her legs wider. "Please…"

He nipped at her mound and kissed his way down her left side, delib-erately avoiding the most sensitive areas.

It felt good.

Correction: it felt *amazing*.

Luanna buried her fingers in his hair. He looked up at her, mischief and lust warring in his eyes.

Lordy, he had the most beautiful eyes and she swore they gazed into her soul and saw things no one else ever had. Maybe desire addled her brain, made her imagine something that wasn't really there, but she was pretty sure he was, as Grandma Beauregard would say, sweet on her. Which was good because she was sweet on him for sure. Sweet on him, and right now, hot and lustful for him. Okay, that was a known, long-term condition, but it was threatening to reach the danger point, just from that little bit of licking.

"Haven't you had enough teasing?" she asked.

"Have you?"

She had to think about her answer. Words seemed tricky, between arousal and emotion. At last, she came up with what felt like the right answer. "Yes and no. I'm not done with teasing forever. I'll probably never be done with it. But we owe ourselves an awful lot of pleasing after the amount of teasing we went through." Then, decisively, she moved his face over to where she needed it.

"I thought you'd never ask," Derek said before he dove in.

Oh my God. The first time had been amazing, but she'd been so ridiculously keyed up, between anticipation and the emotion of seeing her best friend get married, that she'd exploded almost too quickly. Well, not *too* quickly. She wasn't sure that concept applied to women anyway, or at least not to the lucky multi-orgasmic ones like her. But that kind of wild ride was one experience and this was another.

This time, she was aroused, but not riding the edge before he even got started. She could appreciate the exquisite details she'd missed during their first round of sex. The way Derek held her thighs open—as if she were going to close them!—possessive and firm, yet tender at the same time. The way his five o'clock shadow rasped just the right amount. The small noises he made, which sounded like he found her delicious, like a really great dessert. And oh, what he could do with his tongue! There were no words... Luanna didn't think that was just because the articulate part of her brain was rapidly retreating. There might literally be no words in English that could do justice to the way Derek's tongue flicked and coiled and spiraled and shimmied and...

She shattered into something as bright and colorful as the million lights of the Strip. And when she recoalesced, she said the only thing she possibly could: "Wow."

"Yeah. Wow."

She tried to get him to take a seat and switch positions with her.

He laughed. "I'm about ready for a bed."

At her raised eyebrow, he added quickly. "Not for sleeping in. Not yet. But I think I'm ready for a broader playing field."

"Not to mention someplace comfortable to sleep when we do wear each other out," she conceded, "which might take a bit."

He extended his hand and helped her up. She actually needed the hand; her legs were a bit rubbery. She glanced at her dress and Derek's tuxedo, the former on the floor, the latter in a rumpled heap on the settee by the door.

Habit told her to pick them up, at least drape them over a chair if she wasn't going to hang them up.

Oh, screw that. That was why she had a professional steamer with her. Okay, it wasn't why she'd brought it—it was, as Chloe said, more of an obsession not to be without one—but it would solve the problem. Later. Much later.

Hand in hand, they finally entered the bedroom. The elegant duvet and top sheet were folded back and the almost-smooth-as-silk sheets were hidden in what, a few hours ago, must have been a glorious carpet of red rose petals. By this time, they were rumpled and blowsy looking, kind of like Luanna felt after a long day and acrobatic sex. That made them even more perfect.

"Rose petals? Oh, sugar, I love it! I thought that only happened in movies." She'd thought her heart was thoroughly melted already, but the rose petals worked like the sun did on ice cream. How perfect was Derek anyway?

Derek shrugged. "I'm a screenwriter, and my best friend is Sandrine Moss's brother. The line between movies and reality kind of blurs. It's not too cheesy, is it?"

He looked so adorably abashed that she couldn't help laughing. "Of course it's cheesy, as well over-the-top and super-romantic. As a native of Louisiana, I consider those all good things—and just what I'd expect when I'm being ravished by a sexy, sweet-talking pirate."

Then she drew him onto the bed and showed him just how good she thought they were.

And if rose petals ended up in a few places where they really didn't belong, well, peeling them off each other was part of the fun.

Chapter 23

*I*f Luanna had thought she'd been obsessed about sex with Derek before they finally had sex, she now discovered a whole new level of obsession.

The repeated romps of the night before had been followed by the longest, deepest sleep she'd had in as long as she could remember. And that sleep had energized her.

And now everything made her think about sex with Derek.

They discovered, for instance, that the hotel shower had been designed by someone who clearly also had had sex on the brain. The walls, a mottled cream and butterscotch marble, supplied numerous handholds. There were two rain-shower showerheads *plus* a handheld nozzle, which they put to *very* good use. And it didn't hurt that the deep shower was across from a large mirror…

Even getting dressed brought her back to sexual thoughts. Slipping on rose pink, stretch-lace panties that nestled against the puffy, sweetly aching private parts of her (and having Derek make a noise in his throat and cross the room in two strides so he could cup her ass in his hands). Feeling the soreness in her inner thighs as she put on her sandals.

Turning and slipping her arms around Derek's neck and leaning in for a long, slow kiss.

They probably would've fallen back onto the bed if it weren't for the fact that they were both starving. The coffee and oatmeal and fruit they'd ordered from room service had been hours and hours ago.

Luanna was putting on her earrings—silver filigree hoops, a bridesmaid's gift from Chloe—when her phone rang.

The caller ID said Jack Laine, a pseudonym for one of her clients, because the real Jack Laine, a Louisiana band leader, had died in the 1960s.

"Sorry, I need to take this," she said to Derek, glancing at the door between the bedroom and sitting room.

"No problem," he said. "I've got to go over my notes from the interview I did on Friday, anyway. Take the time you need."

Her heart made a little happy *ping* when he dropped a kiss on her forehead and left, closing the door behind him.

Oh Momma, this is even more trouble than I expected. And sweeter, too.

"Jack" wanted to talk about a new commission, and Luanna adored working with him because he had a real fashion sense. A combination of Lagerfeld, Reem Acra, and a hint of Luscious Couture—thankfully a small enough hint that Luanna wouldn't get sued. And Jack was sensitive to that.

Luanna grabbed the hotel notepad and pen and took notes, but half her brain wasn't on the conversation.

It was on Derek. What they'd shared. How that changed things.

She felt a slow, creaking change inside of her, like the lift of the Caddo Lake Drawbridge.

Her loyalty had been to her clients—and it still was. Part of her contract with them was assuring their secrecy.

But she'd been hiding this side project from Derek, and it was getting to the point where that wasn't okay anymore. It felt too much like lying to him. Plus, he'd told her about his mom, which must have been a real struggle considering how private his folks were. It didn't feel right to be carrying a secret of her own. There literally hadn't been a good time to talk about it since his tell-all moment, but she'd had time—granted, it was while she'd been getting her hair done—to ponder how to tell him. She wouldn't—couldn't, per nondisclosure agreements—reveal who her clients were. She wouldn't also because of that loyalty. However, she could tell him the nature of her clientele and what she sewed for them. She owed him that, given the new upshift in their relationship.

She scribbled notes on Jack's project, made suggestions. She'd seen a mouthwatering flowered silk print in the Fabric District that would be as perfect for his design as honey butter dripping off a fresh-baked fluffy biscuit, and told him so.

When the call was done, she stowed the notes deep in her suitcase. Opening the adjoining door to the living room, her heart gave a little squeeze when she saw Derek. He was sitting on the sofa, hunched over his laptop, which sat on the glass-topped coffee table with ornate wrought-iron legs. His dark hair was mussed, as if he'd been running his fingers through it while he read his email.

Oh, my pirate.

Hearing the door open, he looked up, and smiled, and that smile sent her senses ass over teakettle again.

"Hey," he said. "I missed you. Wanna see if Sandrine and Ray want to catch lunch, too? I assume none of us dare to knock on Chloe and Brand's door."

"In a minute," she said. "I have something to tell you, and I want to do it right now. Something to confess, kind of."

His smile faded into a graver expression; not wary or concerned, but the way he nodded made her think he understood the gravity of the situation.

She sat next to him, turned sideways with one leg cocked up on the sofa. She smoothed the pleated skirt of her cabbage-rose-printed linen dress over her thighs. It seemed like a very important thing to do, until she realized she was stalling.

Although she kind of knew she shouldn't, she leaned forward and placed a gentle kiss on his lips. He responded in kind, and the kiss grew deeper—exactly the reason why she knew she shouldn't have done it. But she needed his touch, needed that reassurance.

It flowed through her like a hot buttered rum on Christmas Eve.

With reluctance, she pulled away. "So," she said. "You know I have a side business making clothes."

"I do," he said. His brow furrowed slightly, but his gaze stayed locked with hers.

"I…haven't told you everything about the business," she said. "It's legal and legitimate, but it's also why I got fired from Luscious, even though they didn't know the details, because for good reasons I can't discuss certain details about it."

"Darling," he said, and she shivered with delight at the way he said the word. No, focus. She had to focus. He added, "Whatever happened with Luscious happened. Their problem, not yours."

"Well, not entirely," she said. Argh, this wasn't going the way she'd planned. Granted, she'd planned for all of oh-point-seven seconds, but that was beside the point. "Nothing I do in my side job had any bearing on my job at Luscious. But when they said they knew I had the job and wanted to know what it was, I refused to tell them, and *that's* why they fired me."

He took her hands in his. God, she loved the touch of him. She couldn't imagine ever getting enough of it. "Whatever it is, I know you made the right decision and Luscious—"

"Sweet baby Jesus, will you just let me finish already?"

He fell silent, looking a little sheepish. "My bad. Carry on."

"The reason I haven't talked about it is because I have a nondisclosure agreement with each of my clients because of the sensitive nature of what I'm doing for them."

She was still stalling, she realized. And nervous, because she was talking too fast. As her father always said to her garrulous mother when she veered off topic (which was frequent), "Ease back on track, Annie."

Ease back on track, Luanna.

"But I want to tell you, because I don't like keeping secrets from you. I can't tell you *who*, but I want to tell you what. My clients are all men, and what I do for them—what they hire me for—is to…to make women's clothes for them. They're crossdressers, and some of them are kind of big names, so it's really important that I keep their names secret, and—"

To her surprise, Derek burst out laughing.

"Oh, darling," he said, "you have a funny idea of what a confession means. When you started saying your clients were men and they hired you to do things…"

Faster than green grass through a goose, she grabbed a throw pillow and gave him a solid thump on the shoulder. But she was giggling, too. The very thought! Her grand-mère would have vapors.

"Not that!" Derek said. "I knew it was about making clothes—you'd already said that. I thought maybe something super-kinky. Anyway, it's also funny because—"

As if on cue, her phone rang again. He gestured for her to check it. She mouthed a kiss at him, warmed that he knew it could be work and that was important to her.

This caller wasn't under a secret name. "It's Yancy," she said.

"Go ahead," Derek said. "That could be important. I'll pop over to Sands' and Ray's suite and check on lunch plans."

He got up and headed to the door as she thumbed the phone on.

"Lu! So glad I caught you," Yancy said. "I know you're in the middle of getting your best friend married off, but what are you doing after *Magnolia Road* wraps? Because if you're available, I have more work for you."

For a second, Luanna was stunned into silence. Then she managed to squeak out, "That sounds great! Tell me more." She narrowly managed not to say something along the lines of "Is Tabasco sauce hot? Of course I'm available."

"Excellent," Yancy said. "My assistant costumer for my next job just quit. It's that hot sci-fi novel, *Battle for Resonance*—they're turning it into a movie. Not a huge budget, but they want us to get really creative with the costumes. Oh, and they have this dream of getting Ray to do a tiny part. Like a cameo. I'd understand if you don't want to ask him…"

Science fiction costuming wasn't all that far from runway haute couture sometimes. Plus, *job.*

Plus, *fun.* Luanna had never considered movie costuming as a career, but she'd really enjoyed the bit of work she'd already done for *Belladonna* and the research she'd done for *Magnolia Road*, and the science fiction stuff could be even more fun. No need to worry about authenticity, just make it keep to the spirit of the book—which she'd read and it wasn't rich in clothing details—and look futuristic and cool.

"I'd love to," she said. "Shoot me the contract when you get the chance, and I'll get back to you Monday. And I'll mention it to Ray. The worst he can do is say no, right?"

"Excellent!" Yancy said. "Sorry I had to bother you, but these things need to get lined up super-early. Now, go do something in Vegas that has to stay there."

Luanna ended the call with a grin on her face. Some of the things she and Derek had done last night had been creative, but she knew they'd be continuing in that vein even when they got back home.

She noticed her phone battery was low, and reached for the charging cord on the coffee table. She'd let it charge for a few minutes while they sorted out lunch arrangements, then come back and grab it before they left the penthouse.

The motion nudged Derek's laptop enough that it woke up. The screensaver vanished. She didn't really look at the screen—none of her business—but something caught in her peripheral vision and she froze.

She didn't want to look, but now she had to. She had to know that she had *not* seen the word "crossdressing."

But there it was, big and highlighted after the words "working title":

Fashionable Fops to Hidden Hollywood
A History of Crossdressing

Okay, maybe it wasn't big and highlighted, but to Luanna, it was the same as if it was in flashing pink neon lights with glitter tossed by…

It didn't matter. The bottom line was the same either way.

Derek was researching crossdressing.

Crossdressing.

She wasn't sure if the blood was rushing to or from her head, just that there was a whooshing sound between her ears, and she felt alternatively as if she were going to faint or going to explode.

Maybe this was an attack of the vapors. She'd never been quite sure what that meant.

More importantly, what the ever-loving fried chicken? What had she *done*? She was the one who'd drawn Derek into their close circle. Okay, fine, he'd already been good friends with Brand and would have been best man in the wedding one way or another. But if they hadn't been dating, there'd have been no way she'd have spilled the beans about her other job. No way he could have put together the pieces himself, which he must have.

She wondered when he'd figured out what she was doing. No wonder he'd laughed when she confessed: he'd already known. He'd just been waiting for the right time to…

No, that didn't make sense, a small, rational part of her brain said in a tiny voice. He was kind, and funny, and…and so were serial killers, according to the tabloids her mother read.

Still, okay, maybe he hadn't known what she was doing until just now, didn't know she worked for crossdressers. Maybe it was a coincidence worthy of those same tabloids.

But hadn't he said something once about looking for a straight male crossdresser to interview? Which still meant maybe he somehow knew about Ray, or at least would guess if he had half a clue. Which she'd just handed to him.

Oh sweet infant Jesus in his manger getting gifts, she'd delivered the dress to Ray. He and Sandrine had been out so she'd simply draped it over an overstuffed chair in their lounge area. (The twin to the one she and Derek had deflowered just last night… Oh, she didn't need those thoughts right now. Didn't need them one bit.) What if Ray and Sandrine were out now and Derek saw it? The dress was clearly too large for Sandrine; she'd fit in it three times over.

Oh. No.

What if Ray was wearing the dress right now?

Chapter 24

$\mathscr{L}$uanna had a picture in her mind's eye. It was of Ray in that dress—the satin bridesmaidy one—and Sandrine in the background looking horrified, not at him, but at Derek, who had whipped out a hidden video camera and was cackling "A-*ha!*" like a demented pirate.

If it were a dream, he'd probably have a ridiculous curly mustache and a pirate hat with huge ostrich plumes.

It was just a mental image, though, and it was one she knew was overwrought, but she was Southern, dammit. Southerners did overwrought for breakfast.

But when she yanked open the door to hers and Derek's suite and stepped out into the common area, that mental image was replaced by a memory.

There was the loveseat where she and Derek had necked like horny teenagers just two nights before. Her abandoned water bottle had been tidied away by the cleaning staff, of course, and the potted plants were still probably real and probably fake. Like Schrödinger's Plants. She remembered the sweetness of his kiss, the rasp of his five o'clock shadow against her palm when she cupped his cheek. She remembered how much she'd wanted him, the sweet frustrated desire of it all.

All *that* reminded her of last night (and this morning), and how perfectly they'd moved in sync. She didn't believe in truly bad lovers, as long as people could communicate—but she'd had lovers she simply wasn't compatible with. It happened.

"Compatible" was a poor word to describe how well she and Derek fit each other, both in the bed and, so far, outside of it.

Had he really been playing her all this time? Had she really been so distracted not to see it?

"Well, Momma," she murmured. "Maybe this boy *is* more trouble than I realized."

She knew how Momma would respond. Momma would raise one perfectly plucked eyebrow, raise her sweating glass of mint julep, and say, "I didn't raise a fool, Luanna Marie-Clare Devenaux. Go get trouble out of your hair."

Luanna flipped her long blond hair back, squared her shoulders, and prepared for battle.

There were no sounds coming from behind Sandrine's and Ray's door. That boded well, right? Please, Lord, say yes.

She knocked, and heard Ray's distinctive voice inviting her in. He didn't sound upset. Was that good?

Or was that how he sounded after he and Sandrine had disposed of a body?

*

When Luanna entered the room, Derek felt a rush through his whole body, as if he levitated ever so slightly off the sofa. They'd been apart less than ten minutes, and yet seeing her again just made him…happy.

It had little to do with the fact that he knew what color panties she wore beneath that sexy flowered sundress, and how those lace panties hugged her incredible ass. That was a bonus, no doubt about it. No, it was more about…

Well, if he had to put a word on it, this was probably what falling in love felt like.

Huh. He didn't have a lot of time to process it, but so far, he kind of liked it.

There was a flush on her pale skin, and he hoped it meant excitement—that Yancy had given her some good news. She looked from him to Ray, and caught her lower lip between her teeth in a gesture Derek knew well, but he suspected she wasn't ever aware of doing. He'd figured out that it meant not only that she was concentrating, but that *she* was trying to figure something out.

"Hey, darling," he said, getting up and giving her a quick kiss. She seemed a little stiff, but he put that down to her being distracted about something. He sat back down, patting the sofa beside him.

"We're waiting for Sands to finish getting ready. Could be a few minutes," Ray said in what was no doubt a gross understatement unless Sandrine had started getting ready earlier than Derek imagined. Ray tilted his beer in the direction of the bar. "Help yourself to a libation." He and Derek both had long-necked beers in their hands, which they'd been sipping while chatting and waiting for their womenfolk, their feet on the coffee table.

As in their suite, this one also had a full bar area, stocked with more liquor than a career drunk's liver.

Luanna went over and perused the selection, and chose, to Derek's surprise, bourbon. She poured herself a healthy finger and slugged it back. "Thanks," she said. Leaving the glass on the bar, she came back and sat next to Derek, although as she did, she scanned the room again, as if looking for something.

Okay, so maybe something *was* wrong. If Yancy had put a damper on their weekend, Derek would have to have words with her.

He put a warm, possessive hand on her thigh, and she didn't really seem to respond. His heart sank, and for some reason, he assumed the worst. What if last night hadn't been as amazing as he'd thought? But, then, what about this morning? Wouldn't she have nixed any fun times if last night had sucked? Or had she had time to think after he'd left?

Had he done something heinous? He didn't think he was the type to not realize when he'd done something heinous—and Luanna had seemed like the type of woman who would try talking it out first.

Not knowing what to do, he took a long swallow of beer.

Of course, Ray, ever the host, tried to keep the conversation going.

"Derek was just telling me about the upcoming episodes of his on the ScHis Channel," Ray said. "Some really interesting topics, especially this new one."

Beneath his hand, Derek felt Luanna's thigh—her whole body, really—tense as she stared at both of them again.

"Uh," she said, and her voice sounded a little off, a little high. "Yeah. He's run the gamut."

"What did Yancy want?" Derek asked her, hoping to save the day. "If it's something you can talk about, that is."

She looked relieved, and he breathed a little easier. She told them about the independent science fiction film Yancy had just signed on with, and that she'd asked her to be assistant costumer, which Derek knew was a big deal, two movies in a row like that.

"That's wonderful!" he said, kissing her temple, smelling the minty hotel shampoo in her amazing hair. "I'm so proud of you."

"Oh," Luanna said, looking flustered. "Yancy said the producers would love to have you for a cameo, Ray, if you're interested. I don't have any details."

Ray sat forward, his beer temporarily forgotten. "Would I get to be an alien?" he asked with undisguised enthusiasm.

"I really don't know…" Luanna said.

"I hope so," Ray said. "I want to try something different. Have them send me the script, okay? Straight to me, not to my agent."

"So you might end up doing Ray's costumes," Derek said. "That could be fun, huh?"

Her big green eyes grew wide and she sucked in her breath, as if he'd said something awful.

But then Ray said, "Well, she already knows my measurements; that'll speed up the process."

"Oh, that's…" Derek saw the puckering look on Luanna's face, something akin to finding half a worm in her apple. "…convenient?"

She let out the held breath. "Can you come back to our room with me for a sec?" she said to Derek suddenly. "There's something I need to run by you." She glanced at Ray. "If Sandrine's going to be a few more minutes, that is."

"She's probably almost ready, but you have some time," Ray said. "C'mon back when you're done, or we'll knock on your room."

As Derek let her lead him away, he found himself wishing he'd had a bourbon instead of most of a beer.

Better yet, a double.

*

As she pulled Derek into their rooms, Luanna made one last effort to hold on to rationality. Something in the back of her mind told her she was overreacting, overlooking something important about the situation, but the front of her mind was full of righteous rage and she was having trouble seeing back to that bit of rationality.

She took a deep, calming breath.

Oh, forget that noise. Yoga had its merits, but sometimes a deep breath just gave you lung-power for a more impressive rant.

Especially if you're from Louisiana.

Especially when the guy with whom you'd spent the most erotic night of your life—the guy with whom you suspected the spark was something more than sexual—might just be a snake in the grass slithering after your clients' secrets.

You can put bunny ears on a cottonmouth, but it's still got fangs.

"Crossdressers? You're working on a show about crossdressers?" She took a lesson from Grandma Beauregard and projected without actually yelling. The neighbors didn't need to hear your family arguments, but by God, your target needed to pick up every word as well as all the cussing you weren't actually saying.

Derek nodded. He looked as stunned as if an alligator had just crawled in the door and was preparing to chomp on his ass.

In a penthouse suite in a five-star hotel in Vegas, not in the bayou country, where such visitors were alarming, but not absolutely unheard of.

"As of when?" she continued. "This morning when I told you about my other job? Thought you could get the scoop on crossdressing celebrities because you'd screwed my brains out?"

Derek opened and closed his mouth a few times, but no sound came out.

The expression in his big blue eyes, usually so merry and sexy, reminded her of Evenrude after the corgi had been reprimanded—guilty because she must have done something to provoke her human, but utterly bewildered as to what it was.

For half a shake of a coonhound's tail, Luanna felt sorry for him. That look, from Evenrude, was usually enough to diffuse the situation from a scolding to pets and cuddles while Luanna muttered, "What am I going to do with you, girl?"

But Evenrude was a dog, so if she looked clueless, it was because she was. Derek was human and not at all dumb. And he wasn't an actor, but anyone in the media had to learn to dissemble a bit, right? So she forged on. "I made promises, Derek. Commitments. I can't break them because it would make a great story for your show. No matter how much fun we had last night." And this morning…

"I would never ask you to." His voice was just above a whisper. He could almost pass for completely calm, but the calm voice flowed over a current of hurt.

It was Luanna's turn to gape like a bass in the bottom of a boat and wonder where her fine rant had gone.

Derek drew a step closer, close enough he could have touched her easily. He didn't, though.

Her traitorous body would have melted at the touch and he probably knew it, so she gave him big points for holding back. Even if a soft, squishy part of her (no, *not* that squishy bit, though it shared the opinion of that sentimental bit of her soul) would have preferred to give up the fight or even the rational discussion it might become.

She struggled for words. She'd been so full of righteous rage and the rant that went with it, but the way Derek spoke, like it was a foregone conclusion, obvious, that he'd never ask her, took all those words away.

In the silence, Derek looked past her to stare out the big window that overlooked some of the more fabulous bits of Las Vegas. Luanna took the opportunity to study their suite's version of Schrödinger's Plant, because staring at Derek, who still looked like the tastiest pirate ever, was just going to make the moment even more awkward. The plant was fake at the moment.

She hoped it was the only fake thing in the room.

She prided herself on being good at reading people and the lines of Derek's body told her he was genuinely upset and rattled.

The silence lasted only a second or so but she couldn't stand it. Had to blurt something out. "But your story… You laughed when I told you about my clients, and when I saw the story, I figured it slipped out because you already knew."

"I laughed because it was an odd coincidence. I've been working on that story since we met." He turned back to her, his eyes still serious, but not quite as forlorn as Evenrude when her human scolded or her peacocks wouldn't play. "It's the one that started out being about the history of men's fashion and changing images of masculinity, only it's morphed over time, and it's been crossdressing and fashion and gender roles for weeks now. It's all kind of stuff I'd been pondering because of Mom and her new butch style, only it seems more comfortable to focus on guys for the show—less personal." He extended a hand.

She hesitated, then took it. "But the timing…"

"I started to tell you right after you told me what you do. Then Yancy called and distracted us. And I'd had my notes open while you two talked because our conversation gave me ideas of a few things to investigate."

She thought about pulling her hand back at that, but she didn't want to let go. Not yet. Not until and unless she absolutely had to. Instead she shook her head, tight and emphatic.

"I told you I wouldn't nose into your relationship with your clients and I mean it," Derek went on. "Privacy is a big part of your working relationship with them. I respect how protective you are of them even more because if I've learned one thing doing this research, it's that society doesn't make things easy for people who are gender-variant—or just creative in the way they dress. But I did think you might know about specialty shops I might have missed…or even have a perspective I haven't thought of. I was excited to talk to you about the topic."

He got it. At least, it sounded like he did.

She squeezed his hand and felt a huge knot of tension loosen between her shoulder blades.

Derek smiled. "I'm not a saint. If in the next couple of weeks, one of your clients tells you he's sick of hiding and would love to talk to the media about being a crossdresser, please pass on my number. But I don't expect that to happen, and I absolutely don't expect you to ask them."

"Sugar, I'm so sorry I jumped to conclusions. It was such strange timing and…" She caught herself before she spoke Ray's name. "I'm probably functioning on about three brain cells between lack of sleep, champagne, and really great sex," she added hurriedly. "The bourbon didn't help."

Derek pulled her in for a kiss that melted her last doubts and at least one of her three previously functional brain cells.

Then he pulled back and shook his head. "There's one more thing. I noticed a dress in Ray and Sandrine's room that looked like it could fit three Sandrines."

Chapter 25

*L*uanna froze, waiting for the other shoe to drop—a great, huge, clunky shoe fit for Frankenstein's monster.

Surely this would be when Derek would plead or cajole or threaten. Outing Ray Stark wouldn't just make Derek's show, but give him a story he could sell to someplace like TMZ for a major chunk of change…

But…he'd promised. He wouldn't go back on that, would he?

Derek shook his head again. "I'm not asking," he stressed. "For all I know, the pretty tent is a style that all fashionable women will be wearing soon—though I hope you don't follow that fashion if it's the case. I'm not asking you to tell me anyone's secrets and I'm certainly not going to ask Ray. But I had to say something to you because if I've guessed right, you're going to be wondering if I noticed. I swear this stops now, between us, and I'll never mention it—to anyone—again." He smiled. "Even though I have to admit I'm really curious. The whole idea shatters stereotypes that I didn't realize I still believed—and that right there is a good thing."

Luanna had no idea what to say at first. The beautiful, posh, ridiculously expensive room blurred. She blinked away tears. "I…I…" *I think I love you* was what she wanted to say. What she actually said was, "Thank you. Thank you for helping me honor my commitments to my clients. I just wish…"

She thought about it for a minute.

She didn't need to wish. She could do it, or at least make the overture.

Derek was right that Ray had the power to shatter a lot of harmful stereotypes. She trusted Derek to tell the story that way, not in some sensationalist gossipmonger way.

She didn't want to let go of Derek. Not now, when they were just resolving the near explosion. But they'd kind of left Sandrine and Ray hanging. She'd offer to run over first and check in with them, so that would give her a chance.

In a few minutes. First she owed Derek another apology—and a few more kisses….

A few more kisses inevitably became a lot more kisses, and enough caresses that Luanna felt the need to change her panties to ward off chafing and keep dogs and cats from going into heat. When Derek offered to go across to Ray and Sandrine's without her, though, she stalled him, using the excuse that she knew Ray and Sandrine much better than he did and besides, she was the one who'd come in all storm clouds and dragged him away, so she was the one who ought to go back and offer a few embarrassed words to their friends.

Sandrine had emerged by the time she got there, wearing a cute little sundress that must have cost the GNP of Guatemala and silver gladiator sandals with heels so high real gladiators would have considered them weapons. She was lounging up against Ray on the suite's loveseat.

They were both petting Ray's new dress.

Luanna smiled. When Sandrine first realized Ray liked pretty frocks almost as much as she did, she'd freaked out, but over time, it had become another bond between them.

It probably helped that there was no way on earth Ray could borrow Sandrine's size 0 wardrobe.

"Beautiful work as always, Luanna," Sandrine said. "I'm tempted to order one in my size, only in emerald green."

"Do it." Ray kissed the top of her head. "I just wish we could wear them out together. Maybe someday." The big man sounded wistful, and his hand bunched the fabric of his new dress. "People aren't as weirded out about it as they used to be. I mean, Derek's show is doing something about crossdressing and it's not some exposé."

Perfect lead-in. She'd tried to mentally rehearse the perfect way to ask, but Derek's delicious lips and clever hands had cut that attempt short. So she kept it simple. "Derek doesn't know I'm asking this, Ray…but would you be willing to talk to him for that episode?"

He and Sandrine looked at each other. Sandrine actually scrunched her forehead, something Luanna had rarely seen her do (probably for fear of wrinkling her flawless skin). Then she shrugged. An awful lot of communication seemed to take place without words.

Luanna felt a little queasy, though that might have been the bourbon.

Finally Ray turned back to her and spoke in that big, rumbling bass voice that seemed so at odds with his fondness for pink silk chiffon—but in the end, both were part of what made Ray the man he was, the man she was proud and delighted to call a friend. "I started asking myself about that when Derek mentioned he was working on the story. I'm not ready to go public yet, but even an anonymous interview might be good for his show. Might be good for me." He pulled Sandrine closer. "That is, if…"

"I'm not ready for public yet either," Sandrine said slowly. "But it's just miserable that we even have to think that way when it's just an issue of you dressing the way you like to dress. And we're luckier than a lot of people in this situation because we're rich and famous. People in our position can get away with literal murder, let alone eccentric fashion. Maybe this show will help everyone." Sandrine could come off as a ditz, but her brother swore she was an actual genius; this was one of the rare moments she let her intelligence show when she wasn't working.

Ray leaned forward, which was kind of like watching Mount Rushmore lean. "I get a good feeling from Derek, but you know him a lot better than I do. Can he be trusted?"

"Oh yes!" Luanna felt like her smile might be making her face actually glow in some Disney-character way. "Definitely. He doesn't know I'm asking, said he wasn't going to try to use my work or connections at all. He saw the dress, but said he didn't want to know more because he knew

I'd made a promise of absolute secrecy to my clients. But I want to help him if I can because I trust him and he's wonderful and… and I love him."

She clapped her hand over her mouth as soon as she realized what she'd said, but it wasn't like she could push the words back in.

Besides, it was true. She loved Derek. She'd been verging on it for a while, but the way he'd been willing to ignore connections that would help his story to protect her clients and her honor had pushed her from falling in love to in love.

She had a feeling she was supposed to tell Derek before she announced it to mutual friends, but a revelation that big—one that was a revelation to her as well as to others—just couldn't be kept a secret.

Sandrine applauded prettily, beaming.

And Ray smiled—not the edgy bad-boy sneer he'd made famous onscreen, the one that made hearts flutter all over the globe, but one that reflected the gentle farm boy he was at heart. "Cool. If you trust him, let alone love him, that's enough for me, pretty lady. I'll talk to him."

She bounced in place, hugged Ray, and then excused herself. She had a few things to talk about with Derek, starting with "I love you."

"We'll just go to lunch without you," Ray said with a grin and a wink.

*

Derek paced around the suite's living room, feeling like a caged animal. And not one of the cool, impressive caged animals that drew crowds around their cages at the zoo. Maybe an aardvark or one of the more obscure ante-lopes that people glanced at and moved on. Luanna had been gone forever.

No, not really. Just long enough to *feel* like forever. Everything had seemed resolved and happy and sexy when she left, but the longer she was gone, the more he second-guessed that. What in the world was she talking about with Ray and Sandrine? Explaining that Derek might have an Agenda and wasn't to be trusted? Asking them to help run interfer-ence—because Chloe wasn't available for that best-girlfriend job—so she could avoid him as much possible until they got back to LA (where she could dump his ass on familiar turf?).

He managed to avoid the temptation to grab a bottle of something stronger than beer and start drinking—he knew that wasn't going to make anything better. Not letting his imagination run wild was proving harder. He was a journalist. He was *trained* to ask "What if...?" and then ask again when he came up with possible answers. Useful in his profession. Not so useful when your relationship had hit a snag just when you were starting to realize how much you cared about the woman.

When Luanna bounced back into the room, smiling that brilliant, open smile he loved so much, he felt like he'd set down a heavy weight he'd been carrying for far longer than she'd actually been out of the room.

"Are they ready for lunch?" he asked, forcing himself to sound casual when he just wanted to scoop her up, say something melodramatic along the lines of *Thank God you came back* and then kiss her until they were both reeling from need.

"They'll catch up with us later," she said.

Then she threw her arms around him, looked up with those ocean eyes, and said, "Sorry I was gone so long. I missed you. Okay, it was like five minutes, but I still missed you."

Not quite as over-the-top as what he'd been thinking, but close enough that he grinned like a fool. They were clearly on the same wavelength.

He only kept the grin for a second, though, because after that they were kissing. He wasn't sure which one of them initiated it. Maybe they'd met in the middle, two great minds with a single dirty thought. In any case, once they got started, neither of them showed any inclination to stop.

Even while he guided her to the sofa, they kept kissing. Kept touching.

When he started to unzip her dress, though, Luanna broke off the kiss and shook her head. "Not yet, sugar. Real soon, but I need to say a couple of things before my brain melts into my panties." She grabbed his hand and squeezed it.

"First off," she said, "it'd have to be anonymous, but Ray says he'll talk to you for your show."

"Wha...what?" About two-thirds of Derek's brains had made the journey into his jeans, but he made the effort to pull enough of them out again that he could talk coherently. It wasn't easy with Luanna's tempting curves demanding all his attention, but he managed. Even at one-third brain power, he knew this was important. "Did he just volunteer? I'd mentioned the story before I'd even noticed that damn dress, but I never imagined..."

She pressed her fingers to his mouth to hush him.

He couldn't resist licking them suggestively. Even when Luanna let out a sweet moan, his mind was still tossing around Luanna's revelation, trying to figure out what to make of it.

"Oh, hush." Luanna's smile was salted caramel, sweet and rich with a hint of something naughty. "I asked him. Y'all will have to work out the details, but I asked. And he said yes. It'll be anonymous, though." She took her hand away from his mouth and rested it on his thigh.

"Luanna, I... Why?" Damn, he was usually more articulate than this, but he didn't even know what questions to ask, what thanks to give, let alone how to do it. The hand on his thigh wasn't helping him think straight.

"I trust you to tell as much of Ray's story as he chooses to share, and to do it in a positive way that'll make other folks who are a little different feel safer. Ray trusts you because I do." She kissed his forehead. It was a gentle kiss that could almost have passed for sisterly, but from Luanna, it sent shivers down his spine and made his cock jump and press against his fly. "I trust you because I love you." She looked thoughtful. "And I love you because I trust you. So I realized I could at least ask Ray if he'd be willing."

Derek's blood sang in his ears. His breath caught in his throat. He'd gone from almost losing her to this gift. Trust. Love.

Luanna.

He was still having trouble thinking sensibly, but under the circumstances, he figured that was all right. And while he couldn't manage to come up with a creative, lyrical way to put what was in his heart, he knew he could start with the basics and it would be just fine. "I love you, Luanna. I figured it out just before we had that argument, so this was the worst couple of hours of my life."

She laughed. "Oh sugar, it's been half an hour, tops. But it felt longer to me too." She squeezed his thigh. "Now about that zipper?"

They ended up ordering room service for lunch.

Chapter 26

The common area of the suite held enough luggage to support a Victorian family on a Grand Tour, because when you flew on a private plane, you could do that. Most of it was Sandrine and Ray's—well, Sandrine's—with the bride running a close second, but Luanna had to admit she'd overpacked because she could. The three couples, waiting for a small army of porters to collect said luggage, all sported a happy glow. Luanna suspected it was also a just-been-fucked glow for everyone concerned. She knew it was in her case and Derek's. Why not take advantage of that big, luxurious bed one more time before they had to check out?

Sandrine leaned against the warm wall of Ray's body, his big arms around her, as he leaned on the one spot of wall not blocked by furniture or luggage. Brand and Chloe, who would be honeymooning according to their originally scheduled plan, were crammed into one chair, even though there were other seats available. Chloe was sprawled on Brand's lap. They made goo-goo eyes at each other even when one of them was forced to speak to someone else.

Luanna wasn't on Derek's lap because she didn't trust either of them not to do something naughtier than their friends really needed to see, but she was snuggled close to him on a sofa otherwise covered with carry-ons and computer bags. His arm felt very right around her. Evenrude was sprawled at their feet, snoring contentedly. She seemed to approve of the latest developments with Derek, but Luanna knew better than to take that as a sign. Evenrude pretty much liked everyone and she'd decided early on that Derek could be one of her bestest friends. (Human friends, that is. If it came to a choice between him and the peacocks, Brad and George would win wings down.)

Luanna felt very much like crowing about how happy she was, how happy *they* were, how they were in love. But that was Chloe and Brand's show at the moment, so she just kept squeezing whatever safe-in-public bit of Derek she could reach and glowed quietly.

No one talked much. Too busy grinning like exhausted, sexually sated, happy Cheshire cats, maybe. Besides, it had been an intense couple of days. She was exhausted, and she and Derek had had a relatively easy time, other than the whole falling-in-love aspect. And pretty soon they'd be on their way to the airport, back to LA and their not-so-normal normal lives. Quiet was good.

When Olive finally emerged from her room—unusual since she should have been organizing things—Sandrine asked, "Will the car be here soon? Someone needs to get the bags."

"Soon. Have you seen Hollywood Ooh?" Before they could answer regarding the popular celebrity gossip website, Olive handed her tablet to Sandrine and Ray.

Sandrine dropped an F-bomb, which she somehow managed to make sound elegant. "That is the worst picture of myself I've ever seen!"

"You look gorgeous," Ray said. "Just a little blurry because someone took it on a crappy cellphone from, I don't know, maybe Mars. They call Luanna 'an unknown blond." He was smiling, so whatever the gossip site had to say couldn't have been too awful.

"Very film noir," Derek commented, running his hand up her thigh. "So that's cool."

"And they spelled Chloe's name wrong again," Ray noted.

Brand hadn't extricated himself from Chloe when Sandrine swore—either he was getting better about his sweet but smothering urge to take care of his sister and anyone else with two X chromosomes, including Evenrude, or he didn't want to start a fight this early in his marriage—but at the mention of his wife's name, they both stood and crowded over to look at the tablet, which looked more like a phone in Ray's big hand.

Chloe sputtered.

"What is it, sugar?' Luanna supposed she should have gotten up too. But frankly, she was used to these media-generated Sandrine-storms by now. If it showed signs of becoming a hurricane, she'd board up her metaphorical windows and look for the ingredients to make a pitcher of the eponymous cocktail. But meanwhile, the others would fill her in. "They did worse than misspell my name. Someone sent in a picture of us girls going into the chapel, and Hollywood Ooh totally suggests that Brand and I were pretending to get married to cover for Sandrine and Ray eloping to Vegas." Chloe managed a smile. "It would be funny if it wasn't so stupid. I mean, I *was* in a wedding dress and it isn't like Sandrine and I could switch dresses in the bathroom, which thank goodness Aunt Rosa the celebrity-gossip addict may realize since she's actually met Sandrine." She gestured down her body, which was notably shorter and curvier than Sandrine's willowy form. "They could at least have speculated that maybe Sandrine and Ray *also* got married."

Sandrine growled like an irate wild boar just before it charged a hunter. Luanna figured most people would have a hard time imagining that sound coming out of that slender body and famously exquisite face. Luanna still did a double take, and she'd lived near Sandrine long enough to know that the actress had a hot temper and some startling ways of venting it.

"They said what?" Sandrine said.

She grabbed the tablet from Ray and obviously read the story instead of just looking at the terrible picture. "Ray, what are we going to do?"

Ray squeezed her close and smiled. "That's easy, babe. We get married."

Sandrine's mouth opened and closed as if she were an especially pretty fish. While she was still gaping, Ray slipped away from Sandrine and got down on one knee in perfect old-movie form. "I meant to do this once we got home, after Olive helped me set up something over-the-top romantic.

But I don't want to wait. Sandrine, will you marry me and make me an even happier man than I already am?"

Luanna squealed. She couldn't help herself. Ray might have thought he needed help coming up with a romantic proposal, but she thought he'd done beautifully all on his lonesome.

Sandrine didn't look so sure at first. Her eyes grew as large as one of those sad-eyed '70s kids displayed right next to the velvet Elvis in Aunt May's tacky living room. "Today?" She actually squeaked, emotion apparently defeating years of professional vocal modulation. "I mean, yes, I want to marry you, but today? Right now? In this?" She gestured at her lovely, but not especially bridal, sundress.

Ray froze and looked around wildly. The look was what people called deer in the headlights, though in his case it was more like a moose.

Olive answered, because she was Olive and thank goodness for that. "If you want to do it now and then have the big shindig later, I can make arrangements. It's not like the plane can't wait. But I think Ray just wants you to say yes now. That way you two can celebrate while I give your publicists a correction for Hollywood Ooh that's even more romantic than what they speculated."

Sandrine's smile blossomed. It looked a little bit like the smile she wore at a similar moment in *Love in a Bubble*, but much better.

Then she was on the floor with Ray, kneeling herself, gripping his hands. "Yes! Yes, of course!"

The kiss that followed was arguably more passionate than anything Sandrine had ever done on screen. It was certainly more convincing than any of Ray's onscreen love scenes, ever. Face it, that just wasn't his acting strength. Anger, honor, and courage he could portray, but romantic, erotic passion, not so much. Kind of funny, considering what a big mushpot he was.

Luanna was relieved when Derek whispered to her, "Do you feel like we should be applauding?" because she'd been wondering that too. This might be as sweet as beignets dunked in praline syrup, but it was two famous actors. Even if they happened to be her friends getting engaged very much for real, it felt a bit like theater.

Breaking off from the kiss, Ray patted his pockets.

Before he could even look in Olive's direction, she handed him a small box in a distinctive shade of robin's egg blue. "This isn't the real ring," he said as he fumbled it open. "I mean, it's real, but it's a ring-ring, just pretty jewelry I'd picked up the other day while you all were looking for bridesmaid dresses. We can shop for your real engagement ring when we get home."

"Who the hell has a practice engagement ring?" Luanna whispered to Derek. "And from Tiffany, no less."

Derek shrugged. "What do you expect? It's Sandrine."

Practice ring or not, Sandrine squealed with glee. "Look! Isn't it beautiful?" She gestured like a queen, showing off a spectacular aquamarine on a narrow diamond-crusted band that looked like silver to Luanna, but was probably platinum.

She had to take a closer look, even if it meant letting go of Derek temporarily. This was fashion, after all.

A closer look told her discerning eye that yes, it was platinum. Practice ring indeed! If that was the practice ring, Luanna figured the actual one would be featured in "World's Ten Most Extravagant Engagement Rings" spreads for decades to come and would cost several years of her hometown's collective income.

But excessive wealth and crazy habits aside, Sandrine and Ray were two people in love and freshly engaged. Luanna hugged first Sandrine and then Ray. "Congratulations! I am so thrilled for you both."

"You'll make my dress, of course," Sandrine declared, proving that bliss didn't temper her tendency to be a gorgeous and usually well-meaning dictator.

Luanna remained outwardly calm, but inside she was flailing like a drunken Muppet. Chloe's dress had come close to shattering her sanity—and Chloe had been a laid-back bride. Bless her heart, Sandrine would give new meaning to the term Bridezilla.

Wasn't there some famous designer with a staff of flunkies who could share the pain as well as the joy and the bragging rights of the commission?

But Sandrine was a friend. You sucked up a lot of pain to help out friends. The fact Sandrine could pay handsomely was a bonus but not a primary consideration.

Most importantly—and most terrifyingly—this would put Luanna on the map. In the news. A star as big as Sandrine didn't go to just anyone for a one-of-a-kind wedding dress. This would shoot Luanna's name into the media faster, and with infinitely more cachet, than a sex tape.

It could be the start of a whole new career for her.

Of course, she still wasn't sure if she wanted a movie costuming career or a haute couture career anymore.

Eh. What was one more option?

Ray looked around at the roomful of trusted friends, then grinned shyly. "I'd love it if you made one for me too. Doesn't have to be on time for the wedding, because I know that'll be super busy, but sometime."

Well, that settled it. Famous-designer flunkies weren't going to create a dress for Ray.

"Of course, sugar. Dresses for both of you." Ray would be a design challenge, but easy to work with. Luanna hoped Sandrine wouldn't change her mind about the design as many times as she did about what she wanted for dinner.

"Why didn't I think of that?" Sandrine exclaimed. "A wedding's all about the dress, or dresses in our case. Right, Luanna?"

Luanna blinked and considered her words. From a designer's point of view, that opinion had a lot to recommend it, and she'd certainly met brides who felt that way, but she didn't think it was a good life plan.

"I mean, a marriage is about the right person," Sandrine added quickly, "and Ray and I have that. But a *wedding*? Definitely about the dress. And the amazing food. Chloe, sweetie, I know you're still buzzing on your own wedding, but could I borrow you from DesJardins for the catering? I guess I could just ask him to do it, but he's got such a sourpuss and I want someone who looks *happy*."

While Chloe was flailing around over the idea of catering the Hollywood Wedding of the Decade, Olive stepped up to being her efficient self. "I'll need to get in touch with your publicity team," she said, "make sure Hollywood Ooh and everyone who steals from them gets the real story, and set up engagement photos. I can do that from here. I'll see you back in LA the day after tomorrow."

"You're not going with us?" Sandrine sounded genuinely panicked. "But…"

At that moment, the door to Olive's suite opened. A handsome African American man, a good decade younger than Olive, poked his head out. "I wanted to make sure the plan was still on, love. I know how these work emergencies can go."

Olive's complexion darkened several shades as she blushed, something Luanna would have bet dollars to donuts the down-to-earth woman never did. "My husband surprised me last night; he's out here on business. We'll be driving back together. Sandrine, the porters are on their way for the bags, and the car's waiting outside—I already texted the driver to say you'd be ten minutes or so. You have my number if there are any emergencies, but I may be slower than usual to get back to you. Otherwise I'll be in touch, but not too soon. I'll see you Tuesday."

As she spoke, she eased toward the door of her suite. Her husband's hand protectively at the small of her back, his fine eyes focused on nothing but her, she made a decisive exit.

In the buzz of chatter that followed, Derek snuck in behind Luanna and slipped his arms around her waist. "I suppose it's too soon, but all this wedding talk…"

She turned in his arms. "For one, it's way too soon. I might say yes, mind you, but it's way too soon. For another, what if Sandrine decides we have to have a double wedding? Having my momma involved is going to be trying enough, but Sandrine too? It would be crazier than Mardi Gras in a madhouse." She clapped her hands over her mouth after the words slipped out. Had she just assumed he was proposing?

Chloe leaned in conspiratorially. "Don't be ridiculous. Sandrine likes you, but she'd never share the spotlight like that."

"In that case," Derek said calmly, "let's start small, which was the original plan. How about looking for a place together? Somewhere big enough for you to have a proper sewing studio. I know nothing will be quite like living in the Moss-Stark compound, but I'd like you and Evenrude to myself sometimes. Given our crazy schedules, it may be at three a.m. when we're both finally done with work, but it'll beat going to bed alone."

Luanna peeled her hands off her mouth to say yes. Then she threw her arms around Derek and kissed him.

Evenrude, who'd managed to sleep through Ray's proposal and all the subsequent ruckus, woke, let out one emphatic "woof!" Then she waddled over to join them, wagging her tail so hard the rest of her body wagged with it.

"I'm not sure what just happened," Sandrine said, "but it looks like we have a wedding, an engagement, and a whatever to celebrate. I'm sure Olive ordered champagne for the limo, but we should have some on the plane, too." Even as she spoke, Ray was reaching for his phone.

*

If Luanna had known what kind of a year she was going to have, she'd have made a special celebration dress.

One with love in every single stitch.

sophie
mouette

author of *Out of the Frying Pan*

POSSESSED
UNDRESSED
& in a mess

haunting has never been sexier!

Fancy a steamy romance with a ghost and some hidden treasure?
Turn the page for a sneak preview of *Possessed, Undressed, and in a Mess*,
available now from your favorite retailers in print and ebook formats.

Chapter 1

*A*ngela balanced on the rickety ladder and prayed she wouldn't fall. The ladder wasn't actually rickety. It wasn't exactly new, and it wasn't fancy, but it wasn't old. But it *did* wobble a teeny bit. And she hated heights, even just ladder heights, and she couldn't shake the nagging sense that the ladder was about to collapse under her, or topple sideways and land her in a rosebush with a broken arm and a disfiguring gash across her cheek from a thorn.

The chill wind blowing in off the ocean, numbing her fingers, was no help at all.

Still, as she drove the nail cleanly into the wood with a single hammer blow, reinforcing the butter-yellow shingle that had come loose in the recent winds, she couldn't help but feel a level of contentment, too. Below her, the blustery breeze goosed the hotel's sign, causing it to swing back and forth on its chains.

Angelika

It still gave her a thrill of pride every time she saw it, thinking about the hard work she and Kari had put into restoring the place and making it into a swank spa and artists' retreat. Last year, their first, had been a bated-breath affair, but they'd gotten a good write-up in several magazines—from the *LA Times* to *Poets and Writers*—and taken off. Some solid Yelp reviews had boosted the signal. They hadn't turned much of a profit last year, but they'd broken even, which was stellar for a new small business. Now they were entering their second year, coming off the post-Valentine's Day lull with weekends, and many of the weeks, booked solid for the first six weeks of the summer.

Which was good and bad, because while the taste of success was thrilling, she and Kari were scrambling to make sure Angelika was ready for the onslaught—on a budget for which "tight" would be a compliment. All those bookings were great, but until the guests actually showed up, the hotel was strapped for ready cash.

With the shingle firmly attached to the house again, she could get off this Ladder of Certain Doom. Her stomach twisted. She had to climb down. She had to move her feet from her relatively safe, stable position.

The face-eating thorns lurked below, waiting for her to slip.

She eased one foot a millimeter off the rung.

"I don't suppose you need any help up there?"

The voice, deep in timbre and unabashedly male, startled her. Gripping the ladder with both hands, she found the next rung with her seeking toes. Only then did she dare to look down.

Her stomach lurched for a different reason. The man down there was *gorgeous*.

His dark blond hair was on the long side—a style Angela always appreciated, because it gave a girl more to grab hold of during sex. Blue eyes, as near as she could tell from here, a rough five o'clock shadow, and an easy smile. Possibly even a dimple.

Hot, hot, hot.

She took a deep breath. "Nope, I'm fine. What can I do for you? Looking for a room?"

"Actually, I'm here about the handyman job you advertised." He graced her with a slow, easy smile. "Although it looks like you're doing just fine on your own."

Somehow, he made that sound dirty. If she wasn't mistaken, those heavy-lidded eyes were appraising her ass.

She used that thought and his voice to distract her, and made it down the ladder without becoming intimate with the rosebush.

He had a very nice voice.

She gave a small, silent prayer when her feet hit the ground, then turned to face Mr. Gorgeous, their potential savior.

She was a tall woman—statuesque, a former lover had said, like the beautiful, imposing marble goddesses her Mediterranean ancestors had left behind—but he was a perfect couple of inches taller.

The potential handyman wore a fitted red T-shirt that had seen more vibrant days, although repeated washings had also softened the cotton so that it molded across his chest, arms, and stomach, revealing muscles more likely gained from healthy outdoor work than from reps in a gym. His faded jeans also clung to his body, not tight enough to reveal his religion, but enough to let the world know his side-dressing preference.

Left, in this case.

Angela resisted the urge to circle him and admire the view from behind. After all, he'd had the opportunity to do that to her already.

In the circular drive she saw a battered blue pickup with a shiny toolbox at the front end of the bed and a ladder across the top that was newer and fancier than hers. Probably less rickety, too.

"Glad you saw our ad," she said. "You come with references?" Oh, like *that* didn't sound like a double entendre.

His mouth twitched, and she had the distinct impression that he'd taken her words the wrong way. Or the right way, depending on how you looked at it.

"I do." He dug into his back pocket and retrieved a folded piece of paper. How he'd managed to get anything into those tight jeans was nothing short of a miracle. He smoothed out the paper and handed it to her.

"I'm impressed," she said after skimming the information. An understatement. He didn't just have work experience—he had training in restoration architecture and architectural history. Made her wonder just a bit why he was looking for work in historic, but isolated, San Sebastian, let alone at the salary she was offering.

But she shouldn't look a gift horse in the mouth as long as the references panned out. Especially when the mouth in question made her think wicked thoughts.

"Thank you," he said.

She looked up from the résumé. He was grinning. She suspected he was grinning because she was all too obviously impressed with more than his credentials.

And yes, there was a dimple. *Damn.*

She grinned back. She had no qualms about fooling around with employees. If everyone was an adult and in agreement, why not?

But she was getting ahead of herself. She needed a handyman more than she needed a hot, hard screw. At this rate, she'd screw him just to never have to go up that ladder herself ever again.

As if reading her mind, he said, "By the way, you've got another shingle loose up there." He pointed to a scallop-shaped piece of wood several feet higher than the one she'd just fixed, toward the end of the building where the rosebushes were particularly vicious.

Angela groaned.

"Tell you what," the gorgeous potential handyman said. "I'll go ahead and fix that one for you. And I'll rescue the hammer you left on top of your ladder."

"I still have to call a couple of your references," Angela warned.

"No problem. This one's on the house—so to speak. It's the least I can do to thank you for the view."

Angela glanced down, following his gaze. Thanks to the chilly spring wind, her nipples were clearly prominent beneath her silk-and-cotton burgundy Henley top.

He was a cheeky one, all right. Just for that, he could do the job. Maybe she could get him to do her, too. Maybe in exchange for figuring out what had gone all wonky with the plumbing in Bathhouse Three? Because the way he looked at her made her insides clench.

She stuck out her hand. "I'm Angela Georgenes, by the way. Co-owner of Angelika."

His hand was warm, surrounding hers in a firm grip, and he didn't let go right away. "Tyler Woodruff."

He went to get his own ladder, and she reluctantly pulled her gaze away from him, pausing before she went inside, as she always did, to admire the hotel.

Victorian houses of this type were called Painted Ladies, and the color scheme she and Kari had chosen, while garish, was nonetheless entirely correct for a late 1800s building: rose-pink, robin's-egg blue, and custard yellow picking out the fanciful shingling details, accenting the ornate gingerbread trim on the wraparound porch.

The wind brought with it the salty tang of the ocean. Angelika's gardens extended back to the cliff side; a short walk away was the path down to the beach. The northern California coast wasn't the warm, tropical paradise of the southern beaches, but it had a windswept, almost dangerous beauty about it, especially on overcast days like today. (They kept extra slickers and sweaters on hand because some of their guests, the artists especially, seemed most drawn to the beach in the worst possible weather.)

Indulging herself in one last glance at Tyler—who looked quite fine up there on the ladder, his biceps flexing as he hammered—she went inside.

She found Kari in the hotel office, on the phone.

Her friend and Angelika co-owner sitting on the floor in a lotus position, her hazel eyes closed. Her blond hair was pulled up into a plastic clip, wisps escaping every which way.

"No, Saturday. *This* Saturday. Not next week. No, not next Saturday. Two-days-from-now-Saturday." Kari lifted the pale pink receipt in her hand as if the person on the other end of the line could see it. Angela, who *could* see it, identified it as being from their towel delivery and laundry service. While Angela handled the hotel end of things, Kari, a massage therapist, ran the spa. Angelika featured natural hot springs baths, various types of massage, facials, manicures and pedicures, and even mud baths.

"Yes. Right," Kari said after a pause. "This Saturday. Read me the date again, please. Exactly! Thank you so much! We'll see you Saturday."

She hung up and pulled the headset off. "Why does everything go to hell in a handbasket the day before we open for the busy season?" she demanded. There was no real hostility in her voice, though. Kari was too mellow for that. Which was why she was such a good massage therapist: she was the most calm and grounded person Angela had ever met, and she was able to impart that serenity to others.

"Not everything," Angela said, doing a quick dance of triumph. "I think we've found our handyman."

"Where?" Kari asked.

It wasn't a strange question. San Sebastian wasn't big, and when their last handyman had buggered off to Kansas or Iowa or Missouri or somewhere to join his partner, the pickings had been slim. There were enough folks with basic carpentry or plumbing or drywall skills, but none who knew the vagaries of old houses. Well, there were a few, but they were busy keeping their own Victorian homes in one piece on top of their other jobs.

"Well, right now he's fixing shingles out front," Angela said. She glanced again at the résumé Tyler had handed her. "Down from Oregon, apparently. And he's gorgeous."

"Really?" Kari's hazel eyes lit up.

"I saw him first," Angela said.

"That's okay. I've got a feeling this one is meant for you."

"You haven't even met him yet."

Kari shrugged, her smile serene. "Doesn't matter. My intuition is telling me this guy's going to be important to you, and I know to listen to my intuition."

Angela shook her head, as always, at Kari's New Age outlook and called the references on Tyler's list. The second one didn't answer, but the first and third gave him such glowing reports that she didn't bother contacting more. Instead, she printed out the various employment forms, labeled a file folder with Tyler's name, stuck his résumé inside, and left the paperwork in a neat pile on her desk.

Kari was on the phone again when she passed, but seemed considerably less stressed than she had from her last call. Her smile and her more relaxed tone suggested she was talking with Cybelline, owner of the New Age shop The Silver Stag, about the séance they were planning to celebrate Minerva's birthday.

Minerva May Fenwick: hedonist, world traveler, scholar, poet, forward thinker, artists' model, artist. She'd had the mansion built in 1893, not only as a home base when she wasn't spanning the globe in search of adventure, but also as a salon and hotel for the free expression of both thought and pleasure.

Angela and Kari had organized a "Minerva's birthday party" last year, with oysters on the half shell, asparagus, and plenty of the champagne Minerva had loved—as well as the legal version of the absinthe she'd also loved. But coffee with their new friend Cybelline, during which they'd mentioned a passage in one of Minerva's travelogues about attending a spiritualist gathering, had inspired a new idea.

Cybelline, in fact, had been the one to point out Minerva's birthday fell on a full moon and had urged them to follow through on the séance. Despite her classic New-Age-flake name and occupation, Cybelline was professional, methodical, and easy to work with—and she wouldn't take no for an answer when it came to organizing the séance. She'd taken over all the details, spending several evenings at the hotel after her shop was closed.

If the séance worked well, they might consider having one as a regular Halloween feature.

Angela grabbed a bottle of water from the industrial fridge in the kitchen, noting that Franklin, their cook, had been out shopping. A huge braided bunch of garlic heads on the butcher block workstation filled the room with glorious scent.

Outside, she found Tyler climbing down the ladder. Quite a few shingles looked more stable now. Now she also finally got the view he'd gotten of her. Damn, even the chamois-colored work belt he wore looked sexy, the way it slung low on his hips and outlined his ass, which was as lusciously firm as she'd imagined it would be.

"Good news," she said, tossing him the water. "You've got the job. We just have some paperwork to deal with."

"Fantastic," he said. "Mind if I leave the ladder for now?"

"Not a problem." No doubt there were even more loose shingles. Try as they might, there always were.

He left the tool belt at the base of the ladder and followed her inside. He gave a low whistle when he saw the lobby, and Angela flushed with pride.

The lobby alone had been featured in several upscale magazines. The pine beadboard, perfectly restored, was stained dark and gleamed with polish. Shield-back chairs with acanthus-leaf trim and matching occasional tables dotted the room. The entrance to the check-in area was framed with spoked trim, painted blue. A wide staircase went up the center to split into two halfway up, each then turning back and heading up to the second floor.

Even the plants were correct for the period: lush maidenhair ferns on delicate stands; a hulking, tropical-looking aspidistra in one corner; and, on the reception desk, small pots of fragrant amethyst heliotrope.

"Upstairs has two wings," Angela explained, seeing the curiosity and appreciation in his eyes. "One history of the building had said they'd been a men's wing and a women's wing—standard Victorian practice—but we know for a fact that the wings hadn't been separated by gender."

In fact, they had mixed as often as possible, except for the guests who preferred the company of their own sex, but Tyler didn't need to know that right now.

Angela, meanwhile, dragged her cursedly vivid imagination away from thoughts of mixing with Tyler. Repeatedly.

As they stood there, a lanky greyhound got to its feet and ambled up to them, toenails clicking on the oak flooring. Tyler held out his hand and the dog sniffed it carefully, then leaned against his leg, gazing adoringly up at him with liquid brown eyes.

"That seals the deal, then," Angela said. "Isabella's acceptance is the final test."

"She's a beautiful dog," he said, stroking the short, soft fur between Isabella's floppy ears. Isabella sighed in contentment and leaned harder into his thigh. To his credit, Tyler didn't have to readjust to brace himself.

"Thank you," Angela said. She hadn't been kidding about Isabella accepting him. She trusted the dog's judgment. "She's a rescue, after two years on the track. Kari found her, but she's definitely our dog. Or we're her people."

Isabella followed them into the office, circled once on a large bean-bag-like dog bed in the corner, and then lay down, thin legs splayed.

Angela passed the paperwork and a ballpoint pen across the desk, and he began filling out the information in bold handwriting.

"Do you have a place to stay?" she asked.

He glanced up. "I've rented a room from a Mrs. Parsons on Spring Street." He went back to writing, but added, "Although I might have to move if she makes another pass at me. Older women are wonderful, but I draw the line at someone old enough to be my great-grandmother."

Angela snorted. Adelle Parsons was known for her healthy interest in men of all ages as well as her complete lack of censure when it came to propositioning them. Apparently Minerva's decadent ways had rubbed off on her—unfortunately without Minerva's reported wit and style.

"Thankfully, you can outrun her," she said. "Just remember to keep your door locked at night, and you'll be safe."

Truth be told, she liked the quirky old biddy, who remembered the mansion as Fenwick House when Minerva May Fenwick was still running it. The more they'd heard about Minerva, from Adelle's tales as well as from the journal, the more affection Angela and Kari developed for Minerva.

Tyler handed the paperwork back to her, and she glanced over the forms before putting them in the file folder.

"Can you start tomorrow?" she asked.

He spread his hands. "I can start today if you've got something for me to do."

Oh, she did, all right. It involved her desk, her naked body, and those hands of his all over her. For starters.

Without looking down, she knew her nipples were hard again—she could feel the lovely, anxious ache—and this time it had nothing to do with the cold.

Still, it was better not to jump the help minutes after hiring them. Better professionally, anyway. Surely some etiquette book covered that.

"I think we're set for today," she said. "I'll sit down for a few minutes tonight and make up a list of things for you to look at tomorrow, though."

She stood and stuck out her hand again, wanting to feel his flesh against hers again, wanting to experience the touch of his hand again to fuel her fantasies later.

He didn't disappoint her. The warmth of his firm, calloused touch heated her blood. His eyes claimed hers as he said, "Don't stay up late on my account."

If he only knew. Actually, he probably guessed—and that thought made her wet.

"With a place this old, there's always something needing fixing," she said with a laugh. "You're the one who'll need a good night's sleep to keep your strength up."

He gave her hand a final squeeze before letting go. "Shouldn't be a problem, unless I forget to lock my door against Mrs. Parsons."

*

With a final pat on Isabella's head, because the dog had followed him to the front door, Tyler left Angelika. When he got in his truck, however, he didn't start it up immediately. Instead, he sat, contemplating the stunning, garish hotel before him.

His paperwork had checked out. He hadn't expected it not to, but there was always the risk that someone would dig too deep, catch a discrepancy he hadn't noticed.

He had a sense that the very tasty Angela Georgenes wasn't usually the type to miss discrepancies.

He shifted on the seat, not a little uncomfortably, as his thoughts about the attractive hotel owner went in a decidedly coarser direction. It had been a pleasure to stand there and watch her tight little ass in tight little jeans as she perched at the top of the ladder. Hell, watching the wind toy with her long, curly, dark hair had made him envy the wind.

Her lips and nails had been the same burgundy shade as the knit shirt that had clung nicely to her curves. The material had been light enough that it hadn't hidden the way her nipples had responded to the cold—and to him. He wondered if the tight buds were the same hue of dark red that she favored.

If he didn't stop thinking about that, driving was going to become rather difficult. He forced his thoughts to other things.

It was a pity, really, that he couldn't get to know her well. He really *did* have an interest in old houses—he didn't have to lie about that part—and it was refreshing to meet someone with a similar passion who wasn't gay, married, or approaching Mrs. Parsons' advanced age.

He'd do a good job for her. That was a matter of responsibility, and he took his responsibilities seriously. He never promised something he couldn't follow through on.

He was just very, very good at not mentioning certain things. Things like the real reason he'd come to San Sebastian, or his actual motivation for seeking out Angelika.

He started the truck. No, the sexy Ms. Georgenes wouldn't be happy at all if she found out about that.

Acknowledgements

Sewing, like writing, is often a solo activity, but there comes a point where it's best to have someone else pin the hem and check the overall fit. A number of smart and wonderful people helped ensure this book hangs together properly.

My beta readers, D.H. Hendrickson and Jennifer Hallock, found the dropped stitches and made sure the manuscript's bra straps weren't showing, and Colleen Kuehne's copyediting prowess means the book's skirt wasn't caught in its panties. If these questionable metaphors had been in the book, they would have flagged them, I'm sure, and rightly so. The mistakes you don't see are because of them. The rest of the mistakes are mine.

Gillian Horvath gave me a peek into how TV and movies get made. Don't blame her for any minor details I added to make the book snappier. (Yes, I know that was Luanna's problem with Derek and Graham. Truth is stranger than fiction!) Seriously, though: Gillian, you're phenomenal. And gratitude to Derek Schepinksi for information on the fashion design industry.

Designer extraordinaire Allyson Longueira perfectly captured the flair and glamor of Luanna on the cover, and I love her for it.

A brief encounter in Hollywood provided the spark of an idea that became the Hollywood Spice series (Sandrine's shenanigans are purely fiction, though); thank you to my friends who hosted the party years ago.

And to Sophie fans everywhere: thank you for following along on the Hollywood Spice ride!

About the Author

Author of the steamy 4-star (*Romantic Times*) novel *Cat Scratch Fever*; the sexy paranormal romp *Possessed, Undressed, and in a Mess*; and more, Sophie Mouette is the brainchild of two widely published authors of erotica, romance, and speculative fiction. Her popular short erotic fiction has appeared in anthologies from Avon Books, Cleis Press, and Circlet Press.

The two halves of Sophie—Dayle A. Dermatis (aka Andrea Dale) and Teresa Noelle Roberts—met more than two decades ago at a writers' conference. Talking nonstop, they closed down the hotel bar and went somewhere else to keep on talking. Although they've always lived on opposite sides of the country (and for a few years, on opposite sides of the Atlantic), they've remained very close friends, and it was only natural that they should start writing together as well.

Visit SophieMouette.com for more information.

www.ingramcontent.com/pod-product-compliance
Lightning Source LLC
Chambersburg PA
CBHW050407260626
47156CB00003B/911